UNSUNG
VILLAINS

MISSY MEYER

Also by Missy Meyer:

WE COULD BE VILLAINS

* * *

UNSUNG VILLAINS

Published by Rocket Hat Industries
Copyright © 2015 by Missy Meyer
All rights reserved.

ISBN-13: 978-0-9862399-2-2

UNSUNG VILLAINS

ONE

There were twenty-seven hours and fourteen minutes left until the end of the world as we knew it, so we figured we had time to grab a burger.

We were on the trail of a guy named Manos, so named because an accidental fall into a chemical bath made him sprout extra fingers on each hand, like some kind of human starfish. The rumor was that he had the nickname "Grabby," thanks to his interactions with a lot of women in the supervillain community. So not only was he a bad guy, but he was a gross, creepy bad guy.

It might be a surprise to hear that we were going after a supervillain, since if you want to get technical about it, my team is also made up of supervillains. The world knows our leader, Nate, as Doctor Oracle, one of the most wanted villains out there. What the world doesn't know is that the Doctor Oracle organization is really headed up by a committee of eight people, all with similar goals: mainly, try to expose the so-called superheroes who are just tools of the government, and do some good for the world at the same time.

I've learned that a lot of the heroes are cut from the same depressing cloth: big ego, small vision. They wait around for crime to happen, deal with it in as public and showy a way as possible, then bask in the adoration of the public and the government. We, on the other hand, see problems with society and try to proactively fix them. Occasionally, that means committing crimes.

You can see how we wouldn't get along.

I'm one of those eight people heading up Doctor Oracle's operation, and if you'd told the Sarah Valentine of a year ago that she'd be entering foreign countries illegally, robbing rich people, breaking into multinational corporations, and living in a secret lair hidden in plain sight on a tropical island, she would *definitely* not have believed it. But as the Sarah Valentine of the present day, I have to admit, I was loving every minute of it.

Just this past spring, I was a desk jockey at a software company, doing graphic design because it was what I'd gone to college for, with no idea what I *really* wanted to do. I played video games so that I could pretend I had excitement and adventure in my life. Who knew that by late summer, I'd be trained in skills like lock picking and hot-wiring cars, several famous superheroes and villains would know me, and my personal net worth would be several million dollars thanks to the work I'd done. Not that the cash mattered, since the Oracle organization provided everything on our island; money wasn't even used.

Back to Manos: he'd been making some threats lately, posting screeds and monologues on various message boards frequented by both sides of the super community. Most people laughed him off, but we were keeping an eye on him. He finally issued an ultimatum a week ago: a billion dollars, or he'd shut off electricity across most of the globe. If he could truly do it, it would plunge the world into chaos. But everybody thought he was bluffing.

Well, everybody but us, I guess. We'd tracked a series of small blackouts and brownouts throughout southern Canada and the northern United States that felt a little too random to actually be random. One of our group's greatest assets is a database of all known heroes, villains, and in-betweeners, which let us know Manos's real name. It was easy for our computer expert, Evie, to monitor his credit cards, one of which showed charges in each city on the same dates as the power interruptions.

That's why we were looking for a burger joint in the suburbs of Toronto, Canada, north of the city in an area called Newmarket. If the superheroes weren't going to try and stop Manos, it was pretty much up to us. We weren't entirely sure he had the power or ability to shut off electricity for the whole world, but we already knew he could shut it off for a city. Depending on the city, that alone could be a huge problem.

After a boatload of research, we'd discovered the location of Manos's lair; we'd scouted the place out earlier in the afternoon and were ready to settle in and make some plans. His deadline to the world was the following night at midnight, so the clock was ticking. We wanted to get in, stop his plan, steal anything worth taking, and get out well before the deadline. Hopefully whatever tech we could steal would be reward enough for saving the world.

"There it is," Nate said, pointing up ahead through the windshield while glancing down at a tablet computer. "The place called Grind. It's on a bunch of Internet top-ten-burgers lists for Toronto."

Jin pulled our rented SUV into the parking lot. She was both our team's mechanic and our regular driver on missions. I was in the backseat with Oscar, whose specialties were climbing, running, jumping, and all sorts of physical things that make me tired just thinking about them.

The four of us went inside, found a nice quiet corner table, and placed our orders for burgers and beers. After the drinks were delivered, Nate pulled his tablet out and set it on the table. We all looked at the map he'd called up, showing a lush, wooded area with a creek winding through it.

"So we have two good ways in," Nate said as he poked at the tablet. "I like the southern road. More cover, even though it's a longer trek. That shorter road to the east was just way too open."

"Agreed," Oscar said. "Plus, if anyone else takes him seriously enough to ferret out his lair and pay him a visit, they'll likely take the short, easy road." Nate poked at the tablet and brought up a series of pictures, mostly blobs of blue and green that were taken with a thermal-imaging camera.

Jin reached over and tapped on one of the pictures, which had some small orange blobs in all the blue and green. "Here's one person, most likely Manos. And this heat signature over here is way too big to be a person. It's probably whatever machine he's going to be using." Jin had both designed and piloted the tiny quadcopter loaded with cameras we'd flown over Manos's lair earlier.

"Alone tonight. But who knows about tomorrow," Oscar said.

"For as long as he's been in the game, he's worked alone," Nate said. "He's one of those guys who's always talking about it—bragging about it, really. We'll keep an eye out for henchmen tomorrow, but I'll bet he's doing this all on his own."

Nate swiped his finger across the screen, replacing the map with a group selfie he'd snapped of us, all grinning like fools, with the CN Tower in the background. I looked up and saw the server coming our way with our burgers. She dropped them off along with a large stack of napkins, glancing at the picture on our tablet and smiling.

After she left again, we dug in. The websites were right: the burger at Grind made me glad to be a carnivore. Conversation came to a halt as we ate, and I looked at the picture of the four of us on Nate's tablet. We looked like any other group of tourists, which was the whole point of having the picture on the tablet. Nate and I were practically a matched pair—both medium height with almost the same shade of brown hair. Nate was wearing his favorite pair of heavy-rimmed glasses, and had the usual three days' worth of stubble on his face.

"I might want a copy of that," Oscar said as he saw me looking. "You got me at a really good angle."

"You are *such* a narcissist," Jin said.

"Is it narcissism if I truly *am* that handsome?" He waggled his eyebrows. "Or is it just *honesty*?"

Jin rolled her eyes and grinned. "*Honestly*, my friend, your big old face looks perfect as usual. But did you notice that your left arm looks like it's been Photoshopped?"

Oscar looked at the picture again thoughtfully, while I looked at Oscar. He actually was really handsome, with thick black hair and brown skin from his Mexican heritage, with bone structure that would make a model jealous. But he wasn't my type—he went around the bend into too-pretty territory, while I liked my men a little more real-world, a little geeky.

I knew he wasn't Jin's type either. Her husband, Mark, was several inches taller than Oscar, and had a blond surfer-dude look, which somehow worked well with the crisp suits he always wore. Jin and Mark Scarborough were an interesting study in opposites, since he was over six feet tall and extremely fair, while she was less than an inch shorter than I was and had straight, jet-black hair. I knew from our many conversations that she'd been born in China but adopted as an infant and raised in Northern California.

Once the plates were cleared and we each got a second beer (no more than that, the night before a job), Nate got back to business on his tablet. He tapped on the glowing envelope icon and read a message.

"Excellent," he said. "Email from Evie: she sent over the building plans and permits." Once we found out the street address of Manos's lair, we'd sent the address to Evie, our computer whiz, so she could scour whatever public or private systems necessary to get us a schematic of the building. A villain's lair isn't always a cave or a fortress—Manos's place looked like an abandoned lumber mill. Not that I have any room to talk, since our lair is disguised as a vacation resort. Which seems way more comfortable than an old mill in Canada, but maybe Manos preferred his solitude with a side order of drafty rooms and sawdust.

We looked over the plans and compared them to Jin's infrared photographs. Whatever his machine was, it was almost smack-dab in the middle of the place. Whether we went in through the front or the back, we'd have to make our way through half the building to get to it.

After the beers were empty, we packed up and headed back to our motel. It was hardly the Ritz, but the sheets were clean and the beds were relatively comfortable. And there was air-conditioning, which was a relief—Toronto's summers were normally pretty mild, but we were there in the middle of an unusually hot week. It was far more humid than I was used to, either from our island in the Pacific or my former hometown, Seattle.

We gathered in Nate's room and spent two hours going over our plan for the following night, refining as we went and coming up with multiple options for any contingencies we could think of. As always, I was glad to be surrounded by a team of professionals. The fact that they listened to my opinions and suggestions continued to amaze me.

Jin and Oscar said their good nights and headed off to their own rooms, leaving me and Nate alone.

"Ready for tomorrow?" he asked.

"Ready as I'll ever be," I said. "At least I get to wear regular gear for this one." In my time with Doctor Oracle, I'd put on a variety of strange and unusual outfits, ranging from a true super-style silver and blue spandex outfit to a massive insulated cold suit designed to keep me from setting off thermal sensors. It was always a pleasure to do a job where I got to wear the comfortable black tactical gear.

"I hear that," Nate said. "I'm going to have to see if Rupert can modify my business outfit; I was sweating like crazy last week at that press conference." What Nate referred to as his "business outfit" was actually a full disguise with a padded body suit. Nate was actually Nathan Hart, owner of the Hart Corporation, an international company that started in real estate, then branched out into more directions than I could name. Nate had inherited the Hart Corporation from his father, and left most of the daily operations to people who were actually interested in running those kinds of things. Although he did have to make occasional appearances to assure the members of the board that he wasn't dead and was still of sound mind and body, for the most part he stayed away and worked on things that interested him.

He styled his billionaire business-owner persona as a recluse who hated the spotlight and only spoke in public when absolutely necessary. It gave him the freedom to be out in public as just plain Nate, an everyday guy who never got recognized as either the portly and balding billionaire Nathan Hart, or the scarred and goateed supervillain Doctor Oracle. You'd think it would be tough to pull off living a triple life, but Nate seemed to handle it with ease.

I yawned and pulled my boots out from under my chair, where I'd kicked them off earlier. "I guess I should be going." I sat on the bed next to Nate and pulled the boots on.

"We *are* on the job," he agreed. Then he rested his hand on my thigh and wiggled his eyebrows.

"Excuse me, my friend," I said, picking up his hand and depositing it on his own thigh. "Don't even think about it. *You're* the one who insisted on promising everyone there would be no funny business when we're out on a job."

"You're right, you're right." He groaned and flopped back on the bed. "It's probably too late for take-backsies on that, right?"

"Most likely." I leaned over to tie the laces on my boots. When I sat back up, Nate put his hand on the back of my neck, rubbing gently. It still felt weird to have stubble on the back of my neck—I'd recently asked the hairdresser on our island base to see what she could do about cutting out some of the bulk in my hair. My goal was to make it easier to wear wigs, and I ended up with a drastic A-line cut. It was crazy different from the plain brown shoulder-length bob I'd worn for years; in a way, it was the outward symbol of the way my entire life had changed over the last few months. Though it still felt way too edgy for me, like it was the hairstyle of somebody much cooler. It was hard to convince myself that I actually *had* turned into somebody much cooler, skulking around in all black and committing crimes for a living.

Nate massaged my neck and shoulders, and I knew if he kept it up I'd fall asleep right there. But we were on the job. I leaned over and kissed him, then stood up before we could get ourselves into the kind of trouble we'd promised the team we'd avoid. He flopped back down on the bed, and I headed for the door.

"Next time I get a great idea like no fooling around on the job, please smack me," he said.

"That I can promise," I said.

"Good night, Valentine."

"Good night, Nate." I blew him a kiss from the doorway, then went to my own room. As I brushed my teeth, I thought about our handshake agreement with the rest of the team to keep work and romance separate while on the job. It was just a drop in the bucket compared to the actual legal paperwork we'd had drafted up and both signed, when we were absolutely sure we wanted to take our relationship to the next level.

Jin had initially brought it up, since I was putting all my eggs in one basket: dating a coworker in a very small, very tight-knit workplace where I also happened to live. She and her husband had signed very similar paperwork when they'd started dating. There was a legal guarantee that nobody would get fired if the relationship ended, with the option of excellent references if I chose to leave the island and work elsewhere (both normal business references, should I choose to go back to the real world, or a specialty reference if I wanted to work for another supervillain). I'd also be able to cash out my share of the profits from jobs I'd participated in, so I wouldn't even have to work if I didn't want to.

In a way, it was like signing a prenup with Doctor Oracle. It was weird, but it made a lot of sense, and I was a lot more comfortable knowing that even if my relationship imploded, I wouldn't be totally screwed. Not that I thought my relationship would implode, since Nate was, in many ways, my perfect guy. But you just never know, and while I love the adventure and excitement of my life, I don't like to take unnecessary chances when I don't have to.

I changed into my pajamas and tried to figure out how to set the motel's alarm clock next to the bed, but it had about a thousand unlabeled buttons and no instruction manual. I gave up and set an alarm on my ChatterBox, the oversized watch-looking device on my wrist that served as my phone, clock, walkie-talkie, and a dozen other household uses. I set the CB down on the bedside table and drifted off, with visions of stealing tech from Manos dancing in my head.

TWO

The next morning we went over our plans again, came up with a few more contingencies, and made sure all our gear was in working order. The sun wouldn't set until after eight that night, and Manos's deadline was midnight, which gave us a pretty tight window of opportunity. Everyone napped (or at least tried), and we headed out to the abandoned mill in the evening.

We pulled up to the spot where we'd chosen to park a little after eight o'clock. It was a beautiful August evening, not a cloud to be seen, so we had to wait patiently as the sky turned from orange to muddy red to dark blue.

As soon as we'd arrived, Jin had sent up her quadcopter to scan the area, checking for anyone in our immediate vicinity. When it finally got dark enough, Jin brought it back, swapped out the batteries, and sent it out again in the direction of Manos's lair. We stood at the back of the SUV and watched the view on Nate's tablet: the quadcopter cruised over lush, green woods; then we saw the abandoned mill come into view. Some small lights were on, but we didn't see any activity outside.

The quadcopter hovered high over the main building, and Jin switched it over from the regular high-definition camera to infrared so we could look for heat signatures. We crowded around the tablet and looked at the orange blobs that indicated heat.

"Damn it, he isn't alone," Nate said. "There's the big blob, which is his machine. Looks like, what, four people total?"

"Looks like it," Jin said. She steered the quadcopter around the rest of the property, but we didn't see any other orange blobs.

"Wait," Oscar said. Jin stopped moving her remote control, and we all squinted at the tablet.

"What do you see?" Nate asked.

"I thought . . . Nah, I guess it was nothing," Oscar said. "Thought I saw something greenish, but it isn't there now."

Jin gave the quadcopter more altitude to get a wider view of the area, but there wasn't any heat to be seen beyond the four figures and one large machine inside the mill.

"Why the hell does he have other people in there?" Nate wondered.

"Everybody gets lonely sometimes," Oscar said.

Nate poked Oscar in the arm. "Not usually when they're adamant about working solo and are about to enact a plan for global domination."

"Investors?" I asked. "An audience? Hostages?"

"It could be anything," Nate said. "So be on guard, everyone."

Oscar nodded and pulled a gun case from his equipment bag. He unzipped the case and took out a tranquilizer pistol with a silencer on it, checking it over with a quick, practiced precision.

"Okay," Nate said. He handed the tablet to Jin. "Keep an eye out, and let us know if anything else pops up." He pulled his own equipment bag out of the back of the SUV, and I followed suit. We were all already wearing our usual tactical gear for missions: black trousers and jackets that were resistant to most cutting weapons and smaller arms fire, oversized hoods, thick but flexible gloves, and goggles that both concealed our identities and switched from regular to night vision with the press of a button. The goggles had built-in cameras so whatever we saw could be transmitted back to whoever was serving as our base. The feeds from our cameras were currently going to Jin, on a second tablet she had propped up on the SUV's dashboard.

We all removed the earpiece from the black ChatterBox units on our wrists and put the transmitters in our ears, then tapped the faces of the CBs together so that we formed a private communications channel. Nate thoroughly checked his own tranquilizer pistol and spare darts—it delighted me that out of the hundreds of missions from before I joined, and the dozens since I arrived, there'd never been a single casualty caused by Doctor Oracle or his organization. Oscar slung a lightweight, expandable backpack on his back, full of a few additional items.

I checked my own equipment, from my lock-picking kit to a multitool knife to a rappelling hook and rope. I had the same nervous energy as with every other mission I'd gone on, but I felt well prepared for anything that came my way.

The three of us headed off through the woods, leaving Jin behind in the van. She'd keep an eye on us from above with her quadcopter, watch the video feeds from our goggles, and let us know over our comms if anything was headed our way. It wasn't full dark quite yet, but the twilight was so dim I already had my goggles switched to night vision. Everything glowed green ahead of me. I glanced over at Nate, who was more of an amorphous black blob than a person; the fabric our tactical gear was made from had a cool way of refracting light, giving us a little more stealth.

We made it to the edge of the woods and had a clear view of the back entrance of the mill. The building was probably a hundred yards away, across a dusty yard lit by surprisingly bright moonlight. I switched my goggles back to normal mode as soon as we reached the tree line. I looked up and saw that the moon was close to full, if not completely there.

"All clear," Jin's voice came over the comms. "Still four people inside. Three of them are grouped near the machine, and one is separate. Maybe on the other side of the room, or in the next room over."

"Roger," Nate said. "Anything around the front entrance?"

"I can't see anything."

"All right. Starting our entry." Nate nodded at Oscar, who sprinted across the clearing and pressed himself against the side of the building. I know that most guys who do parkour are graceful, but it's always kind of a work of art to watch Oscar when he gets up to speed.

No alarms went off; no lights turned on. Jin reported that nobody inside was rushing our way. Oscar turned and ran off along the side of the building toward the front entrance. Nate and I ran across the clearing as fast as we could, and put our backs against the building just as Oscar had.

"All clear, no changes," Jin said. "Three people at the machine, one person off by themselves. The three are milling around a bit, but the one is staying put."

Nate thought about that. "If they're guards, why aren't they out guarding?"

I shook my head. I had no idea.

We both checked the time on our ChatterBoxes. It was just after nine, so we had plenty of time until Manos did whatever he was planning on doing. I waited by the back door while Nate pulled a small black box out of his pocket. He peeled a tab off the back and stuck the box in the upper corner of the back door. He pressed a small button on the side.

"Rear motion sensor in place," he said.

"Got it," Jin said.

"Sensors in place in front," Oscar said in my ear.

"I have all motion sensors live," Jin said. Better to be safe than sorry. If anyone else approached the mill while we were inside, we'd get advance notice from Jin.

Nate and I waited another minute, and Oscar came sprinting back around the corner of the mill to join us. We checked the back door for alarms, but there was nothing. Either Manos didn't have very good security, relying on the secrecy of his lair, or we were walking into a trap. From the research I'd done on him, I was betting on the former; a lot of supers on both sides tended to overestimate their own powers and underestimate the usefulness of technology.

We walked as silently as we could through the back area of the mill, past abandoned machinery and huge chunks of trees covered with dust, searching every nook and cranny for traps or alarms. Some of the floorboards creaked, but according to Jin, none of the four people inside moved toward us. I was reaching for a doorknob to see if it was locked when she told us to stop.

"What's up?" Nate asked.

"Okay, this is weird," she said. "Still four people, three of them grouped by the machine. But the heat signature of the machine is fading."

We thought about that for a moment. "Maybe they're fixing part of it?" Oscar said.

"Letting it cool down, so it's ready for later?" I offered.

"Oh," Jin said. "The three people are on the move, away from your location. They're headed toward the front of the building."

"What about the fourth?" Nate asked.

"They're staying in the same place."

We looked at each other. "How about we wait for a second," Nate said. "Jin, give us a running report."

"They're almost to the front entrance. Yeah, there goes the motion detector. They've gone through the front door and are headed down the road."

"What the hell?" Oscar said.

"Switching the copter to night vision," Jin said. "I'm following them."

We waited where we were, all of us tense. I realized I was holding on to the doorknob. I gave it enough of a jiggle to see that it was unlocked, then reached over and held Nate's hand instead.

"I can't really make much out," Jin said. "They're wearing all black, like you guys. One of them seems a lot faster than the others. Switching back to the infrared. Oh, yeah. I'm picking up a much larger heat signature. Oscar, I think it's about where you saw something earlier. The three people are right on top of it."

"A car," Nate muttered.

"A car," Jin said. "In high-def, I can see the moonlight reflecting on it. Black or dark blue, probably a van."

"Where's the last person? The one left inside?" Nate squeezed my hand.

"One sec, flying back," Jin said. "It looks like they're still in the same place."

"Someone beat us to it," Nate said. "Damn it!"

"So what do we do?" I asked.

"There might be something to salvage," Nate said. "Plus, I just want to know what happened."

We carried on, sneaking through the last rooms before we found the door separating us from where Manos and his machine were supposed to be.

"The last person is just ahead, to the left," Jin said.

Nate and Oscar drew their tranquilizer pistols. We went through the door and all turned left, both of the guys pointing their pistols into the corner.

"Well, now, who the hell are *you* guys?" Manos asked. He was sitting against the wall, securely tied up, his dexterous hands with their extra fingers heavily duct-taped to the arms of the chair.

Nate stepped forward, his face hidden behind his goggles and hood. He put on his extra-deep fake Doctor Oracle voice, the one that anyone in the business would recognize in an instant. "I'd like to ask *you*, Manos, who the hell *those* guys were."

Manos cringed a little bit in his chair. "Oh, hey, Doc! Um . . . not sure? They were dressed like you and your friends here and didn't bother to make introductions."

Oscar and I headed over to a giant cobbled-together heap of machine in the corner while Nate talked to Manos. I didn't know what most of the machine did, so I just looked it over slowly so that Jin could see it through the camera on my goggles.

"What did they want here?" Nate asked.

"What you want, I guess?" Manos said. He leaned to the side so he could see beyond Nate, and squinted at his machine. "Although . . ."

"Something's missing," Jin said. "Sarah, look back to the left a bit, where there's that gap. Yes, right there." I looked at the machine, and sure enough, there was a hole where something had been removed. Not a large something—maybe an object about the size of a large coffee cup. Wires led into the empty space, ending in neatly cut ends.

"Huh," Manos said. "They didn't take my electromagnet."

"So what did they take?" Nate asked in his booming voice.

Manos sniffed. "I should tell you what I told them, which was absolutely nothing. However, I do believe in professional courtesy, since I know who you are. It appears that they stole the power supply that was attached to the electromagnet."

"And you were going to use a single electromagnet to shut down power across the planet?"

"Not just *any* electromagnet," Manos said. "It's the Pederson electromagnet that Discordius stole from MIT a few years ago. I won it in a poker game."

Nate laughed, which was creepy since he was using his phony Doctor Oracle voice. He even threw his head back for the drama. Manos just looked confused. Nate left Manos taped to his chair and came over to where Oscar and I were looking at the machine.

"Something funny?" I asked.

"We already have a bit of a history with this particular item," Nate said. "I'll fill you in later."

"Let's get this baby loaded up," Oscar said. With Jin giving instructions over the comms, he unhooked the electromagnet, which wasn't that much larger than the power source that had been stolen—it was about the size of a loaf of bread. I looked over the bulk of the huge machine and wondered what the rest of it was all for.

Nate went back over to Manos. "So what about this power supply?"

"Courtesy only goes so far, Doc," Manos shrugged. "I've told you far too much already."

"Maybe I could beat the information out of you."

"From what I've heard, that really isn't your style." I could see Nate's shoulders rise and fall in a sigh. His aversion to violence was one of the things I loved about him, but at times it could be a real pain in the ass when everyone knew just how far you were willing to go.

"Fine," Nate said. He came back over and helped Oscar remove the electromagnet, which seemed as exciting as a shoebox now that it lacked a power supply.

"Sarah," Jin said in my ear, "can you cut some of the wires that led to that missing power supply?" I pulled out my multitool and snipped off as much as I could. She directed me around to grab a few other parts that had connected to the missing piece while the guys unzipped Oscar's backpack and shoved the electromagnet inside. They tossed me a second bag, which had been inside the backpack, so I could put the pieces of the machine inside for Jin.

"Hey, so, how about untying me?" Manos asked.

"How about no," Nate said. "Maybe you should stay there for a while and think about what you've done. Seriously, threatening a disaster that could destroy civilization as we know it? Kind of a dick move."

"Well, even though the machine would have *totally* worked, I really just wanted the billion dollars."

"Care to share what you were going to spend it on?"

"Mostly cars, women, and lair upgrades," Manos said. "But I guess I need a new lair now. I've heard there's a skull-shaped cave on the market up north."

"Typical," Nate muttered. I stifled a laugh.

"Red alert, guys," Jin said. "I have a hot reading on the infrared, coming up the front road."

"Another car?" I asked.

"Looks like it," she said. "Moving fast, and so should you."

Nate turned to Manos. "All right, then. Enjoy whatever happens."

"What?" Manos asked.

"Not sure who these next guys are, but good luck with them," Nate said.

"Next guys?"

"The motion detector on the front door just went off," Jin said. "Get out of there."

Nate pulled out one of his Doctor Oracle calling cards, plain white with his logo in thick black ink. The drawing was a winged medical staff with snakes coiled around it, known as a caduceus, but with a flaming sphere at the top. I knew the logo well, since I'd actually designed it in an online contest a decade ago, while I was still in college. It was one of the strangest coincidences of my life.

Nate tucked the card in the machine where the electromagnet had been, a little gift for the group coming in after us. We hustled back out the way we'd come in, through the back of the building.

"Doc?" Manos called after us. "Hey, Doc? A little help here?"

We ran as quickly and as quietly as we could to the back door. Jin kept up a running commentary as she watched the heat signatures from above. Several new people had unloaded from the new vehicle and were heading straight in toward Manos. She flew the quadcopter to the back side of the building and let us know that it looked clear all the way back to her. We didn't even stop to double-check the yard; we just sprinted across the moonlit clearing and back through the woods until we got to the SUV.

Nate and Oscar loaded the electromagnet and the rest of our equipment into the back while Jin steered her quadcopter and landed it perfectly on the hood of the SUV. She grabbed it, we quickly hopped inside, and we took off down the road, away from Manos and his mystery visitors.

"Any idea who these guys were?" Nate asked.

Jin turned the SUV from the dirt road onto a paved road, and we all relaxed a little. "No idea," she said. "Another group in a black van, dressed in black."

"Man," Oscar said. "We had all black first. What a bunch of copycats."

THREE

We didn't want to stay too close to the scene of the crime for the night, so we returned to our motel, packed up everything, and checked out. There were a surprising number of small airfields in the Toronto area, so instead of landing somewhere big and complicated, we'd picked the adorably named Buttonville Airport as the place to park our jet. Less than an hour after checking out, we were in the air with our cargo of a powerless electromagnet and a large assortment of pieces removed from Manos's machine.

Even though we'd all had naps, most of us caught some sleep on the flight. Being from the west coast of the United States, I'd never really thought of how spread out the middle of the country was. If you'd asked me how long it would take to fly from Toronto to Fargo, North Dakota, I would have guessed an hour or so. Turns out, it was a four-hour flight, which gave us plenty of time to rest. It probably would have been quicker to fly straight from one airport to the other, but our pilot had to dodge around into some areas that weren't well-covered by radar so he could monkey with our flight plans to make it look like we weren't crossing international borders. The last thing we needed was to try to get a stolen electromagnet and a most-wanted supervillain through customs.

Before we settled in for a snooze, Jin took me up to the cockpit to go over the flight plans, as well as some of the controls, with me. Besides being a whiz with machines, she was a fully-qualified pilot of small aircraft, and had been teaching me to fly one of our smaller airplanes over the past few weeks. She was neither qualified nor interested in flying the company jet (too much like a bus, she'd said), but it had enough similarities to merit showing me a few things as I learned to fly the same small craft she did.

It was early in the morning when we landed in Fargo. Even though we'd all caught some shut-eye on the flight, everyone wanted more sleep. We grabbed take-out breakfast, got rooms at a hotel near the airport, and set alarms on our ChatterBoxes so we could meet up for lunch before we headed out of town.

Fargo probably seems an odd destination, and it was. But it wasn't our final stop. After sleeping, showering, and having lunch, we loaded up into another nondescript black SUV and headed out into the middle of North Dakota. Our goal was almost two hours away, in a part of the state that could truly be referred to as "the middle of nowhere."

We pulled up next to a tall, windblown fence with warning signs half-hanging off it. Oscar hopped out and held a small device up to one of the signs, and a section of the fence sank down into the dirt so we could drive through. After Jin pulled the SUV inside the fence line, Oscar pressed the device to the sign again, and the fence rolled back up to its normal place.

It was my first time visiting this particular facility, so I thought it was all pretty damned cool.

I'd heard about the Vault at the beginning of my time with the Doctor Oracle team, as part of a huge information dump about the organization and its holdings, but there hadn't been any reason to go there since I joined up. I'd read plenty about the place, but it was exciting to get to see it in person.

Jin drove along the dusty plain until we reached a small concrete building. She stopped with the nose of the car facing a flat side of the building, with no windows or doors. I watched her tap out an intricate code by flashing the headlights. After a minute, the edge of the roof lit up green, as if it was hung with Christmas lights. The rest of the team got out of the car, and I followed suit.

Oscar grabbed the bag holding the electromagnet, and we all went into the tiny concrete building.

"I know I read about how the security systems work, but it feels like there should be a guard or something in here," I said, looking around the empty room.

"Not necessary," Nate said. "Plus, can you imagine what a boring job that would be? We'd never be able to keep people for long, which means we'd never be able to keep this place a secret."

"That's right, it's your first time to the Vault," Jin said. "Would you like to do the honors?" She waved her hand at what looked like a featureless part of the concrete wall.

As with most things, I jumped at the chance to try something new. "Yes, please!"

Jin pointed out one specific concrete block. When I looked at it really, really close, I could see a thin spiderweb of cracks kind of in the shape of a hand. I pressed my hand against the block, which first glowed white, then green. As part of Doctor Oracle's inner circle, I had security clearance to almost everything. It was always a delight to be able to use it.

A chunk of the concrete floor shifted and slid back, revealing a dark hole in the ground. Lights flickered and turned on in the hole, showing a staircase headed down.

I glanced over at the bag Oscar held, the one containing the now-dead electromagnet. If Manos had succeeded in shutting down the electrical power to most of the world, anyone who was down in that hole would have been trapped in the dark. I shuddered.

Nate saw my reaction. "You don't have to go down, if you don't want to."

"No, I should see it," I said. "But I'll tell you right now, I don't think I'll be in a hurry to come back here."

"You and me both, sister," Jin said. "The Vault is necessary, but it's hard to make it less creepy."

Oscar looked around the concrete room we were in. "I don't know, guys. Maybe some bright paint and curtains? A clown painting or two? It'd cheer the place right up."

"Not helping," I said.

"Just think of it like a video game," Nate said, which helped me out surprisingly well. If I could picture myself as just an avatar, being steered down into a dark, concrete pit, it was somehow less intimidating.

We went down several flights of stairs and through a gloomy gray hallway, then came to an elevator. As we headed even farther down, I saw that there were stairs next to the elevator, which made me feel a little less like I was going to get trapped at the bottom with no way up. It'd be a schlep to the top, but it was better than being stuck at the bottom of a giant concrete tube.

Nate pointed out some of the huge letters and numbers stenciled on the wall, identifying the Vault as a former United States missile silo, number US-436.

"There are abandoned missile silos all through the Midwest," I said. "Why did you choose North Dakota?"

"Earthquakes," Nate said. "Or, rather, the lack thereof. North Dakota and Hawaii have the fewest earthquakes of any of the states. Not so many deep, cement-lined holes in the ground in Hawaii, so this was really the only choice."

The elevator reached the bottom, and we went down another gray hallway until we reached a huge metal door. Nate and Jin each put a hand on a concrete block on either side of the door. Just as the one upstairs had, the blocks glowed white, then green. The door made several clicking sounds and a hiss.

Oscar grabbed the door's handle and pulled. Even though the door was massive, it opened smoothly. Lights flickered on inside the huge room beyond the door, and it looked like there were a few things in there already lit up. We went inside, and I had to stop at the threshold to take it all in.

The room at the base of the silo was much larger than I'd expected from my reading and looked even larger because most of it was completely empty. There were a great number of items stored in the Vault, but like in any bank vault, they were all tucked away in boxes, nooks, crannies, and shelves around the perimeter of the room. Oscar carried his bag in and set the electromagnet down in the center of the room.

"You never know what's going to react with what down here," he said. "Best to keep it away from anything else until we know where to put it. Nate?"

Nate typed on his tablet. "Section B, box seventeen." Oscar picked the bag back up and turned left toward the outer wall. Jin wandered to the other side of the room to check on a few things, leaving me and Nate to watch Oscar.

"What made you decide where to put it?" I asked.

"Well, electromagnets are actually a pretty common thing to steal, so they're all in section B together." Nate tapped on his tablet so I could see a listing of everything locked away in that section.

"What makes that section safe?"

Nate grinned. "Remember when I told you how I surround myself with brilliant scientists so I don't have to actually know the hard science? They can just tell me that it works, and that works for me?"

"Yeah."

"So, the lockboxes in section B are lined with something-or-other-ium, which blocks electromagnetic pulses."

"Sounds very high-tech," I said.

"Even better, though, we've been holding box seventeen aside for *this* particular electromagnet: the Pederson electromagnet from the MIT heist."

"How did you know that's what Manos had?"

"We didn't," Nate said. "But we knew it was out there. After it was stolen, we went in and stole all the plans and research files that helped make it. *Fifteen years'* worth of research. That's all tucked away in a different part of the Vault, but we figured we might eventually meet up with this little sucker, so we prepared a space for it just in case."

"Why steal all of the research? Won't they just spend fifteen more years building another one?"

"Two reasons. One: it's really dangerous. With the right amount of power, it's possible that it could actually do the kind of damage Manos wanted it to. Which leads to two: Can you think of any organization or government who should be able to get their hands on something that powerful, that dangerous? Maybe in fifteen years, society will be in a better place. If they build another one, we'll have to see if the world can handle it then."

"What if they just don't build another one?" I asked.

"All the better," he said. "Actually, Dr. Pederson, the guy who headed up that project, passed away a year or two ago. Maybe it isn't as important to anyone else. Which just makes things easier for us."

As we talked, we watched Oscar carefully load the Pederson electromagnet into its little cell. He shut the door and locked it with another palm print.

"What if this place lost power?" I asked. "If, say, Manos had been successful."

"There are backup systems, but . . . well, if all of this stuff was unreachable forever, it'd probably actually be a load off my mind."

Nate took me around the outside of the room, showing a few highlights of what lay behind the locked doors. Objects that were tiny, huge, and every size in between, all designed primarily for death or destruction. The collection included General Payne's giant laser, Hector's bio-mechanical armor, and a number of other examples of the awful things people could come up with, given enough time and insanity.

Oscar joined us as we made it around to section H. "Ah, H—the hocus-pocus," he said.

"Oscar doesn't believe in the supernatural," Nate said.

"And you do?" I asked, surprised.

"Let's just say I'm a supernatural agnostic. I've seen too many unexplainable things to write them *all* off."

"I'll do the writing off for the both of us," Oscar said. Nate showed me some of the items in section H, like a sword that seemed unnaturally sharp and shiny, a creepy clown doll, and a tiny music box sealed in a case made of inch-thick glass.

"What do they all do?" I asked.

"Nothing," Oscar said.

"*Maybe* nothing," Nate said. "But the people we took them from thought they'd do things. Some of them pretty horrible. That music box can supposedly let the person who's holding it control others' minds."

"I listened to it once," Oscar said. "I'm fine."

Jin walked over to join us, done checking on whatever she'd needed to. "You need a mind in there for someone to be able to control it, Oscar."

Nate shook his head, smiling. He turned to me. "Ready to head out? Or do you want to look at more?"

"Since I can browse through the inventory on a computer back home, I think I'm ready to see the sun again," I said.

We made our way out to the elevator, which carried us back to the upper level without a problem. I was glad I wouldn't have to climb the dozens of flights of stairs.

We backtracked through hallways and short stairwells until we made our way back up into the tiny concrete bunker. Nate locked everything behind us, and Jin drove us back out through the secret gate in the fence line. It was dinnertime when we got back to Fargo, but instead of stopping somewhere to eat, we grabbed pizzas and took them back to the airport so we could fly out that evening.

Nate brought a gluten-free pizza back for our pilot, another example of how the team cared for its people. Since I'd only joined up a few months before, I was still getting to know most of the workers (a lot of them preferred to be called minions or henchmen) on the island; there were just over three hundred people there, so it was still taking time for me to meet everyone. I hoped to one day be able to greet everyone by name and know a little something about their lives and interests, just like the rest of the team leaders.

It was an even longer trip from Fargo back to our island out in the Pacific, but the jet had a good supply of reading material and board games. Partway through the flight, Nate browsed the day's news on his tablet.

"Interesting," he said. "We're all over the news for stealing the Pederson electromagnet."

"Anything good?" Oscar asked, setting down his book.

Nate skimmed the story. "Originally stolen by Discordius, MIT lab, plans and research disappeared soon after. They have Manos in FBI custody, and Doctor Oracle is getting the credit for the steal."

"So nothing new." Oscar picked his book back up.

"Well, yes and no," Nate said. "Yes, it's all the same old news. But what's catching my eye is that there isn't a single mention of the first group that beat us there, or of the power supply that they stole. And there isn't anything about the guys who showed up after us either."

We each grabbed a tablet of our own and searched the news sites.

"This is so weird," Jin said. "It has to be a cover-up."

"Yeah," Nate said. "But why?"

FOUR

We got back to our home base around two in the morning and quickly loaded our stuff into the transport balls we'd plugged in to charge up when we left. The transport balls were similar to golf carts, but more like a round cabin mounted on three black rubber balls. They were amazingly agile, surprisingly fast, and a heck of a lot of fun to drive.

From the airstrip we drove around to the main campus, an old vacation resort that had been transformed into a bustling hive of industry and creativity years before I came along. We stopped on our way so Jin could drop off what we'd brought back—the bag full of miscellaneous wires and parts I'd removed from Manos's machine—at her workshop office. Then we all went back to the residential wing and went our separate ways so we could get some sleep in our own beds.

Or at least most of us slept in our own beds. Nate pinged my ChatterBox right after I got back to my little apartment to see if I wanted to sleep alone or not. I texted him to come over in fifteen minutes. That gave me enough time to take a searing-hot shower, throw on some comfortable pajamas, open the sliding doors in both the bedroom and living room to get a breeze, and pour two glasses of wine.

My front door slid open, and Nate walked in. We had access to each other's apartments, which were less than a minute apart at opposite ends of the top floor of the residential building. He was wearing pajama pants and a T-shirt with a cartoon of a pig with a halo and the slogan "Bacon Is My Co-Pilot" on it. When he wasn't being a master thief or an internationally feared supervillain, I'd learned that his wardrobe was mostly simple and comfortable.

We took the wine out to the balcony and stood side by side, looking at the nearly full moon over the ocean.

"Another good job," Nate said quietly. We didn't want to disturb any of my neighbors who might have left their balcony doors open for a breeze. We lightly tapped our glasses together.

"So, what's next?" I asked.

"Nothing big for a while," he said. "Several things are in development, but nothing's ready right now."

"Good," I said, looking back into my living room. "Maybe then I can tackle some of this mess."

I had a number of cardboard boxes stacked in my living room, which I hadn't yet had a chance to unpack. The contents were all from my old apartment in Seattle—nothing I needed urgently, but personal items and creature comforts I wanted with me. We'd been busy over the last few months, and unpacking always took a backseat.

I'd packed up those boxes when I made a clean break from my old life. I joined Doctor Oracle's team in an unorthodox way, in that I got injured while in my office at a software company called WonderPop. I found out later that they'd already had their eyes on me as a future recruit, so it isn't surprising that they took me to their own medical facility (a high-tech wonder) instead of a hospital. The problem was that they had to tell the world I'd been kidnapped by Doctor Oracle while I was recovering, and then kept the ruse going while I was discovering that the island and the organization were the places I was meant to be.

My return was a quiet affair at first; we sneaked back to my apartment, and I packed up the most important things (some clothes, a few childhood mementos, my roller skates, more than a few favorite books, and my video game console) and had them sent back to the island. Then we installed some hidden cameras around the apartment. Most of my furniture was left behind, but it was mainly hand-me-downs, and I didn't need any of it anymore.

The apartment remained mine, paid for by a series of untraceable shell companies owned by Predictive Solutions, one of the many branches under which Doctor Oracle did legitimate business.

After I cleared out everything I wanted to keep, Oracle sent out a press release that I'd escaped their custody. At the same time, I sent emails to my boss and her boss at WonderPop, letting them know that if they hadn't already terminated me, I was quitting. And that I was going into hiding because of the terrible ordeal I'd been through.

Our computer whiz, Evie, received email notifications whenever motion set off the cameras in my apartment, and she kept the rest of us updated. I had a number of visitors just after it was made public that I'd gotten free.

Representatives of one of the super groups, the Ultimate Faction, broke into my apartment several times that first few weeks, and for that first month I could almost always check the feed from the camera on the outer wall of the building to find someone on stakeout outside the apartment. I had actually been in the custody of the Ultimate Faction for two days at one point, though they didn't know (and still don't know) that I was a part of Oracle's team by then. I'm sure they thought I could be a great source of insider information for them.

But the apartment visits eventually tapered off, and we hadn't seen anyone in the last few weeks. I hoped they'd finally given up on me.

Nate and I finished our wine and headed back inside. I put the glasses in the sink and we headed to bed. We were both exhausted from our mission, so after a few kisses we opted to just snuggle down and get to sleep.

* * *

Despite getting to sleep after two, we were both awake around eight in the morning; when your body is wired to get up at the same time every day, it's hard to change. I knew I'd be taking a nap later in the day.

"I have some work to get done today," Nate said, stretching and wiggling his toes.

"I'm definitely going to tackle the rest of these boxes," I said.

"You got the packaging on that microchip done?" I could tell by his tone that he wasn't asking in any kind of official coworker capacity—more of a boyfriend asking about his girlfriend's job. I was glad for it—he always let me do my own thing with my work, the fledgling new Graphic Arts and Marketing Department. You wouldn't think a supervillain would have much to do with marketing, but we made a surprising number of gadgets and products that were released to the general public through another bunch of shell corporations. It's one of the reasons Doctor Oracle was so stinking rich.

"Done, and better than I thought it would be," I said. "Adrianne from the chemistry lab worked on part of it, as her audition to do some work for me. I was really impressed."

"Just don't steal her away from Elliot," he said. Elliot was the head of our science department and usually felt more at home in his laboratories than out in the field stealing things. He'd been on the team for my first jobs and had always done fantastic work, but for the most part he was just happy to let others wallow in all the adventure, while he found his own excitement at the bottom of test tubes and beakers.

"No worries," I said. I'd made arrangements with all the other department heads so that I could find a few people with artistic talent, then use them now and again on a sort of freelance basis. It worked for me, because I was still building the department from scratch and didn't have all that much work to do yet. And it was great for the freelancers: even though we didn't have a payment-based economy on the island, since all food and supplies were included, it was a great chance to step away from their regular jobs for a bit and stretch their legs with something new.

I kissed Nate good-bye, and he headed down the hall to his apartment. I took another shower, dressed for housework in a T-shirt and shorts, and started unpacking. My roller skates were already unboxed, and got quite a bit of use on various indoor surfaces, like our wood-floored gym and the smooth polished concrete in Jin's giant workshop.

I pulled out a bunch of books and arranged them on the bookshelves in the living room. Then I tackled a box full of clothing, things that were favorites I didn't want to part with, but I hadn't unpacked because they were really meant for the cooler climate of Seattle, not the year-round summer we had out in the Pacific Ocean. The clothes smelled a bit musty, so I dumped them in my laundry hamper so I could wash them later. There was a laundry service available, but I preferred to do my own. Laundry time was always good thinking-about-projects time.

Underneath the clothes, at the bottom of a box, was my gaming console. I'd taken a few turns on the old arcade cabinets down in one of the bars and played some racing and party games on Nate's console, but I hadn't played any adventure-based video games since I moved to the island. Probably because I was essentially living in a video game. I didn't need the vicarious excitement of playing when I was getting plenty of real-life thrills.

I hooked the console up to my TV and fired it up. It had the disc of the last game I'd played inside—a stealth game called *Secret Ninja II*. Despite my declaration that I'd definitely get all the boxes unpacked, I decided to take a break and see if I was rusty at playing.

Turned out I was, but the moves came back quickly. I knew I was near the end of the game anyway, and more than one person (Nate included) had told me that the ending was a real thinker, so I started into the final levels.

Two hours later, my little on-screen ninja and his organization had been disbanded, because of the betrayal of an outsider. The dramatic music and cut-scenes hit home the fact that the ninja had been part of a family, and he was now out on his own, perhaps never to see his little ninja family again. It made me think about the fact that I now considered the Doctor Oracle team to be my family. Then it made me think about the fact that the game developer had moved on to some crappy kids' title and had no apparent plans to make *Secret Ninja III.*

"Jerks," I said. I set the controller on the console. Then I looked at the whole setup, unplugged the console from my TV, and tucked it away on a bookshelf. I'd finally gotten that game out of my system and didn't really feel the need to play anymore.

As I worked on the next box full of books, I thought about my career so far with Doctor Oracle. After all, how exciting could a video game be compared to the things I'd done over the last few months? I'd visited several countries I never thought I would ever see. I took part in some really cool jobs, like that high-rise heist in Portland and the treasure hunt off the Florida coast. I was really able to plunge in headfirst and do a lot more jobs than I probably would have otherwise, because Jin got her ankle broken in a fight and Nate broke two toes while on a diamond heist. Things needed to get done, and I was ready and eager to jump in.

It helped that my department on the island was so small and so new. I didn't have to make excuses to my crew as to why I was leaving the island, because I didn't have a crew of my own. I was the easiest person to take anywhere, and I let the team know I was more than happy to let them take advantage of that fact.

After cleaning out another box, I decided to leave the last two for later in the day. Despite my early start, I'd been sidetracked by video gaming, and my stomach told me that it was time for a late lunch.

I went down to the food court on the ground floor and went for tacos, since I'd eaten really good pizza and a fantastic burger on the last mission. I sat and ate with a few of the computer techs; my new department did some work with them, so they were some of the first minions I'd really gotten to know. I couldn't tell them anything about the mission we'd just gone on, of course; as far as the minions were concerned, the eight department heads were just that. We kept them shielded from the knowledge that we were the ones out stealing and scheming; when we left the island, it was under the guise of boring business or seminars or conferences. They're all great people, and trustworthy enough to work for Doctor Oracle, but we wanted to keep up the mystique for all of them. Plus, not knowing the truth gave them all plausible deniability.

It was thought that they'd work harder for a shadowy figure they didn't see every day, that some of the allure would be lost if they knew that Nate, the person who portrayed Doctor Oracle in public, was the head of the administrative wing and was usually seen wearing a T-shirt with a joke about pop culture, the '80s, or meat products. We had a file full of psychological studies showing why the secrecy was better; I'd browsed through a couple, but scientific research really isn't my bag. Elliot, the head of the science labs, had explained it to me in much better layman's terms, for which I was eternally thankful.

After lunch, I headed over to my office in the administrative building. I didn't have any actual work to do as far as graphic arts, but I wanted to check in on a side project. Doctor Oracle had owned the doctororacle.com website for years, but nobody had really done anything ambitious with it. I knew a few things about web design, and enlisted some freelance helpers to work with me to freshen it up.

I added a blog and invited the department heads to contribute whatever they liked. Rupert, who rarely left the island to take part in a job (he was always more comfortable in his studio, working on new costumes, wigs, and prosthetics for assignments in the field), jumped at the chance to take everyone's articles and add just the right amount of evil flair. We all agreed that he had the perfect dramatic tone for blog posts that supposedly came from Doctor Oracle, so everything was filtered through him; then they were passed to me to put online. We'd been picking up the pace, posting a few times per week. There was never a shortage of things to write about—political issues, social issues, mocking things the supers did, and gloat notes about our own work. I made a note to see if Oscar wanted to write up our heist of the Pederson electromagnet, since the news was already giving us credit.

I browsed through some of the blog comments, a fascinating mix of supporters, opponents, know-it-alls, and a few trolls who liked to stir everyone else up. Really, it was the same as any other place on the Internet.

One short comment caught my eye, buried between a rant about how all evil must be banished and a fanboy writing out the top five reasons he should be considered for the job of Doctor Oracle's main henchman, on a post from a few days ago. All it said was, "I have a situation that may interest you." It was signed with the letters *LS*.

I went to the next-most-recent post, and there was another comment from LS: "Please contact me at your earliest convenience." Then on the post that was on the front page, from a few days ago: "I can make this worth your while."

All the comments were simple and really said nothing. But I was intrigued. I wondered if the mysterious LS had tried to contact us any other way. I took a deep breath and opened up the main doctor@doctororacle.com email box, which was even crazier than the comments on the blog.

I scrolled through hundreds of emails, looking for the initials LS. I opened up several possible messages, but they were full of rants and raves, nothing like the simple style of our mystery commenter.

I finally found the email I was looking for: the sender was lstarr@heromail.com. The fact that the sender was a member of HeroMail turned the intrigue up to eleven. You had to prove yourself as one of the good guys to get a HeroMail address.

I read LS's message. Then I read it again. Then I forwarded it to my own email address, called the message up on my tablet, and carried it down to Nate's office.

Nate looked up as I entered. "Hey," he said, smiling. "How's the unpacking going?"

"I took a break to check the blog, and read some emails." I put the tablet on his desk. "You're going to want to read this."

FIVE

Two days later, we held a meeting with all eight department heads in Nate's living room. Nate had me start things off. I told the group about how the blog comments had interested me and how I'd found the email in the bottomless pit we used as a public inbox.

"It wasn't much, but it really caught my eye," I said. "Especially because it came from HeroMail." I plugged a USB memory stick in the side of Nate's TV and used his remote control to bring the first email up on the big screen.

> *Doctor Oracle:*
>
> *I realize this message may seem strange, but I'd like to ask for your help. I've reached out to a number of the superhero organizations, and none of them is willing to assist me. Normally I wouldn't contact a non-hero, but it's my understanding that you never kill, and that you've been known to perform some beneficial acts. If you're interested in helping me save lives and avert a disaster, I have a reward that I hope would make it worth your while.*
>
> *Sincerely, Lucky Starr*

"That was the first message," I said. "We decided to respond and ask for more information, because we were both curious." I clicked on the remote to call up the second email.

Thank you for writing back.

I'm afraid I'm not comfortable discussing the details in writing. As you may have already guessed from my email domain, I'm not exactly on the same side of the law as you are. But I can assure you, the threat is real. I'd be more than happy to meet you or your representative at a mutually-agreed-upon location to discuss both the impending disaster at hand, as well as the reward I'm willing to offer you (information you might find quite interesting) and the ways I can be of assistance to you. I'm sorry to be vague, but I'm sure you can understand, considering that we play for separate teams.

Please let me know if you're interested in meeting.

Sincerely, Lucky Starr

"So . . . the disaster is what, exactly?" Oscar asked.

"We still don't know," Nate said.

"This totally sounds like a trap," Evie said. "I'd like to get my hands on those messages to check on the IP addresses and routing information."

"Absolutely," Nate said. "And yeah, it does sound like a trap. But on the other hand, if a super, someone good enough to get accepted as a HeroMail user, wants our help? That's a huge opportunity for us to get an insider on our side."

Jin's husband, Scar, cleared his throat. "It seems to me that if we can find the right neutral location, a meeting should be relatively harmless. We can assess the situation and see if it's something worth pursuing." We could always count on a sensible response from Scar, who was, for want of a better word, the concierge for our island operation. He kept everyone happy and everything running smoothly and always seemed to know the right things to say.

"Have you looked her up in the database?" Evie asked.

"Yeah" Nate said. I clicked the remote again, and a picture came up on the screen. "Lucky Starr, real name Lucy Culpepper.

She's been a member of at least seven different super groups that we know about but has never stayed more than two years with any of them. Right now, she's a free agent. We're pretty sure she's living back in her hometown: a little town north of Phoenix called Wickenburg."

"Seven groups or more?" I said. "Good gravy, I knew there were a lot of super groups out there, but I guess I didn't realize there were *a lot* a lot."

"Almost a hundred and fifty in the United States alone," Nate said. "And since some of the smaller states only have one group, that means larger states like California and New York have ten or twelve. Lucky Starr has been a member of groups in Arizona, New Mexico, Nevada, Utah, and California."

"It just seems like a high super-to-villain ratio."

"Yeah, but they don't just fight villains," Nate said. "They also keep busy going after your garden-variety crooks: the muggers and bank robbers and such."

I turned to look back at Lucy Culpepper, hero name Lucky Starr, on the screen. I'm confident enough in my looks that I can admit, she was beautiful. My mother, who was the same five foot six as me, had always said that she was too tall to be a jockey and too short to be a model. Lucy was both tall enough and gorgeous enough to be a model, with long, straight black hair and features that might have been too sharp and chiseled on someone else, but somehow suited her perfectly. The picture was from a promotional photo shoot with a group called the Southwest Storm; she was posed in a sleeveless coral-colored costume, with matching silky gloves that went to her elbows.

"Wow," Oscar said. He leaned farther in toward the screen. "*Wow.*"

"Right?" I said. "She's totally hot."

"You ain't kidding. Powers?" Oscar asked.

"Precognition," Nate said.

"Seriously?" Elliot turned to Nate and grinned. As the head of the science labs, he had an interest in both biology and chemistry, and had been studying the various mutations and incidents that caused superpowers to manifest.

"It isn't strong, according to our records," Nate said. "And there's something unusual about it that makes her powers not valued by the teams she's worked with. It isn't clear in any of the paperwork we could find."

"Weird," Elliot said, running his hand over his bald head in thought. "But I gotta say, if meeting her got us the chance to get a DNA sample, I'd love to study someone with mental powers. We've done a ton of research on the physical stuff, but we know so much less about the few people out there with mind powers."

"And we have no idea what reward she's offering?" Evie asked.

"Just that it's information," I said. "For all we know, it's all stuff we have in the database already."

"Here's the thing," Jin said. We all turned to her, as it was the first thing she'd said in the meeting. "We have nothing else really going on right now, and the next month is wide open. If you can find a neutral place to meet, I think the benefits of having a super in our pocket could be huge."

"I agree," Scar said, taking his wife's hand. "Plus, I know how antsy you get with nothing to do, Nate."

"We were thinking we could meet up at the Golden Mask, in Las Vegas," Nate said. "If she's living north of Phoenix, it should be pretty close and easy for her to get to. Rupert could throw together new costumes, and we'd blend right in."

"Who else makes up the 'we'?" Rupert asked.

"Sarah was the one who dug out this whole thing," Nate said. "So it'd be her first lead mission."

"Hell yeah," Oscar said. "I know you'll run a good mission, Sarah."

I felt my neck and face grow warm, and I knew I was blushing. "It's probably just a wild-goose chase."

"Even so, it'd be a great chance for you to put together some plans," Jin said. "Think of it as your master's thesis."

"A master's degree in evil scheming? That sounds a little beyond my skills," I said.

"Nonsense," Jin said. "We're all here for you, for support and advice."

"Remember," Rupert said, "even though Nate wears the outfit and does the voice, we're all technically Doctor Oracle here. Every one of us has run an operation, some successful . . . some not so much. And some of us just aren't that good at the planning part, even though we gave it our all." That kind of explained why Rupert didn't usually go into the field or lead missions, but his skill with creating costumes and disguises more than made up for it.

I looked around the room at the other seven people. Then I looked up at the picture of Lucy Culpepper on the TV screen.

"Okay," I said. "We'll do it." The rest of the team looked at me expectantly.

"Thoughts about our first steps?" Nate prompted.

"Nate and I will make arrangements to meet Lucy in Las Vegas, if she's cool with that. We'll find out as much as we can about her problem and about the reward she's offering. And if it isn't a complete boondoggle, we'll bring the information back here and get to work on a plan."

We brought the meeting to a close, and everyone fell into conversation. I looked around at the team, already thinking about who could do what in the possible mission to come. Elliot and Rupert were sitting on the couch, cracking each other up, a very odd pair of best friends: Elliot was tall, bald, and black, while Rupert was short, stocky, pinker than a flamingo, and his white hair and goatee made him look like a hipster Santa Claus. Even their specialties were miles apart, with Elliot involved in all things science, while Rupert was our master of costumes and disguises. Still, their friendship was more powerful than some marriages I've seen.

I looked over at Jin, who was talking with Scar and Evie. It was almost comical to watch her turn back and forth between them, looking up at her tall husband, then down at Evie, who was barely over five feet tall. Evie pulled out her tablet and tapped around on it to show Scar something, which appeared to surprise him. I was delighted as always that our most tech-savvy person was in her forties and probably knew more computer tricks than all the rest of us put together.

Jin saw me watching them and left Scar talking with Evie, coming over to the kitchen to join Nate and me.

"I like this," she said. "Seems like a nice, easy first mission."

"I hope so," I said. "It'll probably end up being nothing, but it'll be fun to work out a plan."

"Just promise one thing," Jin said.

"What's that?" I asked.

"Don't you two dare get married while you're out in Vegas and not invite the rest of us."

SIX

Nate and I took the jet to Las Vegas the day before our scheduled meeting with Lucy. We figured it would give us a chance to get the lay of the land, and I hadn't been to Vegas for almost a decade. I wanted to see how the city had changed.

Since this was now technically my mission, I'd taken over all communications with Lucy and had proposed the meet-up time and location. She had no problem with the plan we presented, and despite the brevity of her emails, I got the feeling she was relieved that representatives for Doctor Oracle were at least going to hear her out. Even if her problem turned out to be no big deal, *she* thought it was a big deal. And she was desperate enough to reach out to us.

We normally traveled through small municipal airports, because they usually offered more flexibility and fewer security hassles. For Vegas, however, we flew right into McCarran, the big international airport right at the end of the strip. Apparently it's a town that's used to private jets zipping in and out, with occupants who don't want to undergo a lot of scrutiny. At any rate, the steep fees we paid to rent a hangar kept us free and clear of any security.

We rented a car using fake IDs. Nate sometimes went by his own first name, but the driver's license he carried on the Vegas trip identified him as Ethan Wells from Portland, Oregon. My own license was for Beth Cartwright, also from Portland. Thanks to Evie's computer savvy, both Ethan and Beth had social security numbers, full credit histories, and credit cards. We also had plenty of cash, since paper money was the thing that really made Las Vegas run.

The place where we were meeting up with Lucy, the Golden Mask, was in the older downtown area, but we opted to stay in one of the high-rise hotels on the strip. I drove, because Nate hadn't spent too much time behind the wheel of a car in the last few years, especially since Jin joined the team as our head mechanic and getaway driver. I was grateful for the air-conditioning in the car, since the temperature was hovering right around a hundred. At least it was a dry heat. The guy at the rental car counter laughed when I said it was hot and told me that it was nothing; they'd just tied the city's record-high temperature earlier in the month: 117 degrees. Ugh.

I steered us down the strip, marveling at how even though a lot of the casinos had changed names or themes since I was last there, they overwhelmed the senses just the same—lights that dazzled even in the daytime, reflective glass everywhere, and tons of replica world landmarks. The skyline was always evolving and always impressive.

The afternoon traffic was crazy busy, and we crawled our way down the road. It took us at least ten or fifteen minutes to make it from one hotel to the next. The fact that each of the hotels was a gigantic monstrosity may have had something to do with it.

Finally, I turned onto the side street that led to the main entrance of the Bellagio. Given our pick of the hotels on the strip, we laughingly agreed that the site of *Ocean's Eleven* was the perfect place for us to stay. We let a valet park the car and checked in. They insisted on sending a bellman up with us, even though we'd only packed two small suitcases for our short stay. They looked sad and lonely on his giant luggage cart.

After tipping the bellman generously, we were left alone in our two-bedroom suite on one of the higher floors of the hotel. We were on the strip side, so we had a great view of tons of other hotels and the famous water show out in front of the Bellagio. I reminded myself, as I usually did in such situations, to make a note of how grateful I was for the lifestyle I was living. It would probably be easy to start expecting rock-star treatment, and I didn't want that to ever happen. I wanted to remember what it was like a few years ago, when I was eating ramen noodles at the end of the month because that was all I could afford and still be able to pay the rent.

I stood at one of the floor-to-ceiling windows that looked out over the strip. "Man, so much has changed, and yet it's all the same, isn't it?"

"How long has it been since you've been to Vegas?" Nate asked.

"About nine years. Some friends and I had birthdays all around the same time, so we flew down for a long weekend right after we'd all turned twenty-one."

"That reminds me," Nate said. "You do have a big birthday coming up."

"Indeed I do." I was less than two months away from turning thirty and was actually pretty happy about it. When I'd turned twenty-nine, I was in a job that I didn't see becoming a career, I had no boyfriend, I didn't socialize much, and I usually turned to video games to add some excitement to my life. The last six months had brought me an awesome new job, a great boyfriend, and a circle of friends I couldn't imagine being without—not to mention more excitement and adventure than any girl should be allowed to have.

"Have you thought at all about what you want for a birthday present?"

"I hadn't, really," I said. "Maybe I should start looking at some museum collections."

Nate laughed. "We could always buy you something. Though we're always open to stealing something, if that's what you'd like."

"We?"

"Well, yeah, the team knows the big three-oh is coming up, so they want to do something special for you. We all figured a surprise party is off the table, since none of us would really want one either."

I had to agree. In my opinion, a surprise party is more for the people throwing the party, so they get to feel not only generous, but like they did a splendid job keeping a huge secret from you. Most of us were somewhere on the introvert scale; it's part of why we were all happy to work as part of the secret team behind the Doctor Oracle figurehead. All the fun, none of the awkward personal recognition.

"We could just have a party in one of the bars back on the island. Or go to the bowling alley or something," I said.

"If that's what you want. Think about it."

"I will."

"And be warned, I will be watching and lurking to find something to get you myself."

"Such as?"

"We'll have to see," Nate said. "I might catch you staring longingly at something. Who knows?"

"Doofus," I said, and tossed one of the fancy brocade pillows from the fancy brocade couch at him.

Afternoon had turned into early evening, so we decided to hit the town. Or at least stroll up and down the strip a bit and visit some of the casinos, for some touristy gawking and people-watching. I swapped my sandals for good walking shoes, though I stuck with my lightweight T-shirt and shorts. We each tucked a few items in our pockets that most tourists wouldn't carry—a small Taser, retractable batons, and lightweight masks. We were relatively anonymous, since Nate's Doctor Oracle disguise looks nothing like him, but on the other hand, I'd been in the custody of the Ultimate Faction only a few months before, so those guys all knew exactly what I looked like. Better safe than sorry.

We wore special travel ChatterBox units, separate from the ones we wore while at home on the island. These were the same kind we took out on jobs, but these two could only be used to communicate with each other, with no links or information about anyone else in the organization. Like normal smart watches, they told the time and temperature, along with a few other generic functions that wouldn't put the wearer in jeopardy.

It was my first summer not living in Seattle, and it amazed me that the farther south you go, the earlier the sun sets in the summertime. A few days before, in Toronto, the sun had set around eight thirty. In Las Vegas, just a few days later, my CB told me that sunset would be a little after seven thirty. That gave us plenty of time to look around a bit in the daylight, grab some dinner, then enjoy the lights of the strip the way they're meant to be seen: in the dark.

We found a small sandwich place that sounded good for dinner. Because it was Vegas, the place was owned by a big-name celebrity chef, and the sandwiches were twice the price than any reasonable person would expect. Neither of us felt like going to a fancy-schmancy restaurant; it was nice that Nate's tastes were as simple as mine, especially since he'd grown up not just rich, but *rich-rich*, as the sole heir to the Hart Corporation.

As Doctor Oracle he'd become ten times richer, but he kept connected to his father's company, sometimes traveling to VIP events in his business disguise: the frumpier, dowdier version of himself. It was a brilliant plan—he wore disguises as both the reclusive owner of a worldwide corporation and a famous supervillain, so he was able to walk the streets unmolested when he was just being plain old Nate.

We walked down the strip, stopping in at several of the casinos to throw some dollars in the slot machines. Instead of taking coins, the machines had all been converted to accept bills only, and instead of a jackpot spitting out a bunch of loose change, the machines printed out a ticket with your balance on it. The new system took me by surprise, but then again, it had been almost ten years since I'd visited the city. And back then, I'd mostly played blackjack. And gotten drunk. At any rate, it was a much lighter load to carry dollar bills instead of rolls of quarters, which I appreciated.

It took almost as much time to walk from one casino to the next as it had taken to drive past them—traffic was still mostly bumper-to-bumper down the strip, and each hotel was a sprawling small city of its own.

As we made our way down the strip, the big casinos and hotels were thinning out, and smaller ones were interspersed with liquor stores and strip malls. We crossed to the other side of the road and headed back toward our hotel.

Nate pointed out one of the many, many small wedding chapels in Las Vegas, a place called Love's Chapel of Love. Like most of its ilk, Love's had a mishmash of décor out front, from Greek columns and cherub statues to giant neon hearts and bells. It reminded me of Jin's joke, that we weren't allowed to get married while we were in town.

"We could get married for your birthday," he said.

"Right here, sure," I said. "With a dozen Elvis impersonators for good measure. And maybe a Liberace or two."

"I'm serious," he said.

I stopped walking, and looked at him. "Is that a proposal?"

"Do you want it to be?"

I squinted at him. "I can't tell if you're joking or not."

He put his hands in his pockets and smiled at me.

I sighed. "Then no, Nate, I don't want that to be a proposal. What kind of proposal is that, anyway? Do you even have a ring?"

"I . . . uh . . . no, I don't." He looked down at the sidewalk, then back up at me with a grin. "But I bet I could steal one tonight."

"Even worse," I said, taking his hand and starting to walk again. "I mean, I know that stealing's totally your thing, but I would hope that you'd actually *buy* me a ring, if you were really serious."

"But that's so *easy*! Walk in, throw down some cash, walk out with a ring. I would think you would appreciate the work that would go into stealing your engagement ring, since you're leading this particular job. You'll see how much of a pain in the ass all of the planning can be."

"Look," I said. "I love you. You know that. But we haven't even known each other for a year. Hell, we haven't even known each other for six months. Everything's still so new and different. I don't think getting married would be the wisest move."

"We could just get engaged," he said. "One of those long, drawn-out engagements that make people wonder." He flashed me a sly half smile.

"Oh my God," I said, rolling my eyes. "Fine. If you ever get a ring, I'll let you propose."

"Would you say yes?"

"I guess you'll just have to wait and see, won't you?"

We walked on for a little while in silence, the topic stewing its way around my brain.

"Imagine the news coverage," I said.

"For what?"

"If we got married," I said. "Despite all of the disguises, you're a billionaire business owner. And I'm a nobody who was held hostage by Doctor Oracle. Someone would be sure to ferret that information out of some public registry somewhere, no matter how careful we were."

"Those would be some interesting headlines," he said.

"Plus, it would be a link between Doctor Oracle and Hart Industries. A small, weird link, but nevertheless, it could be just the crack in the organization that people need to figure the whole thing out."

"We could get married with fake IDs. Ethan and Beth could get hitched, no problem."

"That kind of defeats the purpose," I said. "Who wants a fake marriage?"

"We'd figure something out."

We were getting close to the Bellagio again. "Let's table this conversation for the time being, shall we?"

"Fine," he said. "But I just want it on the record that you're the one with cold feet."

We played a few slot machines on the way back through the Bellagio's casino and made a brief stop at the roulette table, where I made a surprising win when I put twenty dollars on the number four, since my birthday is October 4. The payout was thirty-five times my bet, sending me away with $700.

"I guess the rest of the trip is on you," Nate said as we rode the elevator up to our suite.

"I *am* feeling lucky tonight."

"Oh, are you?" He opened our door but left the lights off. They weren't really necessary anyway, since the room was lit by the glow of neon from the hotels across the strip and the fountain and light show going on outside the huge windows.

"How about you, Nate? Feeling lucky?" I kicked off my shoes and tilted my head toward one of the bedrooms.

"I don't know," he said. "Aren't we technically on a job? I'd hate to break the rules."

"As the leader of this particular job, I feel confident in saying that it doesn't *technically* start until tomorrow, when we meet our contact and find out if it's even a job we want to take."

"Well, as long as the boss is okay with it . . ."

"She is. Besides, as they say, 'What happens in Vegas stays in Vegas.'"

"Then by all means," he said, "I'm all in."

SEVEN

The next day, Las Vegas remained hot, gross, and fascinating. We had an amazing breakfast buffet, which was included in the exorbitant room price. After stuffing myself with bacon, eggs, pancakes, and two mimosas, I felt ready for either a vigorous exercise session or a hearty nap. Or both.

Instead, we went for a drive downtown. There were far fewer tourists around in the morning, and it wasn't as hot as it was going to get later in the day. We parked in the lot of one of the larger downtown hotels and headed out on foot to scout out the area. We played the tourist role as we went, depositing more dollar bills in slot machines here and there. Even though it was breakfast time, the big casinos were all open and eager to receive our money.

We covered a number of blocks in a grid pattern, just looking over our possible entry and exit routes should things go sour at the Golden Mask. Fortunately, there were plenty of alleyways and side streets in the downtown area. We walked past the front entrance of the Mask itself: a plain, unmarked doorway that was hidden away around a corner from most of the hustle and bustle of the regular tourists. It was closed in the morning, one of the few places in town that wasn't open twenty-four hours. We couldn't get inside until after six in the evening, unless we broke in.

Maybe some other time. For this trip, our visit was going to be on the level.

Satisfied that we knew where we'd park and what routes we'd take later that evening, we headed back to the Bellagio. It was around lunchtime, but neither of us was hungry after our enormous breakfast. We changed into our swimsuits instead and headed down to the pool.

We settled in to our curtained and shaded cabana, included with our suite, which gave us a bit of privacy. There was a fresh-fruit plate for nibbling and a refrigerator fully stocked with soft drinks, beer, and wine. In the shade, the heat didn't feel too bad. Because the air was so much drier, it felt cooler in Las Vegas at a hundred degrees than it had in July in Florida, with ninety-degree temperatures combined with 90 percent humidity.

Nate must have been thinking the same thing. "Not as bad as that treasure hunt, right?"

"I don't know if I'll ever want to go to Florida again," I said. "Certainly not in the summertime. That air felt like soup. But on the other hand, when it's this dry, I feel like I need eight pounds of lotion on my skin. If only everywhere was as perfect as home."

"We did find a pretty nice little island," he said. "And I'm always happy to hear you call it 'home.'"

I looked over at him. "We aren't going to get into another marriage discussion, are we?"

"Not until your cold little feet want to."

"All right, then," I said. I opened an ice-cold bottle of beer, promising myself to only have the one, since we'd be meeting Lucy in a few hours. "Tell me about the Golden Mask instead."

He sat up straighter in his lounge chair. "Okay, the Mask. You remember Chalmun's nightclub?"

"Where we were ambushed and had to leave through the secret tunnel out of the manager's office? And where your ex-girlfriend threatened to mess up my face for showing up with the great Doctor Oracle? How could I ever forget?"

"I'm telling you, Catalyst was never my girlfriend. She didn't even know my name, as you may well remember, since she called me Jeremy. Heck, she wouldn't even recognize me right now, since I was in full costume both times we went out. We just went on three dates, until I saw just how deep her crazy rabbit hole went."

"If she wasn't your girlfriend, maybe you shouldn't talk about her rabbit hole," I said with a laugh.

"Very mature." Nate rolled his eyes at me. "So Jimmy, the owner of Chalmun's, set it up for just villains. Which is why every year or two someone busts in there and tears the door off the joint, and they have to move to a new location. You'll be happy to know, by the way, that Jimmy reopened the club in San Diego. And I sent him that *Star Wars* action figure I promised him for letting us use his back exit."

I giggled again.

"Yes, that's right, I said *his back exit*," Nate said, lowering his sunglasses and raising an eyebrow at me. "My, you're an easy audience today."

"Breakfast mimosas, afternoon beer," I said. I put the half-finished beer aside. "You'd think I'd sweat the alcohol out as fast as I could drink it."

"At least you're a cheap date."

"With a less crazy rabbit hole, I hope," I said.

Nate just looked at me. "I'm not going near that comment with a ten-foot pole."

"Fair enough," I said. I leaned back in my lounge chair. "Do go on."

"So, back to the Mask. Unlike Chalmun's, the place has been around for *years*. Actually, decades, now that I think about it. It was opened sometime back in the early seventies, when downtown was the place to be and the strip hadn't been built up yet like it is now."

"So what makes it different? And how can they allow supers and villains and everyone else?"

"Instead of a likeable fellow who loves *Star Wars*, the Mask is owned by a guy who just calls himself the Legitimate Businessman."

I snorted. "Can I assume with a name like that, he's affiliated with some sort of mafia?"

"You assume correctly. So not only do you not want to mess with him on that side, he apparently has powers of some sort."

"What powers?"

"We have no idea. Even with our huge database, we don't know everything about everyone. That guy is just one of many gaps in our research—we've never even found out his real name."

"So nobody wants to mess with him?"

"Not anymore," Nate said. "Early on, some guys tried. And those guys ended up either permanently mangled or dead. Which is why, to this day, the Golden Mask is one of the few pieces of neutral ground in this weird shadow society we live in."

We took a swim in the pool, went up for a nap, and then had a late lunch at one of the hotel restaurants. We prepped all the gadgets and items we wanted to take to the meeting, and Nate gave me some pointers about what to look out for when leading a mission.

"Remember that you're the boss here. If you want me to take the lead in anything, just pass it off to me. I'm there to support you."

"I might take you up on that," I said.

"I'll be constantly scanning the room, but it's always smart to have everyone on the lookout for anything unusual. We'll try to sit so we're not side by side, so we can always see behind each other's backs."

"Got it."

"And most important, don't be afraid to just get up and leave if you think it's right. We're all taught from childhood that it's rude to interrupt or be abrupt, but trust your gut. If your gut says to get out, get out. I'll be right on your heels."

According to Nate, there was no official dress code at the Golden Mask besides the usual no shirt, no shoes, no service. We'd told Lucy that we'd be the couple in blue and that I'd have blond hair. Part of our prep time was spent getting me outfitted with one of Rupert's beautiful wigs. I put on a full face of makeup, which wasn't my usual look, but I'd learned enough basics from Rupert to be able to muddle through.

Nate wore a pair of navy cargo shorts with tons of pockets, each one holding a tool or gadget that might come in handy. He opted for one of his jokey T-shirts, a blue one with the Windows "blue screen of death" error text printed on it. I opted to go a little classier, and wore a sleeveless blue sundress with deep pockets. I had a purse with the strap slung across my body. The top compartment of the purse contained mundane things: a lipstick, a small wallet with my fake driver's license, and some cash for gambling. The secret pockets underneath held all the fun, including my Taser, my favorite multitool, and a coil of thin, strong rope. I buckled a small utility knife in a sheath around my thigh; I had to slap Nate's hands away while putting it on.

So far since we'd arrived in town, we'd been nothing but the perfect tourists. Now we were about to step into a place where we could actually meet up with some enemies. On one hand, Nate wasn't in costume, so even if someone overheard our conversation at the Mask, they wouldn't know he was Doctor Oracle; we were presenting ourselves to Lucy as Oracle's representatives. On the other hand, some guys out there would kidnap a supervillain's representatives just as readily as they'd grab the villain himself.

We attached safety devices to the car: a motion detector that would alert us if anyone touched the car while it was parked, and a small black box containing a tiny computer chip and an even tinier camera, which fastened to the rear window with a suction cup. I could see its display light in the rearview mirror. The computer chip analyzed the traffic patterns behind us, and the light changed from green to red if the device noticed another vehicle tailing us.

Of course, we kept on the lookout the entire time, too. But when you have a gadget that can back you up, use it.

The drive downtown was uneventful. We took a winding route of side roads all the way so we wouldn't have to deal with the traffic on the strip. The light in the back window stayed green, and neither of us spotted anyone following us. Not that we expected to be followed from the hotel to the Golden Mask; any real danger of a tail would come later, when we were heading back.

I pulled the car off into a side lot several blocks from our eventual goal, and we put on our masks. It was far enough from the casino that nobody attending that night would be around, but close enough that we'd only be driving a few blocks wearing masks, something that could make people nervous. Nate's mask for the evening was a deep shade of purple, in a style very different from the black mask he wore as Doctor Oracle. I stuck with the same type of mask I'd worn before in the field—bright blue, with feminine details.

The last time I'd worn that color mask, the club we were in got invaded by one of the super squads, we barely made it out the back way, and I'd given myself up to the supers so that Nate could get away. It helped that at the time, the supers thought Doctor Oracle was holding me hostage. As far as I knew, they still didn't know I was working for Oracle's team. I didn't want to be superstitious after just one wearing of the mask, because I loved the color, so I was giving it another chance.

We parked the car in the public lot we'd chosen earlier, the one with multiple exits onto multiple roads. I backed in for an even easier time getting out. I flipped down the visor and checked my makeup in the mirror, then pulled out the bright-red lipstick and put on a fresh coat. Nate went over the inventory of gadgets in his pockets, and I made sure I knew where everything was in every compartment of my purse.

I locked up the car, and we headed around the block toward the main entrance of the Golden Mask. I thought we'd stand out since our faces were disguised, but the street was mostly empty. We were only a block and a half down from Fremont Street, the main drag in downtown Las Vegas, but none of the tourists were taking chances walking too far off the beaten path.

The front door of the Mask looked pretty much the same as it had earlier in the morning, except now that it was dark out, a single light was shining on the door. Otherwise, there was no way to know that the place was open. You had to know it was there to know it was there.

Nate knocked on the door, and a small panel opened. I could barely see someone's eye looking out at us.

As the leader of the job, it was on me to say the password. Nate had asked around for it from a few sources who were regulars at the Mask and were on friendly enough terms that they wouldn't immediately swoop down to Las Vegas in order to get revenge.

"Sweet-potato pie," I said.

The little panel closed, and the door opened. The person who had been looking out at us stood in the doorway. I was surprised that it was a woman, but she was definitely a woman I didn't want to mess with: well over six feet tall, with more muscles than I even knew existed on a person, male or female.

"Cash only, no credit," she said.

"No problem," Nate said. The woman stepped aside so we could enter. We passed her by and walked down a short hallway toward a set of double doors inset with frosted glass panels. Whatever was on the other side of those doors was well lit and had to be a more pleasant place than this tiny entrance hall.

As opposed to when we visited Chalmun's, the villain nightclub, there was no coat check and there was no weapon check. We were free to carry in anything we wanted to, and the threat of the Legitimate Businessman was apparently enough to keep everyone in line. It made me even gladder we weren't breaking into the place.

We pushed the double doors open, and I was surprised at the casino that lay beyond. Almost every other casino we'd seen so far was a semidark, cavernous room full of flashing neon lights and tacky décor from years or decades gone by. This place was the exact opposite in almost every way. It wasn't garishly bright, but you could see everything clearly. Instead of one huge room, there appeared to be several side rooms where you could go to play the games of your choice. There was a large restaurant and bar off to the side, and everything was done in a clean, modern style.

If his casino was anything to go by, I kind of liked this Legitimate Businessman guy. At least he had taste.

We were a half hour early for our meeting with Lucy, so we took a slow stroll around. Everyone wore some sort of mask, ranging from those just covering the eyes to a number of people in full helmets, including a beautifully made Boba Fett replica. That alone would have made the people-watching amazing, but the lack of dress code meant that people wore things as casual as a T-shirt and shorts or as formal as a tuxedo or ball gown. It was a crazy mishmash, and it took all my willpower to not gawk.

I didn't see Lucy on our stroll, but for all we knew she would be visiting us in disguise. We made our way around past all the gaming areas and ended up in the bar area, our appointed meeting place. The modern design continued in there, with lots of glass shelves and underlighting. We settled in and ordered soft drinks.

"Nice place," I said.

"Much nicer than a lot of the other neon festivals we've seen here," Nate said.

"I've been wondering about a casino for supers."

"How so?"

"Well, how can they be sure the supers won't use a power to cheat?"

"Good question," Nate said. "But think about the powers we know about—they're almost all physical. Someone with superstrength like Commander Alpha, what's he going to be able to do? Rip the cash box out of a slot machine? That would be very unwise in this place."

"Are there really so few people with mental powers?" I asked.

"New ones pop up now and then, but they're in the vast minority. Elliot thinks with the DNA changes he's seeing, we'll have way more people with full mental abilities in ten years or so."

"What about Firewolf? He can light fires. Isn't that . . ." I searched for the word. "Pyrokinesis?"

"Not exactly. He makes the fire on his skin, usually his hands. So it's some sort of spontaneous combustion happening to him physically. We think."

"Yeesh. This is a crazy world."

"Truth."

We sipped our drinks and looked around and waited for Lucy. At five minutes to eight, I saw her come in through the double doors. There was no mistaking her, as she looked exactly like the photo we had on file. Long, straight black hair, about as tall as Nate, and wearing a formfitting dress the same color as the uniform in her file photo: a flattering shade of coral. Her mask was the same shade and looked perfect against her skin.

"My goodness, she really is *that* beautiful," I said. Nate just turned to me, put his hand on my knee, and kissed my cheek. It was a nice gesture of reassurance.

Lucy came straight over to the bar and looked around, spotting us right away. We were the only couple in the area both dressed in blue, so we were pretty easy to spot. We both stood up to meet her.

As she approached us, she tugged at one hand with the other. I realized that she was wearing beige cotton gloves. I hadn't really noted them when I first saw her; I was already used to seeing plenty of people wearing lightweight cotton gloves in Las Vegas, to keep their hands clean as they dealt with cash, one of the filthiest things we touch every day. She took one off and reached out her bare hand toward me, smiling. She shook my hand. "Beth," I said.

She turned to Nate and they shook. "Ethan," he said.

"I'm Lucy," she said as she put her glove back on. "But I'm sure you know that already. You don't need to use fake names with me, but I understand why you feel it's necessary."

She sat down across from us with the same serene smile on her face, while I stood there startled by her absolute confidence about our names. I realized that while I was used to supers with physical powers, someone with mental powers was in a whole different league.

EIGHT

I couldn't tell if Nate was as weirded out as I was by the fact that by merely shaking our hands, Lucy had known we were lying about our names. Whatever he felt, he hid it well. We sat back down in our seats.

"I'm so glad you were willing to come and hear me out," she said.

Since I was the boss on this mission, I took the lead. "We'll listen to what you have to say with open minds, then report back to Doctor Oracle."

"I expected as much," she said. Her brow furrowed. "I only hope I can get across to you how serious this situation is and that he'll see how important it is that he help me."

That was a relief, in a way. Either she was a great actress, or she hadn't somehow figured out when shaking Nate's hand that he was actually the person everyone knew as Doctor Oracle.

"Oracle is a reasonable man," Nate said. "If help is genuinely needed, he may be able to arrange something."

"I hope so." Lucy shook her head sadly. "Nobody else will take me seriously."

A cocktail waitress came up to our table. Nate and I ordered fresh soft drinks, while Lucy ordered a glass of wine. I'm sure Nate wanted to get to the nitty-gritty of Lucy's problem, but her order intrigued me.

"I'm sorry if this is intrusive," I said. "But you have me interested. You're sitting down with representatives for a well-known supervillain, and yet you're willing to let your guard down by drinking alcohol. You already don't strike me as foolish, so I'd like to know why you're so comfortable with us."

She smiled again. "Let me ask you this. You already know some things about me, correct?"

"Yes," I said, not getting into how much of her history we knew.

"I've never really been that secretive about my past," she said. "Primarily because nobody has seen my powers as much of a threat. Or much of a help, really." The cocktail waitress brought by our fresh drinks, and Lucy took a sip of her wine. "My name is Lucy Starr Culpepper, but since I was a baby, my parents called me Lucky Starr."

"Were they Asimov fans?" Nate asked.

"No, but my mother was really into Madonna."

"Asimov?" I asked, looking at Nate. "As in *I, Robot*?" I was familiar with some of his work, but clearly there was a gap in my pop culture knowledge.

"He wrote some young-adult sci-fi stuff in the fifties with a hero named Lucky Starr," he said. "I think I have one of the paperbacks I can loan you later."

"Cool."

Lucy laughed. "I like you two already."

"Go on," I said. "Your mother nicknamed you after a Madonna song."

"Yes, she did. But the nickname was for another reason. According to her, even when I was a baby, I was incredibly lucky. Never sick with any of the stuff other kids caught. One time, she was about to put me down on a blanket and I screamed. She lifted up the blanket to show me that it was harmless, and a scorpion ran out from underneath. And that's just one of the small brushes with danger that I always seemed to just *know* about."

She sipped her wine again before continuing. "Once I started walking and talking, I was able to articulate the feelings I got. I don't get pictures in my head about things or see the future in any concrete way. But I feel emotions when I touch things. It was by following the good emotions, and steering clear of the bad ones, that I was so lucky."

"So you touch something, and what? Get happy, or sad, or scared?"

"Basically, yes. Though sometimes it's a range of emotions, and it can be hard to figure out what exactly they mean. I've been this way for thirty years, and some feelings still confuse the heck out of me."

"The gloves help to block your power," Nate said.

"Yes, they do," she said. "But I wanted to know if I could trust you, so I took my glove off to shake your hand. That's how I knew you were using fake names; I felt a twinge when you said those names. But those brief feelings were just blips in a sea of relief and trust, which I felt as soon as I saw the two of you, and grew much stronger when we shook hands. Every part of me is telling me that you're going to help. Thus, the glass of wine."

"That's amazing," I said.

"Thank you," she said, smiling. "Very few people seem to think that."

"Seriously?"

"Seriously. If you've researched me, as I suspect you have, you may know some of this, but I've been a member or conditional member of eight different super groups. I quit two, was let go from five, and one disbanded. The ones that let me go never really figured out how to use my powers, and as for the rest, well, life's too short to work with jerks."

I leaned back in my seat and thought about it, then repeated, "They never figured out how to use your powers."

She smiled and raised an eyebrow but said nothing.

"But *you* know what your powers can do," I said. "Surely you've tested their limits."

"Of course," she said. "That's how I know the threat I'm bringing to you is real."

"And yet you've taken the information about this threat to, what, the five groups that weren't jerks?"

"Plus a number of other groups where I have contacts."

"Then I don't understand why they won't listen to you."

"Because nobody trusts mental powers," Nate said. We both turned to him. "The question is, did they ever *ask* you to show them the extent of your powers, the range and scope of them that you'd figured out for yourself?"

"They did not," she said, beaming. "And that's the problem with all of them."

"Since you know that we've read up on you, I'll tell you how you were classified by at least one of those groups," he said. "Mental powers: limited precognition. That's it. That's the extent of your listing."

"And that's why they never knew what to do with me. I've always tried to explain what I can do, but it's hard to get across. Some of them wanted me in some sort of isolation so I could shout out predictions to them, like in that film *Minority Report*. One group even threw around the idea of building me a tank to float in."

"Okay, that's creepy," I said.

"It sure was. Those were some of the jerks. They were pretty cruel about the fact that emotions are involved; I heard more than one guy comment about how every single woman has stupid emotions, so why should mine be any different. As soon as they proposed the tank, I let them know that it just doesn't work that way and got the hell out."

"So tell us, Lucy," I said, "how *does* it work?"

"I'm glad you asked. I can get general feelings about things by just being near them, but my power really activates when my bare hands are touching something. It doesn't need to be a person; it can be an inanimate object. When I'm touching something, I feel either an emotion or combination of emotions, and then have to interpret what those emotions are telling me. Sometimes it takes several exposures to be able to truly form a picture of what my feelings are trying to tell me."

"Like you felt you could trust us when you shook our hands."

"Exactly. But humans can be complicated—with a lot of people, yourselves included, I feel a lot of different things all at once. My best source for information is one that I learned to use very early: the printed word."

"It's easier to understand?"

"Usually, yes. When I was a child, my father would take me to the racetrack down in Phoenix. All I had to do was run my finger down the list of horses' names and tell him which one made me happy. We didn't go often and we didn't go crazy, so they never caught on. My father was sensible about that, and he didn't get greedy. But it's thanks to those trips, and a few up here to Las Vegas, that my college education was paid for by the time I was thirteen.

"Newspapers, magazines, books, even the Internet can help me *see* the future in my limited way. Because news stories and articles are usually so specific about just one thing, there isn't a lot of other detail in there to get muddled up. And if I do get confused feelings about one story, I can find other stories about the same subject matter, written in different ways, to try and figure out what part of the story is the part I react to."

"Incredible," I said.

"Thank you."

"So this is how you've come across the situation you want Doctor Oracle to help with?"

"Yes," she said. "But now that I've told you that my power can be a bit vague at times, you may understand another reason why everyone else has laughed me off. Because right now, I'm getting very, very bad feelings about a specific thing. But I can't tell yet what's going to happen with that thing, and I can't tell you *when* it's going to happen. All I know is that it's going to be big, and it's going to be awful. I have a worse feeling about this than I did when that tidal wave hit Australia two years ago." I remembered that disaster; hundreds of people died.

"We're all ears," Nate said.

"The thing that terrifies me is a combined energy plant and water reclamation system that's being built out in the desert.

From what I've read, they found a volcanic area and are digging a deep shaft, with the goal of reaching or getting near a pocket of magma. They're also digging down to reach groundwater—we may be relatively dry on the surface here in the Southwest, but there are massive underground aquifers full of water. If those could be tapped, it would help millions of people." She paused to drain her glass of wine and patted her mouth with a cocktail napkin. We nodded to show that we were following her.

"The system will be two parts, working symbiotically. The groundwater meets the magma, which causes it to turn to steam. The steam is funneled up to the surface, where it can be used to create electricity. They've been successful with a similar system in Iceland, so they know it can be done. Then, as the steam cools, the water condenses aboveground, so it can be used for drinking water and irrigation."

"That's kind of brilliant," Nate said.

"I agree," Lucy said. "And normally, I'd be all in favor of it. But every story I read about the project fills me with complete and utter dread, the likes of which I've only felt a couple of times before."

"But you don't know what part of the project is the problem?" I asked.

"Not yet. But it should just be a matter of more research. The more news stories and articles I find that give me that same feeling, the more I can narrow down what exactly is going to happen, and when."

Nate tapped his finger to his chin. "You're sure this thing, whatever it is, can be stopped? Could it be that you have such strong feelings about it because it's destined to happen, no matter what?"

"Everything can change," Lucy said. "That I've learned. What did they say in *Star Wars*? 'Always in motion is the future,' something like that. I've learned to only take events as hard fact once they've already happened and are safely in the past." The fact that she was quoting *Star Wars* bumped her up even higher in my esteem.

"I can see why the supers didn't take you seriously," I said. I looked at Nate, who nodded. "But to be honest, Doctor Oracle is between projects right now, and I'm sure he'll be interested in helping with whatever he can."

For having a superpower involving emotion, Lucy wasn't very good at hiding her own—she practically sagged in her chair with relief. She reached into her pocket and pulled out a USB thumb drive.

"Here are all of the news articles that have triggered me so far," she said. "There's one on there you may have seen already, as it's about a recent theft from some guy called Manos."

"We're familiar with it," Nate said, smiling.

"The odd thing is, it gave me mixed feelings: the same dread as the digging project, combined with a feeling of hope. That's why I knew I'd done the right thing by getting in touch with you."

"Why did it give you the dread?" I wondered.

"Possibly because you're going to be involved in stopping it," she said. "Or there's some other aspect that I haven't figured out yet. I'll continue researching so that I can figure out more of the details."

I reached out for the thumb drive, and she put her gloved hand over mine.

"You haven't asked about the reward I offered," she said.

"You're right," I said. In truth, I was so fascinated by her powers and the problem she wanted us to solve, I'd forgotten about the promise of a reward. "I suppose I should find out what it is, to see if that will sway Doctor Oracle one way or the other."

"That drive also contains a very small portion of the information I've been holding on to, from one of the organizations that I belonged to. For all I know, this is all information you already have, but I picked out some things that I thought might interest you."

"That's . . . a little bit evil," I said. "Stealing information from your employer?"

"The way they treated me was a little bit evil, too," she said.

Nate leaned forward. "What did they do to you?"

"A lot of very unpleasant things," she said. She took a deep breath and let it out slow. "We're here in Las Vegas because it's a place I can drive to. I don't fly, because I have fairly severe anxiety. That's why every group I've belonged to has been within driving distance of my home. Somehow driving my own car doesn't trigger a panic attack, maybe because I feel like I'm in control.

"With all of the groups I've belonged to, I've tried to avoid going into the field, spending my time instead behind a safe wall of books and research materials. Most people just didn't understand and thought I was either dumb or somehow unhinged for not wanting to charge out into the unknown where I knew I'd have a panic attack."

"I get it," I said. I'd known more than a few people with anxiety, depression, and a host of other mental disorders. I'd worked in a creative field, after all. It occurred to me that mental illness and creativity often went hand in hand. "Trying to tell someone with anxiety to stop worrying about things, especially things they know for a fact will trigger their anxiety, is like trying to tell someone with a broken leg to stop limping. It just can't be helped."

"Exactly," she said. "So, anyway. The group I was with was called the Nightsiders, led by a guy named Nimbus. I'd disclosed my diagnosis and medication needs on all of the application forms, but I guess nobody really looked at those. It wasn't until they bullied me into going out on a mission and I had a panic attack in the back of the van that it was really out in the open. At first, there were just some mean-spirited jokes. But then Nimbus decided that I was soft and weak and that he'd toughen me up. He took away my medications and told me they weren't necessary, that I'd 'get over it' soon enough. Then he made me go on every field mission for two weeks straight, even though every one ended with me curled up in a corner, a crying mess."

"Seriously?" I said.

Lucy nodded. "The team wasn't united, and a number of them felt really bad for me, but nobody felt like they could go against Nimbus. And he was one of those leaders with enough charm to make you see past the abuse he heaped on almost everyone."

"How did you get out of that group?" Nate asked.

"Nimbus died," she said.

"Oh," I said. I couldn't think of anything else to say.

"The group disbanded almost immediately; without Nimbus, there was nothing else really holding them together. Most of the equipment was slated to either be split up among a bunch of other hero organizations or sent to the junk pile. So while I had full access, and was a full member of the Nightsiders, I copied everything I could find in the database. I stayed away from organized groups for a while after that. The Southwest Storm invited me in a few months afterward, and I gave them a try. But once again, they had no idea what to do with me."

I thought about her story for a minute, then asked the obvious, awkward question. "Did you know Nimbus was going to die?"

"I did," she said. "And he did, too, because I told him several times. Though I'm not sure he ever believed me, or at least he didn't until just before it happened. So if we are going to work together, I hope you'll be smart enough to listen to me when I have a feeling."

"You can count on it," I said. I put the thumb drive away in my purse.

She looked at the drive as I put it away. "Even with everything I went through, it's hard to justify stealing that information. But at the time I had full and legitimate access to all of it, and I figured it was probably going to be scrapped anyway. I had a gut feeling that it would come in handy someday, and believe me, I *always* trust my gut feelings. At the time I took it, I figured I'd end up using it for blackmail."

"You don't have to justify yourself to us," I said. "We're bad guys. We steal things all the time."

We sat back in silence for a moment. She'd hit us with a lot of very personal information in a short amount of time, and it was a lot to take in. It was true, she didn't have to justify stealing things to us, but it was kind of nice to know that she had a good reason to go against her hero nature.

"So," she said, "please let me know as soon as the Doctor has made his decision. Is there anything else I can tell you?"

"If it isn't too much trouble," I said, "I wonder if you could show us a bit more of a demonstration of your powers? Just so we know how to describe things to the Doctor."

"It would be my pleasure," she said. "This is actually the perfect place. Let's visit the slot machines."

We stood up and headed toward the gaming areas. On the way, she put her gloved hand on my arm.

"I should let you know," she said, "though you'll find out when you look at my research. There's one other big reason the super groups didn't want to hear my warnings: there are rumors that several of them are investing in and helping to operate the digging."

NINE

Lucy led us to the cashier cage near the slot machines. She exchanged pleasantries with the young man behind the counter, then asked to see Sam. The young man made a call, and a minute later, a tall, thin woman in an impeccable suit walked through a door at the back of the cashier area. She grinned broadly when she saw Lucy.

"Hey, Lucky! How goes it?"

"Things are going well, Sam. Thank you."

"The usual, Tito?" Sam glanced at us.

"Yes, please," Lucy said. Sam opened a drawer, pulled out a white paper ticket about the size of a credit card, and slid it across the counter toward us.

Sam looked at me and winked. "Good luck." She chuckled to herself and went back through the mystery door. Lucy grabbed the ticket and led us over into a deserted corner of the slots section.

"That was . . . strange," I said. "Did she just call you Tito?"

Lucy laughed. "No, that's an acronym. It stands for 'ticket in, ticket out.'"

"Oh, okay," I said. "No more coins in the slot machines."

"Not for a few years," Lucy said. "We have a shorthand, Sam and I, for when I'd like to show my powers to someone. I'm sure you know this place is run by someone you don't want to cross."

"I've heard."

"Well, I have something of a special arrangement with the management. They let me have the run of the slots; I just have to return everything that comes out of the machine to them. In exchange, I'll sometimes deal or sit in on table games for them, to catch cheaters."

"So it sounds like they appreciate your talents here," I said.

"They do, but house detective seems like more of a hobby than a career."

She set up in front of one of the dollar slot machines and put the ticket in. The digital readout went from zero to one hundred, so we had a hundred bucks to play with.

"May I try the machine first?" I asked.

"Please do," she said. "You're one of the few who have asked to do that. Wise, to make sure it isn't rigged." She pulled a spare pair of cotton gloves out of her purse and handed them to me. I didn't have to ask what they were for; even though the filthy coins had been taken out of the equation, the machines were still grubby from all the hands that touched them.

I put the gloves on and tapped on the "Bet One" button. It was a hybrid machine—you could still call it a "one-armed bandit," because it had a pull arm on the side, but it also had a full set of modern push buttons on the front. I opted for the arm, betting and pulling it at regular intervals, then at irregular intervals. I had a few small wins, but mostly losses. I felt convinced that, unless there was someone behind the scenes triggering jackpots, the machine had roughly the same odds of winning as any other slot machine we'd played since arriving in Vegas.

"Now, I'll play with the gloves on," she said. She tapped on the betting button and pulled the handle a few times, with roughly the same rate of return as I'd had.

"All right," I said. "I feel pretty secure that this machine isn't rigged."

"Then I'll take my glove off. I'll wait for a good feeling, then hit the 'Spin' button. I do like the arm, but the button gives a much faster response." She tapped the "Bet One" button five times, the largest amount you could bet. Our original stake of a hundred dollars was down to seventy-three, and I wondered if we'd have to pay back the hundred to the casino if we lost it all.

Lucy slid her right glove off and rested her hand gently on the "Spin" button, ready to press. She closed her eyes and took a deep breath. After a moment, she twitched and pushed the button.

"Not a huge jackpot, but pretty good," she said as the wheels spun around. The machine had a fruit theme, and we watched as the three spinning reels landed on an apple, an apple, and a third apple. A bell in the machine clanged, and it made a digital beeping sound as the counter showing our credits went from seventy-three up to ninety-three. Without the sound of coins clinking into a tray at the bottom of the machine, it felt almost more like a video game than gambling. Since I loved video games, I was totally cool with it.

She placed another five-dollar bet, rested her fingers on the button, and closed her eyes. She twitched but didn't spin the reels yet. I looked up at the lighted display that showed the payouts. The best possible result on this particular machine was three sets of cherries.

Without a twitch this time, she pounded on the "Spin" button. She opened her eyes and grinned at me. "That one felt really good. Maybe cherries good."

The reels spun, and landed one by one. Cherries, cherries, and cherries. The machine gave out a more enthusiastic whoop, with more clanging bells, and the credit counter beeped fast and furious, adding two hundred more dollars to our total.

"That's . . ." I searched for words.

"Amazing," Nate said. "Incredible."

"Thank you," she said. "Now, Beth, would you sit in front of the machine?"

"What are you going to do?"

"I've shown you how I can feel my own luck. But I want to show you how it works with other people, how I can feel when *you're* going to be lucky."

We swapped places, and I sat in front of the machine. I pressed the "Bet One" button once, then figured, *What the hell,* and pressed it four more times to place the maximum bet. "Do I need to take the gloves off?"

"No," she said. "All I'm going to do is rest my hand on your arm. I'll tell you when to spin."

"Okay," I said. She lightly rested her fingertips on my bare shoulder.

"Please try to clear your mind of any strong emotions. They can cloud what I pick up from you." She glanced at Nate, then looked back at me, and one of her eyebrows twitched. Great.

I took a deep breath, let it out slowly, then rested my hand on the "Spin" button. I figured I didn't need to look at anything in particular, since she was just going to tell me when to push, so I looked at a label stuck to the machine that told the world when the machine had last been inspected by the gambling commission. I tried hard to concentrate on nothing in particular, then worried that I was concentrating too hard on not concentrating and might throw her off.

"Now," she said, and I pushed the button. The reels spun around. "You're a good conduit. This is maybe not as good as cherries, but it's going to be decent."

The reels stopped on three plums, causing the machine to have another jangling celebration, and more credits appeared on the machine. We were over $300, and I was suddenly glad that we didn't have to deal with coins, since they'd be a heavy and dirty load to deal with in comparison to a little paper ticket. We repeated the whole thing, and once again, I had a moderate win.

"Would you like to try?" She looked at Nate.

"Hell yeah, I would," he said. I switched places with him, and he rolled up his sleeve so she could touch his arm. He got three plums again; then on his second try, he'd barely placed his bet and put his hand on the button when she told him to spin.

"Sorry, but it was a good one. I had to take advantage of it."

The reels spun, and again, three sets of cherries appeared. The old slot machine had hit six good payouts in a row, an astronomical feat. The jangling bells were starting to sound a little tired, and we had over $600 in credits on the machine.

I didn't know about Nate, but I was convinced that her power was something real. And I was more than a little spooked, since it was the first mental ability I'd ever come into contact with. I pressed the "Cash Out" button and retrieved the ticket the machine gave us, and we went back to the cashier cage. Sam was there waiting for us, smiling.

"Cool, isn't it?" she asked.

"Unbelievable," I said as I slid the ticket back to her.

"Believe it," she said. She looked over at Lucy. "I'd bring her in full time if she'd let me."

Lucy blew Sam a kiss, and we walked back toward the bar. I stopped in the restroom on the way back, since my hands still felt grimy even though I'd been wearing gloves. After a thorough wash, I rejoined Lucy and Nate at the same small table we'd sat at earlier, just as he was thanking her.

"So," she said, "any other questions?"

"I can't think of anything," I said. I looked to Nate.

"One thing," he said. "You said you got a hopeful feeling when you read an article about Doctor Oracle's theft up in Canada, but that article came out *after* you first tried to contact him. What made you decide to try him in the first place?"

"He always gets results," she said. "Plus, the whole not killing thing is a real draw."

"Good to know."

"You know," she looked at him with a strange expression. "Doctor Oracle could be a good guy, if he wanted to."

"Nah," Nate said. "Enough of the goodies hate him by now. He wouldn't get invited to any of the cool parties."

We shook hands and promised that we'd be in touch as soon as Doctor Oracle made his decision on whether to help her. Nate and I left and walked down the deserted street to our car. We looked the car over on the outside, then checked on Jin's gadgets we'd set up inside. The car hadn't been touched since we left it.

I drove us back to the Bellagio, taking another roundabout route. The side streets were quiet, there was nobody behind us for much of the drive, and the camera mounted in the back window didn't detect anyone following us. But I'd learned my lessons well and drove as if I was being followed anyway. It was a good habit to get into and let me practice a few evasive maneuvers.

We didn't talk much in the car, both lost in thought. Once we got back to the hotel and into our suite, we collapsed on the couch and sat in the dark, looking out the giant windows at the lights of Las Vegas.

"That was something," Nate finally said.

"It sure was. It was like . . . this one time, I saw a magician do a show up close. Sleight-of-hand stuff. He took a regular metal fork, shook it in front of me, and the tines spread out like a bird of paradise. The rational part of my brain knew it was a trick, and he'd probably spent years perfecting it. But the other part of my mind was freaked out, because I just couldn't understand how it could possibly be done."

"Unsettling."

"Exactly," I said. "That's how she made me feel. Off-balance."

"I've heard of a few other people with mental abilities," Nate said. "But this was the closest I've ever gotten to one. Man, Elliot will love to learn about her."

"What, are you going to ask her for a blood sample so he can study her DNA?"

"Hopefully, this will do," he said. He reached into one of the cargo pockets of his shorts and pulled out a cocktail napkin. "It's the one she wiped her mouth with. There's DNA on there he can use."

"Wait a minute," I said. "She came to us for help, generously gave us a demonstration of her powers, and you stole this so we could study her?"

"Just so you know, even though I'm excellent at stealing things, I didn't steal *this* particular thing," he said. "While you were in the bathroom, I asked if I could take it."

"And she was fine with that?"

"Seemed that way," he said. "She even asked for a copy of any results we found."

"Huh," I said.

"That's what I was thanking her for when you came back."

I looked at him, then at the napkin. "You *could* have stolen it, though."

"Not without the okay of my team leader. This is your operation; you decide what gets stolen. I only asked for it because I know how crazy Elliot gets for DNA samples of the supers. I didn't expect you to know that, and I figured it would be awkward for me to ask you to ask for it."

"Ugh," I said. "This team-leader thing is a pain. How am I supposed to think of everything?"

"You aren't," he said, scooting over on the couch so I could rest my head on his shoulder. "That's why you have a team."

I looked at my ChatterBox; it was after ten in the evening, and since we'd had a late lunch and skipped dinner, I was hungry. We ordered up some room service, partly because it was easy and partly because I wanted to see just how fancy the Bellagio could make chicken strips with fries.

It turned out they looked just like any other chicken strips with fries but tasted *much* better.

"I should shower; then I think it's bedtime," I said.

"Want help?"

"That depends."

"On what?"

"On whether Doctor Oracle wants to take on this job of helping Lucy," I said. "Because if he does, we just might *technically* be on the job right now."

"Hmm." Nate thought about it. "Well, since you're team leader of this research expedition, technically *you're* Doctor Oracle right now."

"In that case, I bet Doctor Oracle would insist on a bit more research before making a final decision."

"Would that research happen to have something to do with soap?"

"See? Mental powers aren't so uncommon," I said. "You just read my mind."

TEN

We returned to the island the next day, after one final gigantic buffet breakfast. As the project leader, it was up to me to deliver the few things we brought back with us.

First I visited Elliot in his science lab. It was one of the only times I'd seen him in his natural work environment, and I was startled that he was actually wearing a white lab coat, which stood out against his dark skin.

"Looking good," I said. "I've never seen you in your full scientist uniform before."

He twirled around for me. "More pockets and coverage than an apron, and I can wear whatever I want underneath." He opened up the coat and showed me the T-shirt and board shorts he had on.

"I do believe that's the first time I've ever been flashed by a scientist."

"Well, a good scientist should always be ready to help others have new experiences."

"I'll keep that in mind," I said. "So, I've brought you a little something from our field trip."

"What is it?"

"A cocktail napkin that Lucy wiped her mouth on. Hopefully you can get some usable DNA from it."

His expression lit up. "I'm sure I can. Saliva isn't the same as blood, but it can give us some good information."

"Great," I said. "Anything you need from me?" I wasn't entirely sure how much supervision I was supposed to offer as team leader.

"I'm good," he said. "I'll get on this right away and should have some results in a few hours."

"Perfect, because we figured to do dinner and a recap around seven up at Nate's."

"I'll be there."

I left him to his work and went upstairs to Evie's office near the computer labs. I found her hunched over a tiny circuit board with a soldering iron in her hand, with her face just inches away from the delicate work she was doing. I waited in the doorway for her to notice me. She finally looked up and smiled when she saw me.

"Sarah, my love," she said in her charming English lilt. "Back from the continent, I see."

"That we are, and I come bearing gifts."

"By all means, let's see what you have." I handed her the thumb drive and sat next to her.

"I'm not sure if you need to scan it for viruses or what," I said. "Apparently it contains documents pertaining to the impending disaster she's predicting, and a few select files from her collection of material that she stole from a super group she used to belong to."

"Oh, I like her already," Evie said. "Saucy."

"I like her, too, but that's no reason to trust her too much."

"Right you are. Now, so you know, what I usually do with something like this is scan it with two different computers, each with different load-outs of virus- and malware-detection programs. Those computers aren't connected to anything on our network, so if there is a problem, it can't spread."

"Good to know, thank you," I said. "I didn't want to assume what you'd do."

"You're doing fine," she said, then ruffled my hair. It felt motherly, even though Evie wasn't quite old enough to be my mother.

"We're thinking dinner at seven, up at Nate's. Do you think you'll have something by then?"

"Indeed I shall. I'll ferret out what I can and have it ready to present."

"Perfect. Thank you, Evie."

"It is my absolute pleasure, my dear." She headed straight to one of her computers. There was no reason for me to stick around; she'd tried to teach me some computer-code tricks a while back, but I was pretty hopeless. Making images pretty on a computer was something I could handle. Anything more detailed than that under the hood was beyond my abilities.

I visited a few other team members to let them know we'd returned and to make sure the meeting time worked all right for everyone. My route took me out to the residential building and the administrative building. I stopped by Nate's office while I was nearby, on my way to my last stop, Jin's workshop.

"Everyone good to go for the meeting?" Nate asked.

"So far," I said. "I've saved visiting Jin for last."

"You know, you could have just sent the meeting time to everyone's ChatterBox."

"I know, but then it feels more like an order."

"Have you ever felt like I was ordering you to go to a meeting?"

"No," I said, "but this is my first lead. I wanted to avoid sounding demanding."

"Just don't go too far the other way, or they'll walk all over you."

That made me worry. "Will they? Oh, crap."

He laughed. "No, they won't. They know you're good, and they know you're new. And they've all been through this exact same experience. Someone may just razz you or give you a little grief. I won't say who, except that his name might rhyme with Oscar."

"Funny thing, I know a guy named Oscar. Which just happens to rhyme with Oscar."

"So it doesn't just rhyme; it's the *perfect* rhyme," he said.

"I wonder about you sometimes," I said. "Maybe they're all right when they say you're a madman."

"I'm mad, all right." He waved a dramatic hand over the paperwork on his desk. "Mad about accounting!"

I went around his desk and kissed him. "Much as I want to help you add and subtract, I have to go see Jin."

"Fine, go, have your girl talk."

"Yes, girl talk. Ponies, boys, saving the world."

"Exactly that fluffy stuff," he said. "And hey, on a more serious note, you should start thinking about who you want as the key members of your field team for this thing. Most important is your second-in-command."

"Won't that be you?"

"Not if you don't want it to be. In fact, it might be better if it isn't me. I tend to lead more than my fair share, and it's entirely possible that if I'm your second, people might look to me as the person in charge. It may be more effective for me to just do your grunt work."

"There are a thousand comebacks to that," I said. "I'm paralyzed by my choices."

"I aim to please," he said. I kissed him again and left.

I headed back to the huge building where most of the actual work got done. Jin was down in her workshop, tinkering with the electric motor on one of the transport balls. She had the round white body separated from its round rubber tires. I looked at the tires from several angles but couldn't figure out how they attached to the chassis—they just looked like playground balls to me.

"How was it?" Jin asked, wiping her hands on a rag. "Glitzy and glamorous?"

"Some parts," I said. "And other parts were grimy and smoky. Typical Las Vegas."

"So it hasn't really changed. I haven't been there for a few years, not since Mark and I got married." Even though a lot of the people on the island called her husband Scar, because of the last name Scarborough, she usually called him by his actual name.

On the walk over from the administrative building, I'd thought about what Nate had said about picking my team. "Do you want to take a walk, talk about where we are so far and what the next steps are?"

"Sure," Jin said. "Though I have a better idea. Let's go over to the airfield, and you can get some practice in while we talk."

"Sounds good," I said. She quickly reassembled the transport ball, cleaned up a bit, and then we drove the ball around to the far side of the island to the airfield. Doctor Oracle had several planes, a helicopter or two, and even some ultralights that I hadn't found the courage to try flying yet. They just looked too fragile.

We signed out one of the small propeller-driven planes, a Cessna 172. It was more of a commuter plane, a little four-seat model with a range of only seven hundred miles or so. But it was more than enough to get us to Los Angeles or San Diego if we didn't have the jet available. Plus, it was the easiest of the island's fleet for me to learn on.

We walked around the plane and did all the preflight checks; then I took the pilot's seat and Jin climbed in on the copilot's side. I taxied down the runway and announced myself over the radio, even though we didn't have an air-traffic-control tower to communicate with. But as with so many things, I did it so that it would be second nature when I flew out of real airports on the mainland. Jin said the responses I'd normally expect to hear from the tower.

I checked over all the instruments, then set the flaps for takeoff and pushed in the throttle. My takeoffs and landings were getting smoother every time, and I thought I was really getting a feel for the airplane. It was exhilarating, like a combination of driving a motorcycle and a sports car, but up in the air.

Jin directed me to do some touch-and-go maneuvers—basically, flying around in a giant rectangle so I could get more takeoff and landing experience. Those were the hardest things; once you were airborne, the flying part was really pretty simple. We talked as I steered the plane around.

"First things first," she said. "You didn't get married out there, right?"

"No," I laughed. "We didn't. But you sure got Nate thinking about it."

"Good."

"Is it? We're so new, really."

"I know," she said. "But I really think you two have something special. So many people here are happy to be alone, married to their jobs. But when the two of you are together, you both light up. Not to tell tales about your boyfriend behind his back, but this is the happiest I've seen him in a long time."

That made me feel a little giddy inside. "I love him, but it would definitely make things more complicated."

"Eh, life's complicated."

"That it is," I said. "I'll tell you what I told him. If he seriously proposes, I'll seriously consider it. But until that happens, I'm happy to just keep on with things as they are." I angled the plane around and headed in for the runway again, checking in all directions for other air traffic. I knew there wouldn't be any, but again, I was building good habits. I aimed the plane down the runway, cut my speed, set the flaps, and gently touched down. Instead of hitting the brakes, I pushed the throttle back in and took off so I could run the pattern again.

"So besides having a romantic weekend away, what happened? What did you think of the mysterious Lucy?"

"I liked her," I said. "And I believe that *she* believes something terrible is going to happen."

"Something?"

"Yeah, it was vague. I know, this doesn't sound impressive, but Nate and I both agree that we should strongly consider helping her. At least until we find out more about what she needs."

"What was the reward she offered?"

"A huge stash of information, from a group she used to be in. She gave us a taste of it on a thumb drive, which Evie is looking over right now. She'll bring what she finds to the meeting tonight. And we got a sample of her DNA, which Elliot is looking at."

"My, you're really getting the hang of this team-leader thing," she said.

"That was all Nate. He was really looking out for me. But on that note, I was thinking about who to bring on as my second-in-command on this one."

"Not Nate?"

Besides Nate, Jin was my best friend on the island. I knew I could be open with her, so I told her Nate's reasoning for picking someone other than him. "I figured you were the obvious choice."

"First," she said, "I'm flattered. Second, hell yes I'll be your second. Third, though, I'd love to know why I'm the obvious choice, instead of Oscar or someone else."

"This thing has something to do with machines, apparently. She's getting . . . I'm going to call them vibes, because that's pretty much what she gets. Bad vibes, based around some project in Arizona where they're digging a huge hole in the ground with some high-tech drill thingy."

Jin laughed. "Now you're *really* taking to this team-leader thing. That sounds like the same kind of ultraprecise scientific explanation that Nate would give."

"Well, he always says I don't have to understand the science as long as someone else around me does. As far as this thing goes, if I had to explain it, I'd pretty much be reduced to 'digging holes, lava meets steam, blah blah blah.'"

"And this is my kind of science. When we get back, I'll do some research to see what I can find about drilling, lava, steam, and especially the blah blah blah."

"Perfect."

"So she was cool, huh? I've never met a super with mental powers."

"She was very easy to like. But the powers were kind of unsettling. Even so, I bet she'd get along well with everyone else here."

"Except for the whole being a super part."

"What do you mean?" I took the plane around one last time, since we both had work to do.

"There's a real pride here among a lot of people," she said. "That we have no supers on the island. That we're a team of ordinary people, doing extraordinary things and taking on extraordinary foes."

"This team is hardly ordinary," I said. "Most of them qualify as geniuses."

"True, but they can't bend a steel girder, or turn water to ice by blowing on it, or run faster than a cheetah. And for a lot of people, that makes them feel like the scrappy underdogs who are getting one over on the big bad meanies. It would be kind of demoralizing to have one of those big meanies in their midst, even if they were a very nice big meanie."

"Ugh," I said. "I thought I left high school behind when I graduated. But it's everywhere I go."

"And it always will be," she said. "It isn't that life stays like high school; it's that high school is just like life."

"That's a depressing thought."

"On the bright side, you're dating the quarterback of Oracle High." I caught a wicked smile out of the corner of my eye. "And if you're really lucky, he'll give you his class ring."

ELEVEN

After landing the plane, we took our transport ball back around to the main side of the island so we could get some work done before the meeting. Jin was going to research the kinds of digging projects Lucy had talked about, and I wanted to get my thoughts gathered and an agenda drawn up.

At around six, I called down and ordered three pizzas so we could pick them up for the meeting. Then I went down the hall to Nate's apartment to help him set up. We moved the furniture around in the living room so that everyone would have a good view of his TV.

"So, thought about your second-in-command?"

"I have," I said. "I asked Jin earlier today."

"Good. She's a great leader but also a great second. And don't forget, the rest of us will have your back."

"I'm counting on it."

Nate went down to collect the pizzas, and I stayed behind to let everyone into his apartment. When he returned, almost everyone else was there; we were just missing Evie, but it was still a few minutes until seven. We dished up the pizza, and she showed up just as we were heading in to the living room.

"Sorry I'm late," she said. "I lost track of time reading some of the stuff Lucy sent along."

"No worries," I said. "Pizza first, meeting second."

"Lovely." She grabbed a plate and a slice and joined us in the living room. After everyone had eaten, Nate collected the plates and put them in his sink. I washed my hands and grabbed my tablet with all my notes. Everyone looked at me expectantly, and despite all the support, I still felt like a disorganized fraud.

"Okay," I said, "please bear with me, everyone. This is my first time."

"That's what she said," Oscar said.

"She certainly did," I said. I took a deep breath. "So, here's what we know about Lucy so far. Her precognition is fairly limited, in that she can get feelings or emotions by touching people and objects with her bare hands. She can't outright visualize the future, so a number of groups didn't really find her useful for their purposes. Most of her research work is done with newspapers, magazines, that sort of thing. I guess the super groups wanted more of a hands-on team member, not an emotional librarian. She didn't do a lot of fieldwork because of anxiety, but I'm not too concerned with that, since it makes perfect sense to me. If I was assaulted with emotions every time I touched something, I'd be a basket case. I'm amazed she's as stable as she is." Several people nodded.

"On the good side, Nate and I both thought she was honest and forthright. On the minus side, she isn't exactly squeaky clean. She stole a bunch of information from one of the super groups while she was a member. It's understandable, given the story she told us of how they treated her. But if we do choose to help her out, we should keep in mind that she's willing to show some moral flexibility."

I described the way she'd demonstrated her powers for Nate and me and the few details we had so far about what the disaster was going to be.

I invited Evie to the front of the room, and explained what we'd be looking at while Evie plugged her tablet into the side of Nate's TV and queued up a document. "She gave us a thumb drive with some information from her secret stash, and some of the research she's been doing on this drilling project."

"And what a good bit of information it is," Evie said. "First, let's take a look at what she sent us about the drilling project.

There are a number of articles, but this one had the most detail. It appears that the digging is being done with a plasma cutter, one of the largest ones in existence. It's going to be more on Elliot and Jin to explain how the whole thing works. They only began drilling three weeks ago, and they're already making great progress."

"Does anyone want to know the details of how a plasma cutter works?" Jin asked.

Nobody raised their hands.

"They're really cool," she said.

Nobody raised their hands.

"Maybe later. Anyone wants to learn, come see me."

"So Lucy believes that something is going to happen with this project," I said. "But she hasn't yet nailed down what. She's working on figuring that out."

"It's a delicate area they're working in," Evie said. "I looked up some geological maps. There's a ton of underground water all throughout the Southwest and a surprising amount of recent volcanic activity. By recent, I mean in the last few thousand years. If they hit a pocket of magma that isn't too deep, and find a good source of groundwater nearby, it'll be a brilliant project. Until whatever problem happens to it, that is."

"If she can figure out what's going to happen, maybe it'll be an easy fix," I said.

"Well, easy or not, the information she has might well be worth it," Evie said. She swiped her finger across her tablet to get back to a list of documents. "Most important for us, one of the folders was named 'Oracle' and had two files in it. One was a text file, a note that Lucy had stuck in there. She wrote that once she knew she'd be meeting with us, she got this file from a friend who owed her a favor. She went on to say that generally, in all of the groups she's been in, there was little to no information known about Doctor Oracle. Which is good, if it's true."

"What's the other file?" Nate asked.

"Here it is," she said, and tapped on the face of her tablet to open the file. We all leaned forward to look at the TV. It was a detailed dossier, issued by the Ultimate Faction, a group we'd tangled with up in Seattle. According to the document, Doctor Oracle's real name was possibly Jeremy. I was glad that Nate hadn't used that fake name when we went to meet Lucy—he'd retired it from his massive list of fake identities when we found out that the Ultimate Faction knew the name.

There wasn't a lot of concrete detail on the document, but a lot of guesses and generalizations. The Faction had obviously been paying *some* attention during our interactions with them. They proposed that Doctor Oracle has a regular crew of at least three people, one of them a woman. They only described approximate height and build, since we always wore plenty of protective gear to hide our identities. Fortunately, Jin and I were roughly similar in size, so in full tactical gear, we could easily be mistaken for each other. The other description they gave was probably Oscar; when we last tangled with the Ultimate Faction, or more specifically Commander Alpha, the head of the Faction, he'd seen Oscar, Nate, and me.

It wasn't terrible, but it was more information than we wanted them to have. We tried to keep our missions as covert as possible. Unfortunately, the Faction got the drop on our people more than once due to information passed off the island by a mole; the information leak had been sealed and steps taken to avoid any future breaches, but the result was several jobs where members of our team came into contact with members of the Faction.

The mole wasn't even placed with us by the Ultimate Faction; she had been sending her information back to a woman named Catalyst, the nasty piece of work who Nate had dated and was hell-bent on getting him to notice her. She passed her information along to the Green Lady, another member of the Faction.

"It's a lot of guesswork," Nate said.

"If that's all they have, I'm pretty relieved," Evie said. "So that part of the information is pretty uneventful."

"How about the rest?" I asked.

Evie backed out of that folder and showed us the contents of another. "This is where things get good. If this is just a small sampling of what she has, I'd love to see the rest."

She tapped on her tablet and scrolled through a number of documents, some of them pages of text, some of them blueprints of buildings, some of them schematics for devices or machines.

"Is that the plans for Major Threat's gravity generator?" Jin asked.

"It is," Evie said. "And several pages of documentation of the additional work that the government has put into trying to get it to work. Without success, I might add." She kept flicking through documents.

"What building is that?" Nate asked as the screen showed a set of blueprints.

"The new headquarters of the Paladin Sector," she said. "You may recall that they moved a few years ago, after a reporter discovered the location of their old headquarters by accident."

"And they stored the blueprints for their new place on the Nightsiders' computer servers?" I asked.

"Why, yes, they did," Evie said with a grin. "Nimbus, the leader of the Nightsiders, is listed as one of the designers of the building. These documents don't have the location of their new headquarters, but for all we know, Lucy's stash of information includes that."

"Is it all this good?" Nate asked.

"Not all of it, no. Actually, a lot of it is information we already have. But even if there are just a few nuggets like these, we can learn a great many things about the other side."

Evie finished up with her presentation; then it was Elliot's turn. He didn't have any visuals to share.

"I was able to get some genetic material off of the napkin you gave me," he said. "Not a lot, and not enough to run all of the tests I'd like to. But I was able to do a rapid DNA test, and she definitely has the standard markers we see in people who are born with physical superpowers."

"So it's the same kind of genetic mutation for physical as it is with mental powers?" Nate asked.

"I can't say for sure without more study. I'd love to get a sample of her blood."

"She was pretty cool about giving us the napkin," Nate said. "We'll see what we can do."

"At any rate," Elliot said, "if I just saw her DNA profile and looked at the right locus, I'd know immediately that she was a super. So as far as I'm concerned, she's legit."

"All right, then," I said. "We have a verified super asking for our help, with something that may or may not be a big deal, but we won't know until either she gets a feeling about something, or we do our own research into that drilling operation. It's a weird situation, so naturally it would be my first lead. Does anyone have any arguments against taking the job?"

Nobody spoke up.

"All right, then. I guess we're on." I took a deep breath. "Meeting adjourned."

Everyone got up to stretch, and a couple went back for more pizza. Scar came over and sat next to me. "You'll do great. It was a good meeting, and Jin told me you asked her to be your second."

"I hope she doesn't mind," I said.

"Are you kidding? She loves being in the center of the action. Me, I'd rather stay back here, run a tight ship, and hear about all of the fun after it's happened."

"Do you worry about her, out in the field?"

"Every day," he said. "But I know she's good at what she does, and she's surrounded by a good team."

"I know," I said. "But she got a broken ankle while on a mission to rescue me. Anything can happen."

"I could get hit by lightning tomorrow. Or a coconut could fall on my head. You can't live your life in fear of what *might* happen, or you'd turn into a hermit. I just have to trust that she'll make safe choices. Although I sense that this line of questioning isn't entirely about me and Jin."

"Jin talked to you, huh?"

"Nate, too, and he had the same questions that you do. You're both going through the uncertainty I had to go through when Jin and I got serious. Was the relationship worth it, with the possibility of the other person getting injured or killed?"

"I'm guessing it was worth it," I said.

"Absolutely," Scar said. "But then again, I've always figured love is more important than fear."

Jin heard the tail end as she came over to join us. "My suit-wearing husband is a secret hippie."

"I live my life like a Beatles song," he said. "All I need is love."

"Or possibly you're the fool on the hill," she said, and kissed his cheek. She turned to me. "Let me know what you want me to take on, and I'm all yours."

"Fantastic," I said. "I have to get in touch with Lucy to let her know that Doctor Oracle is on board and find out if she's been able to figure out any more details about what's going to happen, and when. I'm just crossing my fingers that it won't be anything too crazy."

"It's your first job as leader," Jin said. "It's probably safer to go in expecting crazy."

TWELVE

The next day, Jin and I took the island's floatplane to San Diego. It was good flight practice, and we were able to work on some concepts that we couldn't in the Cessna—namely, water landings both intentional and emergency. Most of my flight training was on land, since for the sake of convenience, most of my landings would be on runways instead of waterways. But because we lived on an island, it was essential to learn how to land planes in water.

The trip got me to a place where I could have a good, long phone conversation with Lucy on a burner phone without worrying about anyone tracing my location. We could make calls from the island, but they had to be brief while the signal was being relayed around. I personally preferred email instead of talking on the phone, but we all figured that Lucy would be more comfortable with the acceptance of her job offer being from an actual human who could answer her questions immediately.

The flight would only have been two hours if we'd flown straight from the island to the airfield, but we took a circuitous route to muddle up our flight plan. We finally landed at a small marina north of the city, and I made the call before we got lunch. Lucy answered her phone quickly.

"Hi, this is Beth," I said, using the same fake name I'd used when meeting her.

"Good to hear from you," Lucy said. "I hope you have good news for me."

"I do. Doctor Oracle has decided to help, if he can. Though he wants more details about what's going to happen."

"Oh, yes," she said. "I've been doing a lot more research, picturing the drilling operation in my head and skimming newspapers and magazines."

"What else have you found out?"

"I have a pretty weird list of things that have triggered my feelings. Some of them make sense, but others, not so much."

I pulled out a pen and a notepad. "Go ahead and tell me what they are; maybe someone on Doctor Oracle's team can figure out the parts you can't."

"All right. First, I think I have the date figured out. I think it's going to happen the day after Labor Day. I've had feelings from an ad for the upcoming rodeo, a Foo Fighters concert, and a number of articles arguing that school should start up the day after Labor Day instead of late August. I can't see any other connection for those, except that they're all about the same date."

I made notes about the events and her conclusion. If the event was going to happen the first Tuesday of September, that was only two weeks away. "Okay, how about the vague stuff?"

"I'm worried that this is going to be about radiation," she said. "I watched a video online where someone flew a drone around Pripyat, that city near Chernobyl. I got a really bad feeling when I watched it. Same feeling when I looked up a few news stories, especially the ones that talked about how radiation had changed the area."

"Is there something radioactive where they're digging?"

"I don't think so, but I don't know all of the details of how their operation works."

"Okay, Chernobyl, radiation. What else?"

"I got a light feeling from Jell-O."

"What?"

"One of those classic ads. Like from the eighties."

I didn't understand, but I wrote it down. "Anything else?"

"I totally understand if this stuff sounds crazy," she said.

"Crazy sounding or not, these are the only leads we have."

She took a deep breath. "I got twinges from a McDonald's ad. And during dinner the other night."

"What was the ad for?"

"A bunch of things," she said. "I'll take a picture and email it to you."

"Good. And was there anything weird about that dinner?"

"No," she said. "It was pretty normal. Pork chops, mashed potatoes, a green salad with ranch dressing."

I wrote it all down; I had no idea what was important and what wasn't. That was for people way smarter than me to figure out.

"Cool, okay. Is that all?"

"So far, but I'll keep trying."

"Please do. I'll pass this all along to Doctor Oracle and his minions; hopefully we'll be able to figure this out."

"I'm so glad you're helping me, Beth," she said. Every time she used my fake name, I felt a little guilty.

"It's our pleasure." Then, to emphasize that Doctor Oracle wasn't in it just to be nice, I added, "Of course, the information you'll be giving us will make it worth our while."

"So should I just email you with anything else?"

"That's fine," I said. "We can set up a time to call if we need to go over anything in more detail. Do you have any questions or anything for me?"

"No—as long as I can reach you by email, I'm good."

We signed off, and Jin and I went for a quick lunch before we filled the floatplane's fuel tanks and flew off on our zigzagging route back home. I filled her in on the list of things that Lucy had given me.

"I bet she's right about the radiation, but I have no idea why they'd put this project anywhere near something radioactive," Jin said. "I don't know if there are any reactors down in Arizona, but we'll look into it. There's probably a ton of buried nuclear waste out there in the desert, but I can't imagine anyone being allowed to dig near it."

"And what about the foods?"

"A Jell-O ad, McDonald's, and a home-style dinner. Weird. Maybe when she sends you the ad, something will click."

"Maybe," I said, but I wasn't sure. It felt like one of those puzzles I never liked in school: *Here are four totally different things: What do they have in common?* Give me story problems any day, with two trains leaving a city at the same time.

When we got back to the island, I called up Nate and Oscar so we could have a mini-meeting to go over things. Even though Nate had practically insisted that I choose someone else as my second-in-command, I wanted him as a part of my core team. Oscar was always a good choice to round out any group; he had a ton of field experience and was almost as footloose and fancy-free from his department as I was. He ran the gym and the intramural athletics programs and headed up entertainment with Jin's husband, Scar. He had great assistants, and a job description so vague and varied, everyone pretty much assumed he was overseeing something else if they didn't see him for a while.

The guys came to my office, and I filled them in on Lucy's list of things. Jin mentioned her concerns about nuclear material, and neither of the guys could think of how radiation would come into play.

Lucy had emailed the McDonald's ad while we were flying back. It looked like part of the giant bundle of ads and coupons that come with a Sunday newspaper. She'd circled a section of it: a picture of a hamburger, fries, and a drink in the classic white cup. She'd included a link in her email to the video of the classic Jell-O commercial. It was a little bit before my time, but the jingle sounded vaguely familiar.

We threw around a few ideas, but nothing made sense to connect the three food-related objects that gave Lucy her feeling of dread. Oscar even ran over to the food court to get a serving of Jell-O, which was the only triggering food item we had on hand at the time. Pork chops wouldn't be on the menu until later in the week.

He pushed the Jell-O around on a plate; then, like you do, he shook the plate to watch it wiggle and see it jiggle.

I went back to looking at the McDonald's ad, trying to figure out what it was about that meal that could trigger Lucy.

After a minute, Nate said, "Oscar?"

I turned back to look. Oscar was gently wiggling his plate back and forth, but he wasn't exactly looking at it. His eyes were a little unfocused, staring off into space.

"You okay, man?" Nate asked.

Oscar blinked rapidly, then looked up at Nate. "An earthquake."

"How do you figure that?"

"The Jell-O wiggles and shakes." He pointed at the ad I had on my monitor. "That meal in that ad doesn't include a soft drink; it includes a milkshake."

Jin snapped her fingers and laughed. "Pork chops. Shake'n Bake."

"All three things have something shaking or something called a shake," Oscar said. "That could be the connection."

"One way to find out," I said. I wrote Lucy a quick email to let her know we'd received her picture, and asked what she thought about the word *earthquake*.

While we waited for a reply, we tossed around what would need to happen next. We knew that the event would have something to do with the drilling operation, but not precisely where. It might be the drilling site; it might be an office related to the site. We knew it would happen the day after Labor Day, the first Tuesday of September, just about two weeks away. And now we suspected it might have something to do with an earthquake. Details were sketchy, but we were making progress.

"If it is an earthquake, I bet the location would be the drilling site," Jin said. "We're talking about a brand new digging technology being used deep underground. A tremor of any kind might cause it to malfunction."

"How rare are earthquakes in Arizona?" Nate asked.

I did a quick search on the computer. "Wow, not as rare as I would have thought. Though it isn't surprising, since they're next to California, and that place seems to be earthquake central."

I read a preview of a news story. "A region where quakes are frequent but usually don't produce much damage or alarm."

"Until the big one hits," Oscar said.

"Thank goodness for the Internet," I said. "Here's a map and a list. Wow, Arizona has had a hundred and forty-two earthquakes so far this year, the largest registering a magnitude of five point one. It looks like they're normally frequent and small."

"Until the big one hits," Oscar repeated.

"True," Nate said. "And maybe it wouldn't take all that big of an earthquake to damage a drill, if that drill is a mile under the surface."

My computer chimed, letting me know a new email had arrived. I opened it up.

> *Beth—*
>
> *YES! I think that's it. Just touching the word on my computer monitor set me off. I knew you'd be able to help me!*
>
> *—Lucy*

"All right, earthquake it is," I said. "Next steps?"

"It looks like we need to dig up some things, no pun intended," Nate said. "We need to find out exactly where this drilling facility is and get the blueprints to it. Then we need to get the schematics for this drill to find out what about it could be so deadly."

"And since the entire operation is under the umbrella of several super groups," I said, "I bet this isn't the kind of information Evie can just slip into a computer system and steal."

"Probably not," Nate said. "But if it could all be stolen remotely, where would be the fun?"

THIRTEEN

We had the when, and we had an idea of the where, and the next day Jin figured out at least part of the what.

She asked me to meet her at her workshop. When I got there, I saw that she had a table covered with all the pieces we'd taken from Manos's machine.

"Lucy got me thinking," she said. "Something about the news from the Manos job set her off, and we knew we were looking for radiation. So I got out my Geiger counter."

She picked up a device about the size of a shoebox, with what looked like a microphone attached to it by a coiled cord. It was like something out of a monster movie in the '50s. She switched it on, pointed the microphone-looking device at one of the parts we'd stolen from Manos, and the Geiger counter made a soft clicking sound.

"Whoa," I said, taking a step back. "Does that sound mean this is radioactive?"

"Only a very little bit, so we're okay," she said. "More to the point, these pieces themselves aren't radioactive, but they've been in contact with some material or object that is."

"Whatever was stolen before we got there?"

"Most likely." She set the Geiger counter down, and we went back to her office. Even though she said the pieces of the machine were safe, I was glad to step away from them. To think, I'd carried those pieces in a bag slung on my back.

"So what was it?"

"We already figured that the missing piece was a power source, since the Pederson electromagnet wasn't running once that part was removed. I did some tests, and what's setting off the counter are trace amounts of plutonium."

"Hang on, now," I said. "I saw *Back to the Future*. Plutonium is strong stuff, or else they wouldn't have chosen it to power a time-traveling DeLorean, right?"

"It's strong stuff, for sure," Jin said. "Fictitious time-traveling car aside, it can power a lot of things. Over a third of the energy from the world's nuclear power plants comes from plutonium."

"But you're okay with having it in your workshop?"

"Really, it's trace amounts. You probably get more exposure to radiation when you travel by airplane."

"I think I'll stay over here," I said.

"Suit yourself. Here's the big problem: I checked around in our database and did some strategic searching of police records, looking for something plutonium related that might be around the right size to fit in this machine." She jiggled the mouse of her computer to wake it up and turned the screen toward me. It showed an alert from Interpol with a photograph of a small, lumpy, gold-colored box with wires coming out of it here and there.

"This," she said, "is a plutonium-strontium battery, developed by a team in Italy. They have a weird relationship with nuclear power over there; they shut down all of their reactors over twenty-five years ago, but they're working on other ways to work with nuclear material. This was one of their more successful projects."

"You think that's the thing that powered Manos's machine?"

"I'd bet money on it. I checked some of the screenshots I took of Manos's machine, from the feed from your goggles—the wires that come out of it are in the exact spots as the snipped wires where our mystery item was removed."

"So we're sure the Italians no longer have their battery?"

"They don't. It was kept hush-hush, but the battery was stolen two years ago. Nobody was caught, and the battery hasn't been recovered."

"Did Manos steal it?" I asked.

"I don't think so. The big suspect at the time was an English guy who went by"—she paused and raised one eyebrow—"Mr. Fahrenheit."

I grinned. "Did he make a supersonic man out of you?"

"Yes!" Jin slapped her hand on her desk. "I was hoping you'd get that!"

"Are you kidding? Queen is one of the best bands ever."

"See?" This is why I'm glad we're friends."

"So where's Mr. Fahrenheit now?" I asked.

"He passed away earlier this year. It appears that his old partner, Miss Celsius, decided to retire after Fahrenheit died. She sold a number of their possessions, but there's no record of the battery."

"I wonder if she sold it off under the table."

"I figured the same thing. After all, Manos didn't steal the electromagnet either; he got it from someone else. It wouldn't surprise me if all the parts in that machine were bought or stolen from other thieves."

"Jeez," I said. "Did the guy build any of his *own* stuff? Or just take other people's ideas?"

"They don't call him Grabby for nothing," Jin said. "However, I think that's mostly for different reasons."

"So I hear."

"If it matters, he put together a lot of stolen items in a really effective way. I wouldn't be surprised if that machine of his actually did have the ability to shut down electricity over most of the planet."

I sighed and ran my hands through my hair, then realized it was a very Nate thing to do. His leadership techniques (and deep-thought techniques) were rubbing off on me. "So can we get in touch with Miss Celsius to find out who she sold the battery to?"

"We could, if we had that kind of time. Unfortunately, she's gone completely off the grid. It would take too long to track her down, and our time line is pretty tight as it is."

"Okay, so. We're assuming someone stole the battery from Manos so they could use it to power their drill."

"If that's what happened, then the team that got to Manos before us was made up of supers. Or sidekicks of supers. Or maybe even just some thieves working for the supers on the side, since the digging project is partially financed by the supers. I can't imagine they'd take delivery of a stolen power source without knowing its origin."

"Great," I said. "Who are the good guys here, again?"

"That's an argument we'll never win. What really concerns me is the fact that I got radiation readings from parts that you took from that machine that were nowhere *near* the battery. I'm not surprised by the readings from the parts that were connected, but I shouldn't be getting readings from pieces from the other side of the machine. The fact that I could get a reading off of those parts tells me that the battery might be leaking. It's probably just a teeny tiny bit, but if we're right about an earthquake, if that thing is miles deep down in a hole, that small leak could turn into a big leak in an instant."

"And what, get radiation into the hole? And down into the magma?"

"Don't forget, they're also tapping into the groundwater, so there's a fifty-fifty chance that right now they're digging into the aquifer instead of into magma. So what happens when radioactive material leaks into an underground source of water that spreads for hundreds of miles under several states?"

"Oh my God," I said. "How bad could it get?"

"Bad," she said. "The plutonium alone might not kill everyone in the area. But the fact that they combined it with strontium is the kicker. They used a synthetic version in this battery, strontium-90. Out of all of the isotopes, it has the longest half-life: just over twenty-eight years."

"So it'll stay radioactive for that long?"

"Radiation isn't the problem with strontium. It's chemically similar to calcium, and the human body absorbs it the same way. It actually replaces calcium in your bones. Funny thing, it's used to treat bone cancer, but it can also cause bone cancer."

"Wait, so they combined something that can give you cancer with something else that can give you cancer, and put them together in a battery?"

"When you put it that way, yeah, it doesn't sound that great. But it's an ingenious design, and would be totally fine, if only it wasn't leaking."

"Surely the guys who stole it would check to see if it was fine before putting it in their drill. They've figured out a way to drill two holes to get power and water to the entire Southwest; they aren't idiots."

"I'm sure they've tested it, but I'm fairly certain that because they're taking readings off of the battery itself, they'll expect a small amount of radiation. They didn't take any of the other parts from Manos's machine, so they don't know how far from the battery the contamination spread."

"So as far as they're concerned, everything is hunky-dory."

"I'm sure," Jin said. "I ran a few hypothetical questions past Bruce, a guy on Elliot's team who's a geology buff, so I could get a better idea of how far the toxic materials could spread. If they dug in just the right place, and the battery failed at just the right time, they could make both the underground water and the drinking water unsafe for around fifty years and slowly kill millions of people."

I pinched the bridge of my nose and sighed. "And we can't just tell them to stop using that battery."

"They'd never believe us," Jin said. "Especially since overall, the project is a good one, meant to help those same millions of people. If Lucy hadn't had this feeling, and if they were using a safer power supply, I'd be cheering them on from the shadows."

"So would I."

I had Jin forward me the information about the stolen Italian plutonium-strontium battery and sent it on to Lucy. She replied quickly that everything I sent gave her the same feeling of dread, so we knew we were on the right track. We had to get that battery out of the drill or disable the drill somehow, and we had to do it by Labor Day at the latest.

We plotted out what we'd need to do in order to complete the operation, working from the end result backward. The very last goal would be to remove the battery from the drill. That meant getting into the secret location where the drilling was taking place. Backing up from there, we'd need to find out the secret location. The odds pointed toward the information being stored at the headquarters where the group of superhero organizations had set up shop to run the whole project.

"Wouldn't they have all of their offices and everything at the dig site?" I asked.

"Probably not," Jin said. "That would mean a lot of traffic going in and out of the dig site, which would draw unwanted attention to a supposedly secret location. Plus, if the dig truly is hidden away somewhere, it isn't likely to be near any major city. And I don't know of anyone, super or not, who would want to go to work every day in the middle of nowhere."

"All right, that means they'll have a separate office near or in a big city."

"So we'll need to find out where *that* is, too."

"Fantastic. So we're, what, two heists deep?"

"Possibly three, if Evie can't get computer access to information about their offices."

I shook my head. "Remind me again why I agreed to lead this one?"

"Because it was going to be easy," Jin said. "Silly girl."

FOURTEEN

Evie wasn't able to dig up plans to the super groups' office building, but at least she was able to find out where it was.

"I can show you the outside," she said when Jin and I visited her. "But so far I'm coming up with nothing as far as interior plans." She pulled up a web page for a company called Exponential Projects; from the pictures on their site, it looked like an ordinary office tower, about twelve stories tall. "It's an older building, so it isn't surprising that the blueprints aren't online anywhere. They're likely just rotting away in a drawer in some storage room."

"You're sure this is them?" I asked.

"Absolutely," she said. "They can hide their own documentation from me, but the government is absolutely rubbish at hiding *theirs*. I found a number of red flags pointing me from the super groups to this Exponential place. Our old friends the Ultimate Faction, the Southwest Storm, the Sentinel League, and maybe a dozen more are all in on this together. It's practically a who's-who of super groups on this side of the country."

"Doing good for the region," I said. "I kind of have to applaud them."

"Except that they're keeping their involvement secret," Jin pointed out. "Maybe in case it fails. Take the glory if it works; sweep it under the rug if it doesn't."

"Well, then," I said, "we'll have to include spilling the beans about their involvement on our agenda."

"Best to save that for the end," Evie said. "We don't want them to know we're sniffing around that project."

"Makes sense."

"So," Jin said, "where do you think we're going to find plans for this Exponential Projects office building?"

"The building itself is on the outskirts of Phoenix," Evie said. "We have two places to look: either the city planning department will have the building schematics in their archives, or the building inspection department will have something in their library. Lucky for you, both offices are in the same building."

"Then I guess we're taking a trip to Phoenix," Jin said. "Sarah, you're doing the flying."

I went over to Rupert's workshop before we left, to pick up a few disguise and costume pieces for our trip. As I got close to the door, which was open a crack, I heard voices coming from inside. I raised my hand to knock, then stopped myself.

"I just don't know," I heard Elliot say. "I'm pretty sure she's going to fail."

I hated to eavesdrop on my friends, but I couldn't help myself. Especially if they were talking about me.

"I'm not so sure," Rupert said. "But you never know. The first try at anything is difficult."

"Want to place a bet?"

I felt a little queasy. The other members of the team were going to bet on whether I succeeded at my first leadership role?

"Why not," Rupert said. "I say she does it. How about a bottle of Scotch?"

"You're on," Elliot said. "A bottle says this first try is a failure."

I didn't want to hear any more. Elliot was one of the team members I knew the least, but I was still shocked that he'd be so unsupportive of my first leadership role. I knocked on the door and pushed it open wider, sticking my head in. "Hey, Rupert, I've come by for those pieces you were going to get ready for us?"

"Of course!" Rupert jumped up and went to one of his locked cabinets, keying it open with his palm print. As he pulled out a box, I looked at Elliot. He smiled warmly at me, which was even more disconcerting. He was betting against me, after all. Although at least he wasn't betting I'd fail straight to my face.

I thought about whether I should say anything for a moment, then made my decision. I'd always gotten my best results when faced with adversity by killing people with kindness.

"Everything going all right in the labs?" I asked him.

"Right as rain," he said. "I'm running some more detailed tests on Lucy's sample, though I'd love to get some of her blood in order to run all of the checks I'd like."

"I'll see what I can do," I said. "No promises."

"No worries," he said. "I'm sure you'll do your best."

Rupert handed me the box he'd prepared for our trip, and I left, saying cheerful good-byes and stewing inside.

I tried my best to put my inner turmoil aside during our trip to Phoenix. I didn't want to discuss any of it with Jin, or even with Nate—as more seasoned members of the team, either one of them might want to handle the situation themselves, which would only make me seem like a weaker leader. I decided that the one thing I could absolutely have control over was doing the best job I could.

As usual, we found a nice, small airfield on the outskirts of town to park the plane, a place called Eagle Point Municipal Airport. The little Cessna took a little longer to get us places compared to the jet, but the trip gave me more time at the controls and more time to talk about plans with Jin.

The nice part about Phoenix was not having to change time zones. Most of Arizona refuses to participate in daylight saving time, which means that in the summer, their clocks are set the same as the Pacific time zone. We followed Pacific time on the island to make things easy, so we didn't have to worry about working by a different clock from everyone back home.

We picked up the rental car that Evie had arranged for us and headed downtown to city hall. It was late morning, and we hoped to get to the Planning and Development Department at lunchtime, when it would be relatively quiet. Evie had done some additional digging to locate where in city hall the older records were kept and the year the Exponential building had been constructed, so we'd have a general idea where to look.

While we were out in the field, Nate and Oscar were working on ideas for how to breach the Exponential Projects headquarters since it was a twelve-story building with nothing else nearby but a busy freeway. There weren't a lot of easy entrances and exits.

I'd emailed ahead to Lucy to let her know that I would be in town, so we could meet up in the afternoon and update her on our progress. I wasn't wearing a mask, but I felt disguised well enough—Rupert had me set up with a new nose and chin, colored contact lenses, glasses, and another blond wig. Jin had some fake latex features of her own, plus a pair of glasses and a wig. We both wore business suits.

Jin drove downtown, and I was happy to navigate and take in the sights. It was my first time to Arizona, and I kind of liked it. Just like Las Vegas, it was made up of dozens of shades of brown punctuated with patches of green. I'd grown up surrounded by the lush greenery of the Northwest, so it was an interesting change. It felt just as hot as Vegas had, but again, it was a pretty tolerable dry heat.

We parked in the public garage attached to city hall, got two slim briefcases out of the trunk, and walked into the building at ten minutes after twelve. The first floor was bustling, but most of the foot traffic was going the other way, leaving for lunch. We made our way to the security checkpoint.

"Good afternoon," Jin said, placing her briefcase on the X-ray scanner's conveyor belt. We only had a couple of gadgets on hand, disguised as ordinary objects. We easily passed through the metal detectors. We gathered up our briefcases and walked toward a guard in front of the elevators.

"Afternoon, ladies," the guard said. "Can I help you find where you're going?"

"We're good," Jin said. "Just heading up to Planning and Development on six." She stepped past him and pressed the button on the elevator.

"Great," the guard said as the elevator doors opened. "You have a good day, now."

"Thanks, you too," I said as we stepped into the elevator. Jin pressed the button for the sixth floor. No reason to lie to the guards if it wasn't necessary; we'd come up with a plan to get in and out without taking anything away with us and without raising any suspicion around the Exponential Projects building.

We got off the elevator on the sixth floor and walked down the hall to the Planning and Development offices. Thanks to Evie, we knew the layout of the building, so we looked like we knew where we were going. Not that it mattered; just as the first floor had been busy with a flood of people leaving, the sixth floor was practically a ghost town.

I opened the door, and we went inside the office. It was a small area with two computer workstations, and another door behind the desks. There was one lonely-looking guy sitting at one of the desks, halfheartedly tapping at his keyboard.

He looked up at us and smiled, which delighted me. We had a solid plan in place to get into the records room, but it was always easier to talk to someone who wanted to talk to you back, instead of someone who was surly and doesn't want to be bothered.

"Can I help you ladies?"

"You sure can," I said. I pulled a business card out of my pocket and handed it to him. "I'm Ellen, this is Sue. We work for Twin Palms Architecture and Design. We just need to check on past plans and permits for a building we're working on. The stuff the client gave us doesn't exactly match the building itself." I rolled my eyes and smiled.

"Oh, no problem! If I could just get you to sign in right here." He pushed a clipboard across the desk, and both Jin and I signed our fake names and wrote down our fake company name and the fake phone number associated with it.

"I'm not sure how the records are stored here," I said.

"By address," the man said. He pulled his computer keyboard over and tapped away. "Where's the building you're working on?"

"Fourteen fifty, Charleston Drive," I said as he typed the address into his computer. It was a small warehouse two blocks away from the Exponential Projects building.

"That's going to be in . . . aisle D, section twenty-seven," he said. He made a note of the section on the sign-in sheet. "Right this way."

He opened the door and led us through. The room beyond the small vestibule was surprisingly large and well lit, full of rows and rows of file cabinets. It was like an office version of the warehouse at the end of *Raiders of the Lost Ark*. We followed him past a set of coin-operated photocopiers to aisle D, then down the long row of cabinets to a half dozen or so with the number "27" stenciled on them.

"Great," I said. "Thank you so much."

"Just let me know if you need anything," he said. "My name is Brian; I'll be right out front."

"Excellent. Thanks, Brian."

"Oh, and just to warn you: our records are pretty good, but they aren't perfect. So you may have to peek over in sections twenty-six or twenty-eight to find what you're looking for."

"I'm sure we'll find exactly what we need," I said.

"All right, then. If there isn't anything else I can help with?"

I got the feeling he was stalling out of loneliness, not mistrust. Jin stepped between us and stuck her hand out to Brian for a handshake. "We're good, thank you for your help. We'll let you know if we need you."

I shook his hand, and then he finally left, looking back at us as he made his way out of aisle D. We watched the top of his head bob along over the tops of the filing cabinets until he went back out through the door.

Jin looked around the room. "Yeesh. This place is massive."

"I'm glad we're doing this through the front door," I said as I opened one of the drawers in section twenty-seven. "I'd hate to have to figure out where things are on my own."

"Evie could probably get into Brian's computer. But this way, we need a much smaller team."

A few of the files were out of order, but Brian was right: their records were pretty good. We found our warehouse address in the first filing cabinet of section twenty-seven, then backtracked to the middle of section twenty-six and found the address of the Exponential Projects building. There were a ton of documents in there.

I opened my briefcase and pulled out a smartphone. In the spirit of disguising things in plain sight, we didn't need secret cameras hidden in other objects. The only thing making the phone different from any one you could find on the street was that it had been upgraded with an ultrahigh-resolution camera. One by one, we pulled documents out of the file folders, spread them flat on the floor, and took pictures of them. There were blueprints, applications for permits, and architectural drawings spanning back at least thirty years.

We took extra pictures of the most recent stuff—drawings and plans for interior renovations of the building from about a year ago. Every document went back into the files in the same order we'd found them.

When we'd taken enough pictures of everything, we closed the drawer in section twenty-six and went back to our warehouse address in section twenty-seven. Jin pulled out one of the drawings of the interior of the building and went to the photocopiers, spending a quarter to make a single copy. If we'd opted to copy all the Exponential stuff, we'd be out a lot of dollars, and we wouldn't have had enough room in our slim briefcases for all the paper. She returned the drawing to its drawer, and we headed back out.

Brian was tapping at his keyboard again but spun on his chair when we came back through the door. "Find everything?"

"We sure did," I said. I waved the photocopy at him. "Looks like the client didn't have the plans for this expansion on hand." I tucked the copy away in my briefcase.

"Happens all the time," he said. "Is there anything else I can help you with?"

"No, thank you," I said. "You've been a great help. And everything was right where it was supposed to be."

"You need anything else, just let me know," he said. "I'm here every day."

"Fantastic," I said. Sensing that we were going to get caught in another conversation loop, I held out my hand for another handshake. Finally, we were able to break free and go back out to the elevators.

"Poor Brian," I said.

"The loneliest man in the world," Jin said.

We went back to the car and ran the standard set of security checks on it, then connected the phones to a portable wireless hot spot to upload all the pictures to our secure server in the cloud so the team back on the island could get their hands on them. As the files were uploading, Jin drove us back to the airfield so we could grab a change of clothes out of the plane. It was a relief to get into a T-shirt and shorts after wearing a suit and pantyhose. It was still uncomfortable wearing a wig and a full set of prosthetics on my face, but at least my arms and legs were cooler.

I called Lucy to let her know we were on our way. I knew that she lived in her hometown, Wickenburg, which was to the northwest of Phoenix, but she said she was running errands in the southern end of the city, so she'd meet us there. I was amused to note that the restaurant she chose for lunch was barely a mile away from the Exponential Projects building.

We met up with Lucy at a small mom-and-pop sandwich shop; since it was well past one o'clock at that point, we had the place to ourselves. I felt like I should be wearing a mask, but with our fake faces on, we were just as well disguised. As far as I could tell, Lucy came to meet us wearing her normal face, completely uncovered.

She had her beige cotton gloves on but took one off to shake my hand. "Beth, it's good to see you, even though I'm pretty sure you're wearing a different kind of mask."

"Can't be too careful, running with the crowd we do," I said.

"I understand."

"You know I'm not really Beth; may I introduce not really Sue," I said as Lucy shook Jin's hand.

"Pleased to sort of meet you," Lucy said.

"Likewise," Jin said.

"Someday, I'd be honored to know your real names."

"That's certainly possible," I said. "Maybe after we stop this impending disaster."

Over sandwiches, we filled Lucy in on as much information as we felt we could divulge: the leakage problem on the plutonium-strontium battery, our thoughts about how the disaster would go down, and a general outline of our plans for how to access the location and schematics for the drilling site.

"You were right that several of the super groups are helping to finance the operation, all very hush-hush," I said.

"Good," Lucy said. "My source wasn't absolutely sure, but it felt like good intel."

"We've found out where they're doing business, so we can break in there to get the information we need."

"I get why you won't tell me what that information is right now," she said. "But would you let me know afterward?"

"Sure," I said. "I'll have to run it by Doctor Oracle, but I bet we could give you most of the research we've done, after all of this is through."

Once the business was discussed, we turned to small talk. It turned out that Lucy and Jin had a number of things in common, and lunch passed with a nice conversation about books and bands.

According to the clock on the wall, it was almost three in the afternoon. "We should get rolling," I said. Since we'd be doing a fair amount of work in the Phoenix area in the next two weeks, Jin and I had plans to buy a pair of nondescript black SUVs with cash and fake IDs and rent out a private hangar at Eagle Point

Municipal Airport, where we'd parked the Cessna, before we headed back to the island.

"Thank you," Lucy said, "for the work you're doing. And be sure to thank Doctor Oracle for me. I hope to be able to meet him someday."

"That might be something that could be arranged," I said. She took her glove off to shake hands good-bye, and gave me a sort of sideways smile. I tried to clear my mind; I didn't want to think about what kind of vibe she would get from me when I was thinking about Doctor Oracle. She shook hands with Jin, then smiled broadly.

"This is going to go well, I think," she said. "I'm feeling very positive about both of you."

"I hope so," I said. "We'll do the best we can."

"I'm sure you will."

We parted ways, and Jin drove a roundabout route out of the area. It was a convenient way to drive past the Exponential Projects building so we could give it a look. Just as described, it was a twelve-story office building that stood apart from any other structures. The next tallest building in the neighborhood was only six or seven stories anyway. We drove two full laps; then Jin merged onto the freeway that passed near one side of the building.

"It's like they picked the place specifically because it would be hard to breach," Jin said.

"Wouldn't you?" I asked.

"Hell yes, I would."

FIFTEEN

Two days later, Oscar and I walked into the Exponential Projects building. It was broad daylight, and the building was hustling and bustling. We'd found out a lot from the blueprints and architectural plans but needed a reconnaissance mission to pinpoint the location where we could find the schematics for the drill and the location of the dig site.

We were both wearing dressy clothes; Oscar cleaned up surprisingly well and looked dapper in his suit and tie. I had on an elegant pencil skirt and a blue silk blouse that felt like I was wearing a cloud. I didn't even want to think about how much a shirt like that cost. I had an expensive leather purse slung over my elbow, and Oscar carried a full-sized briefcase. We'd actually made an appointment with another business that rented space in the building: a law firm on the eighth floor.

Nate could have come along, but for these little two-person missions, I wanted to change up who I traveled with so I could get more one-on-one time with the members of the team. Oscar had no poker face whatsoever and was pretty much an open book with everybody, so at least I didn't have to worry that he (unlike others) was placing bets on whether I would succeed. With Oscar, what you saw was what you got.

Plus, our plans for checking out the building involved climbing a lot of stairs. When it came to physical activity, Oscar was usually the best choice. He barely broke a sweat, even in the scorching Arizona summer heat.

I looked over the directory of businesses in the building. There were a surprisingly large number of companies renting space there, but it looked like Exponential Projects had the top four floors and a number of spaces scattered around the other floors.

We checked in with security on the ground floor. One of the guards, whose name tag read "Rodney," looked up the fake names on our fake IDs on a clipboard and handed us plastic visitor badges.

"You can scan this in the elevator," Rodney said. "You're going up to eight."

"Gracias," Oscar said. He was playing up his ethnicity on that particular visit. I, on the other hand, had a long blond wig on and was playing the part of the ditzy woman with more money than brains. We both had prosthetics on our faces, and Oscar wore a dapper little mustache. We definitely didn't look like us anymore.

As we passed the security desk, I looked back to see if I could get a look behind it. They appeared to have some security cameras in the building, because there was a monitor displaying four feeds. The monitor was small, but in my quick glance, the four feeds all looked similar to each other. We rounded the corner to a vestibule with four elevators, and I realized that the feeds must have been from cameras in each elevator.

We waited for a group to get on an elevator ahead of us, then caught the next one so we could have it to ourselves. I touched my visitor pass to the sensor on the panel, and a green light lit up. I pressed the button for the eighth floor, then tried to press the button for the twelfth. Eight lit up, but twelve didn't. Eleven didn't either, but I was able to select the tenth floor. So the top two floors had extra security; I figured that's where we would hit pay dirt.

I looked up into the back corner of the elevator, and sure enough, there was a smoked-glass dome. I turned my back to the camera and watched the floor number slowly change. Some modern office buildings had high-speed elevators, but this one was a plodding classic from decades ago, when the building was constructed.

We got off on the eighth floor to have our meeting with the lawyer. It was worth the half hour or so we'd spend in the law offices to give us a valid excuse for being in the building, in case we got caught snooping around. We were quickly led into a small conference room, where we waited for the lawyer to meet us.

I looked down at my cleavage, which was being shoved upward and inward by a brassiere that I'd swear was one of Jin's crazy inventions. I considered the view, then popped another button open on the blouse.

"Too much?" I asked Oscar.

He took a quick glance, then looked away. "No, it's probably just right."

"You're sure?" I leaned forward a little bit.

"Okay, now you're just making it awkward on purpose. This is like looking down my sister's shirt."

I snorted. I knew that from the neck up I wasn't Oscar's type, but I knew that *all* breasts were Oscar's type.

"Get used to looking," I said. "You have to sell the character."

"Yeah, but I don't have to look *now*," he said. "Believe me, I'll get an eyeful soon. And I'm gonna have to tell Nate all about how this went down when he takes me out for a casual beer later. I'd prefer to be able to look him in the eye."

"That's so sweet," I said.

The conference-room door opened, and the lawyer, Mr. Franklin, came in to sit down with us. I explained that my new lover (and I made sure to use the word *lover*, which I find just as creepy as some women find the word *moist*) wanted to start a business and that I wanted to finance it. I tossed my blond hair around and did my best to sound like an idiot. Oscar answered the lawyer's questions in broken, heavily accented English and spent a lot of time gazing at my cleavage. Mr. Franklin gave us a number of forms to take home and fill out and spent a lot of time gazing at my cleavage.

All in all, the bra was a rousing success.

After thirty billable minutes of pushing papers around and explaining our next steps, we both shook Mr. Franklin's hand and headed for the elevators. We looked around to make sure nobody was nearby, then opened the door into the stairwell next to the elevator instead.

Once inside, I pulled off my high heels and rebuttoned my blouse.

"Good-bye, friends," Oscar said. I smacked him with the expensive purse.

Checking for cameras and any security along the way, we climbed up from the eighth floor to the twelfth. I'm sad to admit, I had to catch my breath at the top of those four floors; the flights of stairs were impressively long. The door up there was locked, but that wasn't a problem. I pulled a manicure set from my purse and separated the metal nail file into three nesting lock-picking tools, then got to work. Oscar kept a lookout through the slender window in the door as I worked.

"Nothing really going on up here," he said.

"Good," I said. I popped the lock, put my heels back on, and opened the door. Sure enough, there wasn't anyone nearby. We made sure our visitor badges were clearly displayed, then walked down the hall together with a sense of purpose. We passed some people, but nobody gave us a second glance. We didn't see anything that looked like a room where they would keep secret project plans—most of the doors were glass, and we could see all the way to the outside windows through most of them. It was a classic example of showy offices for people to see and be seen, whenever they decided they needed to be there. On the plus side, the doors all had names on them, so the group was into labeling things.

I paid close attention to the ceilings, looking for cameras, but didn't see anything. I guess they only monitored the elevators, not the hallways or stairwells. Shoddy security, if you ask me.

We backtracked to the stairs. Once we were inside the stairwell, I re-locked the door. Anything we could do to keep people from suspecting that something was happening, we were going to do.

We went down to the eleventh floor and went through the same routine: Oscar kept lookout while I picked the lock. There were more people on eleven than there were on twelve, in that two people passed by the stairwell door while I was working on the lock. We were able to pop out of the stairwell without being seen. We did a lap of the floor, the same as we'd done up on the twelfth, but hit pay dirt near the far end of the hall. There was a door with "RECORDS" stenciled on it, and it had a key-card slot next to the doorknob. I knew there wasn't a point in trying our visitor passes in the slot: they were made for a quick scan, while the key-card slot was built for a thicker, more permanent plastic badge.

Like the stairwell doors, this one had a slender glass window set into it. It wasn't even large enough to get your arm through, if you could break the glass, but it was plenty large enough to see through. The room beyond had a number of filing cabinets, including the wide, flat ones commonly used to hold blueprints, and a pair of computers up near the front. It felt like the right kind of place to keep secret project plans. Oscar pulled out a smartphone and took a quick picture through the glass, then bent down to take a close-up shot of the key-card slot.

We finished our lap of the eleventh floor, then went back to the stairwell. I re-locked the door, waited while Oscar made some notes on his smartphone about the location of the records room, and then we headed down to ten. Just as the elevator was willing to allow visitors to go to the tenth floor, so was the stairwell—the door opened easily, without me having to pick the lock.

We walked a lap of ten, but there was nothing even remotely as interesting as the records room a floor above. It was nice to be able to just go into the stairwell and not have to lock the door behind me. We were making sure that nobody saw us use the stairs, but the three floors of Exponential Projects we'd seen so far were practically deserted.

We went down to the ninth floor, where we actually had to wait a minute for people to clear out of the area in front of the door. It was by far the busiest hall we'd seen so far.

Finally, the way cleared and we stepped out of the stairwell. We walked a lap of the floor, but we were both pretty convinced that what we wanted was up on the eleventh floor. There were more people walking through the halls, but nobody asked us what we were doing there; our visitor badges kept us in a bubble of safety. I accidentally bumped into a redheaded woman as we headed back toward the elevators. "Excuse me," I murmured as we kept walking.

We waited for the elevator, and managed to get one just to ourselves, but it looked like someone tried to catch it at the last minute just as the doors were closing. I saw a sliver of motion through the crack as the doors shut, but the person wasn't fast enough to catch a ride with us.

"All good?" I asked Oscar.

"I think so," he said. The elevator chimed and stopped at the ground floor. "Anything else before we go?"

I thought about the ride back to the airfield, which would take anywhere from fifteen to thirty minutes, depending on traffic. Then I thought about the fact that I'd had a rather large coffee on the way over. "You know what, I could actually use the facilities while we're here." I looked around for the restrooms and spotted a sign pointing around a corner from the elevators.

"I'll be over by the front doors," he said. "I'll upload these pictures so the team can take a look."

"I'll be right out," I said. I made my way around the corner and went inside the women's room. It was a pretty small space, considering the size of the building, but I figured that most floors had their own facilities; this tiny bathroom was out of the main traffic pattern and was probably only handy for visitors or people who just couldn't wait until they got to their own floor. There were four stalls, and a small door right behind the entrance that I figured was a storage and supply closet.

I checked my wig and prosthetics in the mirror: everything was where it was supposed to be. I went into the stall and did what I'd gone into the restroom to do. While I was finishing up, I heard the door swish open and the tip-tap of high heels on the tile floor. I heard the door shut, then a metallic sound I couldn't place. The person didn't walk over to one of the stalls; instead, it sounded like they headed to the storage closet. Sure enough, I heard the door open and some clunking and rummaging around.

I was suddenly on high alert. Someone with a reason to get into the storage closet wasn't going to be wearing high heels— anyone who was coming in to clean was going to be wearing sensible flat shoes. I finished my business, got my clothes where they needed to be, then quietly sat back down.

The person walked slowly along the line of stalls, stopping briefly in front of each one. I watched as the shoes appeared under my door. They were bright red and glossy and probably cost a pretty penny. The person's posture shifted; maybe she was looking underneath the doors to find out which stall was occupied.

She finished her stroll along the stalls; then I heard her shoes clicking to the other side of the room, where they stopped. The door didn't open again, so the person was staying in the room with me. Standing there, waiting.

I opened up the top of my expensive purse and took stock. There were a number of filler items, things only there for show, but I had a few useful tools in there. I flushed the toilet to give myself some cover noise and slid my hand into the bottom of the purse, grabbing my expandable baton.

I made sure that my hand was dry and my grip was sure; then I unlatched the stall door.

The woman with the bright-red shoes was standing by the sinks, watching me come out of the stall. It was the redhead I'd bumped into up on the ninth floor. She smiled when she saw me.

"I *thought* that was you," she said. "How *nice* to see you again."

Her hair was styled in a conservative manner, and her makeup was muted, except for bright-red lipstick. She had, I'm willing to admit, an absolutely rocking body in a skintight black business suit with a red satin blouse underneath. She was beautiful, but it was a deadly beauty, like a snake that's about to strike. I wouldn't exactly say I thought it was nice to see her again, because the last time I'd seen her, she'd made some not-so-pleasant threats. Then she called in the enemy for an attack.

Her name was Catherine, also known as Catalyst. She'd dated Nate once upon a time and didn't seem to care for any other woman being seen with Doctor Oracle.

She was holding the thing she'd taken from the storage closet: a very large, very heavy-looking wrench.

SIXTEEN

"Hey, Cat," I said. I flicked my wrist, and the expandable baton sprung out. I set the expensive purse down on the floor and pushed it out of the way with my foot.

Her smile twisted from vaguely wicked to downright evil. "Excellent. *Amy*, wasn't it?"

"Um . . . yeah?" I thought about it, and yes, that was the fake name I'd given her when we met before at Chalmun's, the supervillain nightclub. She'd threatened me for appearing with Doctor Oracle and made it sound like she had some sort of claim on him. Despite the fact that they'd only gone on three dates, he'd been in costume the whole time, and she didn't even know his real name. I wondered if following me down from the upper floors to confront me in a bathroom meant she was still hung up on Nate, or if she just wanted to get information.

"The hair is a little different but just as slutty. I had trouble placing you at first but figured it out soon enough. Same crappy dye job, and you have a very distinctive walk, like you have a stick jammed up your butt. Came in with someone new, though, didn't you? I wonder if you've moved on from Doctor Oracle. Greener pastures and all that."

She quickly turned toward the restroom door and lifted the wrench, smashing it down on the little twist knob of the deadbolt lock. The knob popped right off. I realized that the metal-on-metal sound I'd heard right after she'd come in must have been her locking the door. Then I wondered what kind of crazy public bathroom had a deadbolt on the inside of the door.

She spun back around and stared at me some more. "Wow," I said. It was about all my brain could muster. It felt like half my thoughts were about curling up and crying, while the other half were frantically remembering the layout of the room to see if there was a window or other avenue of escape behind me. There wasn't.

"Yeeaaaaaah," she said. "Though I don't really think your name is Amy at all, now, is it?" She lightly tapped the wrench into the palm of her hand. She had perfectly lacquered fingernails: bright red, naturally. I wondered if she'd worry about breaking one if she tried to use the wrench as a weapon.

"Well, I have a driver's license with the name Amy on it," I said. I gripped my baton tighter.

She laughed out loud, but there was no humor in it. "Very funny."

"Thanks?"

"But I get paperwork from some of the same places as Doctor Oracle. I could call him Jeremy, but I suspect that isn't his real name either. I'm sure you both have convincing documents in a variety of names."

"So do you want me to tell you a few of them, and you can pick the one you like the best?"

"No, I don't think so," she said. "I have a name in mind for you."

"Oh? I'd like to hear it."

"Not right now," she said. "I believe I'll keep that my little secret." Her mouth twisted around again; I had no idea that one beautiful woman could have so many different ugly smiles. But then again, this woman was a special kind of awful. She'd somehow planted a mole on our island, getting a girl to spy on one of us by threatening to kill the girl's mother. And at that moment, she appeared to know something about me I probably didn't want her to know.

"Really," I said, trying to show some bravado. "I guess we all know some little tidbits about each other here."

Her eyes narrowed. "What do you mean?"

"I believe," I said, "I'll keep that my little secret."

She straightened herself up even more and inhaled sharply. "You bitch."

"If that's the name you had in mind for me, it's been used before," I said. "Plus, it'd be so awkward for us to both have the same name. Maybe one of us should go by our middle name instead."

I could tell I was getting her a little riled up but wasn't entirely sure that was a good idea. We were trapped in a bathroom with a broken lock on the door, and she did have a large wrench. I knew I had some fairly good training with the baton; I just didn't know how well *she* could fight.

She breathed in deep and relaxed her features, trying to calm herself. She looked over my stance and the grip I had on my baton. "Oh, you're good. Someone has taught you well. And in such a short time, if my hunch is right."

The fact that I had, actually, been taught in a short time made me more nervous. I did some measured breathing of my own to try and stay calm. "I have no idea what you're talking about."

"Not that I'm terribly concerned for my life," she said. "After all, if you're working for Oracle, you probably have his silly attitude about not killing anybody. Someone really needs to talk him out of that, or he'll become a laughingstock."

I adjusted the baton in my hand. "As you said, I came in with someone else. So be careful, Cat. Maybe I don't have the same concerns about the sanctity of human life as he does."

"Ha," she said. "The fact that you used the tired old phrase 'sanctity of human life' tells me otherwise."

She walked slowly along the line of sinks. I mirrored her movement, walking in the opposite direction along the front of the stalls, trying to keep distance between us.

"Perhaps I will tell you," she said.

"Fine. Tell me. Don't tell me. Makes no difference to me."

"Oh, I think it will," she said. "*Sarah.*"

My heart stuttered for a second. Then my brain kicked it back into gear. "Yeah, I probably have a fake ID with that name on it."

She smiled again, showing enough teeth that it felt like she wanted to bite my face off. "Oh, I'm sure you have an ID with that name on it. But I don't think it's a fake one."

I was glad in a way that I'd been in a state of panic since I stepped out of the stall. Hopefully my panic that she knew my real name was hidden underneath the smothering blanket of all the other panic I was feeling.

"Eh," I said. "You can think what you want, I guess."

She squinted. "You're actually *quite* good. But I know the truth."

"Well, then, how about a deal?"

"Do tell."

"You tell me the truth you know about me, and I'll tell you the truth I know about you. And then I can soothe my itchy baton hand here by using it to beat you up a little."

She laughed again, but this time it almost sounded genuine. "Oh, this is such a *shame*! The funny thing is, I think I might actually *like* you a little bit." She pursed her lips and shook her head. "Of course, I loathe you far more."

"Of course," I said.

"I'm interested to know what you think you know about me," she said. "So let's play."

"Great," I said. We were slowly circling each other, holding our weapons out in ready positions.

"I figured it out eventually," she said. "Once I heard the whole story you told the Ultimate Faction."

"Yeah? What story is that?"

"The story of how Sarah Valentine escaped from the clutches of Doctor Oracle."

"The name sounds familiar," I said, my mind racing to come up with how many actual facts she could know. The one night she and I had met, I'd entered a nightclub as a blonde supervillain, and left through the secret back exit as Sarah Valentine, kidnap victim of Doctor Oracle. "Wasn't she that mousy hostage who escaped?"

"According to Commander Alpha, Sarah Valentine told him that she was taken into Chalmun's nightclub and stashed in the manager's office. Then she attacked a blonde and stole her outfit, which allowed her to escape. But, funny thing, I saw you and the Doctor come into the club, and there was no hostage along for the ride. And the outfit she stole was the same one you were wearing."

It was unsettling, hearing my real name come out of Cat's mouth. "Huh," I said. "Doesn't sound familiar. But Doctor O never tells me all of his plans. Maybe he stashed this Sarah girl in there earlier, before he picked me up. And maybe she stole an outfit from someone who just looked like me, since I jumped out a window as soon as Commander Alpha barged in through the front door."

She shook her head. "No, I don't think there ever was a hostage there. I think you walked in the front door on the Doctor's arm, and walked out the back door as yourself, *Sarah*. But you escaped from the Faction before I heard anything about you, so I wasn't able to warn them that Doctor Oracle's little blonde friend and Sarah Valentine were one and the same." She smiled in triumph.

"Cool story," I said. "I like the part where I get to be two different people."

"Once I figured it out, I tried to tell Alpha, but he didn't believe me. Said that there was no way that the irritating little hostage could keep that kind of information from him. But no matter. Once I've beaten you senseless in here, I'll give him a call, and we can find out who you really are under that disguise."

"That," I said, "is the most fascinating thing you've said."

"What?"

"That you tried to tell Alpha and that you can just give him a call. Last time I checked, Cat, you weren't on the same side as the supers."

"Well," she said, "I . . . I have contacts. Go-betweens."

"Like your mom?"

Her eyes widened, and I hoped I'd been better at hiding my surprise than she was. "I beg your pardon?"

My feet were getting tired of the high heels I had on. I kicked them off behind me and flexed my toes on the cool tile. Much better. I took another deep breath. I was guessing, but it was pretty educated guesswork. We'd discovered that Cat was passing her information off to the Green Lady, a member of the Ultimate Faction. I'd found a portrait of Cat on the wall of the Green Lady's home while we were there to steal a diamond; we didn't know for sure that they were related, but their powers felt too similar to be a coincidence.

"Yeah. You know, your *mom*. About your height, elegant as hell, a little bit green."

Her eyes grew even wider, then narrowed into a vicious glare. I'd hit a serious nerve.

"What do you know?" she demanded.

"Come on," I said. "You both metabolize poisons. It wasn't hard to figure out. You had a deal to pass secret information along to her, and she had a portrait of you on the wall of the salon right across from her art gallery." She blinked rapidly, taking it all in. I pressed on. "I don't know if she's as much of a cast-iron bitch as you, but she's probably pretty pissed that she lost her favorite diamond, am I right?"

"How *dare* you," she whispered. Her grip tightened on the wrench.

"And that portrait isn't at your mom's house anymore, is it? Seems to me the last time I saw it, Oracle had it hanging in the men's room, just above a urinal." We'd stolen the portrait, but had actually stashed it away in a closet, since none of us wanted to look at the thing. Not that she needed to know that.

Catalyst twitched when I mentioned both the diamond and the portrait, so I continued on. "At least she got you a job here. It has to be nepotism, right? Otherwise, what kind of office would need a chick with a crappy attitude and slutty fashion sense?"

She glared at me. "I will never take a handout from her. I'm here as a consultant, on my own merits, thank you very much, and I have a good thing going. I'm definitely not going to let *you* mess that up for me."

"Watch out, Cat," I said. "That's dangerously close to a villainous monologue. Plus, you just confirmed my guess."

I swapped my baton to my left hand and wiped my sweaty right palm on my skirt. She took advantage of the opportunity and leapt toward me. She didn't have a good windup, so I was able to use the baton to knock the wrench away from my face. My instincts kicked in, and while she was off-balance from her thwarted attack, I punched her square in the face. She wasn't ready for it, so she probably hadn't expected much of a fight out of me.

She let out a squawk and staggered back, blinking furiously and breathing hard. She wiped at the blood coming out of her nose, looked at her bloody hand, then looked at me with the most fury I've ever felt in my life.

She kicked off her bright-red shoes, and it was on.

I swapped the baton back to my right hand and lunged at her, swinging my arm down toward her head. I tried to change up my attack at the last moment to throw her off, but I was too late. She whipped the wrench around and knocked my baton out of the way. I started to step back, and she surprised me by bringing the wrench back around toward my side. I jumped back and dodged the blow by a hair. So far, she was a better fighter than I'd hoped for, but not out of my league. So far.

We circled each other some more; then she lunged again. She thrust with the wrench with one hand, and while I was busy blocking it with my baton, she swung her other arm around to backhand me. I jerked my head out of the way, but she managed to hit me along my jawline, and it hurt like crazy. I retreated as she had and gently felt around the side of my face. Nothing felt broken, but my hand did come away bloody.

She grinned, blood from her nose staining her teeth, and held up her left hand, which had an impressively large ring on it. She'd cut me with the stone, which was kind of poetically just, since we'd stolen a precious stone from her mother.

"Now we're even," she said.

I tried to keep her off-balance. "You know, Cat, seeing that blood on your face? It has me thinking. Red just isn't your color."

As a woman, I knew that I'd hit home. An insult from another woman about your appearance, even if it wasn't a woman you liked, was pretty unpleasant. I gave her as much of my focus as I could, but kept looking around the bathroom, trying to find something I could use to my advantage.

She came in for another attack, swinging the wrench in a wide arc. I waited for the right moment, just as Oscar had taught me, then dropped below her swing, bringing up the baton and giving her two solid whacks to the ribs. She grabbed a handful of my hair, but since it was a wig, she just ended up tearing out a bunch of strands without hurting me *too* much. At least it was only the pain of having my hairpins pulled, instead of the much worse pain of having my own hair pulled out at the roots. The fact that she went for my hair buoyed my spirits a little bit; it was such a teenage-girl move in a fight.

I grabbed her arm and twisted, trying to get it pinned behind her back. She swung her other fist and managed to catch me on the cheek, right below my eye. Thank goodness she didn't have a lot of momentum, or she might have broken my cheekbone. That said, the punch was still a doozy, and it hurt like hell.

We backed off from each other again. I didn't think I'd broken any of her ribs, but I was pretty sure she'd be bruised in the morning. I was also sure I'd be developing a massive bruise on my own face.

We were both breathing heavily, circling each other again. "You," she panted, "are going to regret everything you've said and done here. I'll make *sure* of that."

"Oh, Cat," I said between deep breaths. "That's adorable. When I get out of here, I'm going to alert the entire villain community that you've been working with the heroes since day one. And that you're the daughter of one of the biggies. I'm sure some of the psychopaths and madmen will be happy to hear it."

"And you, Sarah Valentine, will be on every super's most-wanted list."

"Good thing I'm not Sarah Valentine, then," I said.

Then I spotted my chance.

I lunged forward, bringing the baton down toward her shoulder. She raised the wrench to block my blow, but I hadn't put that much strength in it anyway; the baton was a diversion. I used my free hand to shove her backward. She grabbed at me, staggered backward, then smashed her bare foot down on one of her own high-heeled shoes.

She shrieked and fell to the floor. She dropped the wrench, which clattered over into one of the stalls. I ran over to take advantage of her position, and she kicked hard and caught me in the shin. It didn't hurt as much as the cut on my chin or the punch in the face, but it hurt enough to make me stagger and fall to the floor myself.

We both struggled to get up. She put her hand on the floor near me to push herself up, and I whipped my baton around and smashed it on her fingers like a nun with a ruler. She let out another yelp and went down again but thrashed her uninjured fist around and caught me in the stomach. I coughed out with the pain, and it felt like it was really hard to suck in more air.

She pushed herself up onto her hands and knees, then got to her feet. I was on the floor and didn't want her to gain the high ground. I mustered my strength and swung my baton around, hitting her in the ankle as hard as I could; I heard an awful cracking sound when I made contact. She squawked again and collapsed backward to the floor.

Her head hit the tile with a louder sound than expected, and she stopped trying to get up.

She actually stopped trying to do anything.

I crawled over to her, trying to catch my breath, baton raised in case it was a trick. But no, she was out cold. I checked her pulse, which was strong, and felt the tile floor around her head. No blood, so she hadn't whacked her head open on the hard floor. She'd just hit it hard enough to knock herself out. I was immensely relieved—the last thing I wanted was to have the first Doctor Oracle–related death to be by my hands.

I slowly and shakily got to my feet; my heart felt like it was pounding a mile a minute. I made my way over to the mirrors and looked at my jaw: the cut from her ring was at least three inches long, and it was weeping blood. The prosthetic cheek on the other side where she'd punched me was peeled half away, so I tore it off completely. I wet some paper towels and held them to the cut on my face. I dragged my purse over near the door and found Cat's purse tucked in the corner.

I rummaged through her bag to see if there was anything worth taking. There was a hard plastic key card with her picture on it, identifying her as Catherine Junkett. I wondered if that was her actual name as I put the card into my own bag. I found an iPhone with a cracked screen and tried to look through its contents, but it needed an unlock code. I buried the phone at the bottom of her purse, under some makeup and tissues, so that she'd be able to call for help when she woke up. There was nothing else of value in her purse, so I tossed it in a corner.

I dug into my own bag and pulled out a tiny travel package of Band-Aids. I wiped down my face, neck, and chest with wet paper towels, pinched the sides of the still-bleeding wound together, and slapped three bandages over it to try and hold everything together. I looked over the rest of my appearance. My wig was slightly askew and missing some hair, but mostly in the right place. I adjusted it, then brushed the blond hair forward so it would shield my haphazard bandage job and the redness growing on the opposite cheek. I washed the blood off my hands and checked my clothes. Fortunately, the intricate padded bra had absorbed most of the blood that ran down from my jaw. There were some dark red spots on my blue blouse, but they couldn't be helped.

With the lock on the bathroom door broken, and no window, I had to figure out another way to get out. I checked on Cat again to make sure her pulse and breathing were fine. When I was convinced that she wasn't going to be dying anytime soon, I looked around the room. The one thing that caught my eye was the acoustic ceiling tiles, but even standing on top of a toilet, I couldn't quite reach that high.

I stopped and closed my eyes, picturing the room in my mind instead of looking at it. I opened them again and looked at the little supply closet. I went over and opened the door and found a tiny room with a mop bucket and a number of shelves stacked with rolls of toilet paper. The shelves were exactly what I needed. I grabbed my shoes, stuffed them in my purse, and carefully hooked the straps of the bag over my arm. I climbed the shelves, using them like a ladder. I pushed one of the acoustic ceiling tiles up and out of the way, and hoisted myself up so I could see.

The tiles were dropped down about two feet from the concrete ceiling—more than enough room for me to crawl up there. I got my bearings, remembering which way I'd come in when I'd entered the bathroom. I pulled myself up and tried to distribute my weight across several tiles, since I didn't really trust them to hold me. Fortunately, I didn't have that far to go.

I reached forward and got my fingers under another tile, pulled it out, and pushed it off to the side. I shifted myself forward so I could see down through the hole and was delighted that my guess was right. There was an identical supply closet that backed up to the one I'd come from, attached to the men's room. I removed another tile so I'd have the best angle, slowly turned myself around, and lowered myself feet first into the men's supply closet, using the matching set of shelves as another ladder.

I put the tiles back in place, made it to the ground, and listened at the door for a full minute, but I didn't hear anything.

I turned the knob and pushed the closet door open and found myself in an empty men's room.

After another check in the mirror to make sure that my blond hair was covering the bandages on my jaw, and noticing how much blood had already saturated those bandages, I slipped my shoes back on and went to the bathroom door. I opened it a crack to peek out, but there was nobody outside. I wondered if these secluded bathrooms ever saw a visitor on a normal day.

I walked as quickly as I could to the front of the lobby, limping slightly because of the whack I'd taken on my shin, looking for Oscar. I spotted him near the front doors, where he was tapping on his smartphone. He looked up and saw me coming and tucked the phone away. As I got close, I saw him glance at my face, then at my slightly wobbly walk, then my bandaged jaw, then back at my face.

When I got close enough, he whispered, "What the hell happened to you?"

"Had a little visit with an old friend," I said. "We need to get out of here, *now*."

He put his hand around my back in a protective way, and we turned toward the front door of the building.

I looked over at Oscar just in time to see someone put a hand on his shoulder.

"Excuse me," said Rodney the security guard.

SEVENTEEN

I stayed turned away so Rodney wouldn't see the blood-soaked bandages on my jaw or the hot area on my cheek that was likely turning majestic colors with every passing minute. Oscar turned to him with a broad smile on his face. I knew him well enough to see by the set of his shoulders that he was ready for action.

"Si, señor?" Oscar said, cranking his accent up to eleven.

"Your visitor badges," Rodney said. "If you're leaving, I'll need to collect those."

I let out the breath I'd been holding and unclipped mine from the front of my blouse. I glanced at it and quickly wiped it on my skirt to get rid of a spot of blood. I handed it to Oscar. He took his own badge off and held them both out.

"Please to forgive her," Oscar said. "The lawyer, he say very bad news."

"I'm sorry to hear that," Rodney said. "I hope everything works out, ma'am."

I made some snuffling sounds and nodded, keeping my face pointed at the floor and my blood-spattered blouse turned away from Rodney.

"Gracias," Oscar said. "Perhaps we will see you again."

"You folks have a good day, now." Rodney turned and walked back toward his post. Oscar quickly turned, put his hand around my waist, and hustled me out the front of the building. We made our way to the car as fast as we could without drawing any extra attention. We checked everything over and got in, and Oscar hopped behind the wheel.

He drove toward the nearest exit and got caught behind a car waiting to turn left across the busy street. He drummed his fingers impatiently on the steering wheel. "So, who did this to you?"

"Catalyst," I said. "She's working there, or at least has a key card."

The car in front of us finally moved. Oscar turned right out of the parking lot and headed for the freeway on-ramp. "I hope she looks worse."

"Well, she's definitely a lot more unconscious than I am," I said. I opened my purse and pulled out my burner smartphone. "On that note, I better call nine one one."

"What?" Oscar merged onto the freeway headed toward the city.

"She's knocked out, stuck in an out-of-the-way bathroom with a broken lock. I don't like the woman, but I don't want her dying in there or anything." I dialed the nine, and then a beeping sound behind me startled me. I turned toward the back of the SUV and saw the little gadget stuck to the rear window that watched for tails. Instead of green, the light on the little device was flashing red.

"I guess someone found her," Oscar said.

"Maybe," I said. "But I'm still calling it in." I finished dialing the emergency number and let them know that someone had fallen and hit her head in the bathroom and that the lock on the door was broken. I gave them the address and hung up before the questions got too in-depth.

Oscar, meanwhile, was changing lanes on the freeway like a fiend. At the last moment, he took an off-ramp toward downtown. I watched out my side mirror as a generic black SUV, much like the one we were in, took the ramp at high speed. I turned and looked out the back window, but I couldn't see who was driving or how many people were in the vehicle. At least it looked like we only had the one car following us.

"I kind of wish Jin was here," Oscar said. "It's a joy to watch her get away from these kind of guys." He wrenched the steering wheel hard enough to make me thankful for my seat belt, taking us down a side street. I fired up the map application on my burner phone to see where we were headed.

"You want a big street, or something small?" I asked. I'd been taught a few evasive driving maneuvers, but there were still a lot of things I didn't know.

"Big," Oscar said. "It'll probably be slower, but easier to get some cars between us."

"Then take this next right. Two blocks over we can grab what looks like one of the main roads."

Oscar made the turns, and we ended up on a wide road in the middle of downtown Phoenix. There were three lanes of traffic in each direction, and with some strategic lane changes, we managed to get a few cars ahead of our followers. The gadget in the window continued to beep sporadically.

"Any nice and wide cross streets coming up?"

"Two blocks up," I said. "Left is a quicker shot out of the downtown area; right will take you back through the concrete jungle."

"Right it is," he said. "More buildings mean more options."

"Got it."

"How's your face?" Oscar asked.

I flipped down the sun visor and looked in the mirror on the back. The fabric pads in the middle of the Band-Aids were all soaked with red, but nothing appeared to be dripping out. I gently prodded the bandages and was rewarded with a stinging pain.

"Good, I guess? It hurts, but it isn't gushing blood."

"Okay. Not gushing is good. Don't worry, we'll get you back and fixed up in no time."

"Will I get the gray slime?" The island's medical doctor had a concoction they called nanogel, some thick slurry of nanobots and antibiotics and heaven knows what else. I'd seen her slather it on Nate's arm one time, when he got cut. There wasn't even a scar there anymore. I looked at Oscar; he'd gotten his chin busted open at the same time Nate got injured, and Oscar didn't have a scar either.

I hoped I'd have the same luck. If, that was, we got away from the guys following us.

"Had to happen eventually. We've all been slimed at one time or another."

"Great."

Oscar put a few more cars between us, then had me get the map out again. "There's a parking garage in that building up on the right."

"We're going in there?" I asked.

"Eventually. First, I need you to make a note of where we are right now."

I looked at the phone. "Cool, all of the named streets are presidents. We're on Van Buren, between Second and Third."

"Now, can you help me take a bunch of turns, like six or seven, and get us back here?"

"Heck yeah," I said. "Okay. Left up here on First." I proceeded to give Oscar a series of directions that took us in a series of figure eights around the downtown area. We passed the courthouse, a big theater, and the train station. With every turn, our lead grew on the car behind us, but we could see it a few cars back.

We made it back around to Van Buren, and Oscar turned into the parking garage. We had a good lead at that point, and as we took the turn into the garage, I couldn't see the car behind us anymore. Oscar had his window down already and grabbed a ticket from the machine in record time. He barely cleared the underside of the automatic arm and whipped the car up the ramp at a speed that probably wasn't entirely safe. Then, in a surprise move, he turned hard into a parking spot on the first level and shut the engine off.

"Duck down," he said. We both slouched in our seats, and I watched the side mirror. After a moment, a black SUV came around the corner up the ramp, tires squealing. It rushed past our parking spot and continued on up, farther into the garage.

Oscar sat back up, quickly started the car, backed out, and turned in the opposite direction, toward the entrance of the garage. The exit lane was manned by a bored-looking guy in a booth, on the other side of the building from where we'd come in. Oscar handed over his ticket.

"Dude," the guy said. "You just got this ticket, like, a minute ago."

"My wife forgot something at home," Oscar said. "You know how it is."

"Boy, do I ever," the guy said. "I'm not gonna charge you. Have a good day." He pressed a button in his booth and the arm raised, letting us out.

Oscar asked me to look up the nearest car rental company. Finally, I could be of more assistance, because of my excellent Google-fu.

"Okay, teaching time," he said. "We're going to drop this car off on the street and rent another one to get us back to the airfield. They may have called in the plates on this one to the police or some other agency, so I don't trust it to get us very far."

"Makes sense," I said. "Looks like there's a rental place just up ahead, in the lobby of the Grand Western Hotel."

We parked on a side street and took our things out of the SUV. Oscar went to the rental counter while I went to the lobby-level bathrooms to look at my jaw. I gently pulled one of the bandages away; the cut was starting to crust over. I stuck the bandage back down and arranged my wig a little better, combing the hair over the side of my face. I swept the hair across my cheek on the other side, since it was indeed getting redder by the minute. I was on high alert, since the last time I'd been in a public restroom, unpleasant things had happened.

I met Oscar back out in the lobby, and we made our way to the hotel's parking garage, where our rental car waited for us. We installed the rear-window camera and took off, headed on a roundabout route back to the airfield.

"So I get almost everything you did back there, but why park on the first floor of that garage? It worked, but I wonder how you *knew* it would work," I said.

"Garages are tricky," Oscar said. "Everyone's instinct is to go up, up, as high as you can. But when you get up there, it's easy to get trapped, with nowhere else to go. If you can hide in plain sight, nine times out of ten a pursuit vehicle will keep going, assuming you're headed for the roof. For that one time out of ten that they spot you, you're on the ground floor already, so it's easier to get out of the garage on foot and hide somewhere else. Much better than having to run if you're on the top floor."

"Sharp," I said. "I'll remember that."

We made it back to the airfield without any more incidents. We dropped off the rental car there, and called Evie so she could scrub the rental records.

Onboard the plane, where we had better first-aid supplies than a travel-sized package of Band-Aids, I gently peeled the bandages away and cleaned my wound the best that I could with hydrogen peroxide, then slapped a big piece of gauze over everything and had Oscar tape it down for me. It would have to suffice until we got back to the island.

I took an inventory of my other aches and pains, which were really settling in now that the adrenaline rush was fading. My jaw really hurt, my face slightly less so. I had no idea what kind of damage had been done to my cheek, since I'd never been punched in the face before. I ran my tongue around and poked my teeth on that side. At least none of them felt loose.

My shin hurt and was turning the same red as my cheek, so I figured I was in for some nasty bruises. The pain in my abdomen was more of a dull ache deep inside, and I hoped there was nothing ruptured. I was looking forward to a thorough inspection by Dr. Adams when we returned.

Plus, Nate needed to know that my real name was likely going to be attached to Doctor Oracle as an associate, if it wasn't already. That was going to be the part that hurt the most.

EIGHTEEN

Nate had a pair of transport balls at the airfield waiting for us. We'd called ahead to let him know that I was all right but that I'd need to visit the doctor when we returned. As soon as the plane came to a stop, he rushed over and met us at the stairs.

"Easy, buddy," Oscar said. "She's fine."

I limped down the stairs slowly, since my poor calf was now red and swollen where Cat had kicked me.

Nate caught my arm to help me down, and his gaze flicked between the bandage on my jaw and the bright-red spot on the opposite cheek. "Fine? This is fine?"

"This is fine," I said. "I don't think anything is broken."

"Oh, well, as long as nothing is broken," he said. He was gentle in helping me into the transport ball, but I could tell he was really upset. Oscar took the other ball and loaded our gear into it while Nate drove me around to the medical wing.

"Nate," I said, "I've seen you cut up and bloody. I've seen you with broken bones. This is no different."

He tightened his grip on the steering wheel. He took a deep breath and let it out slowly.

"You're right," he said. "But I'm used to me getting hurt. This is the first time I've had to experience *you* getting hurt."

"At least now I'll get to experience the nanogel."

He didn't laugh. "When the doctor is done, I want to hear everything."

"Of course," I said.

We made it to the medical wing, where Dr. Adams was already waiting for us. Jin was there, too, so she could make sure I was okay. She apologized for not being there for me when the action went down, though she'd admitted to me more than once that she was pretty useless in a fight.

Dr. Adams scanned me with several devices and poked and prodded both my leg and my abdominal area. She declared that both were bruised, but nothing was broken or ruptured. She pulled the bandages off my jaw, cleaned the wound, rubbed some kind of numbing solution around the edges, and gave me six neat stitches. Besides when I'd had my wisdom teeth removed as a teenager, they were my first stitches ever. It wasn't necessarily an item on my bucket list.

She followed that up with a hearty dollop of the gray nanogel, sealed a watertight bandage on top, and ordered me to return in two days for an inspection.

"Eurgh," I said to her. "That stuff feels as gross as it looks."

"I'm also going to put some on your cheek and your shin," she said. "It will accelerate the bruising process."

"Why would I want that?"

"The faster the bruises appear, the faster they'll disappear."

"Then by all means, bring it on," I said. She slathered a thin layer of the nanogel on my cheek, which felt just as cold and slimy as the thick layer she'd put on my cut. It felt just as disgusting on my leg.

"That should do it for now," she said.

I felt a warmth growing in the places she'd put the nanogel. "Should it feel this way? Kind of warm and weird?"

"The tingling means it's working," Dr. Adams said with a smile as she made one last inspection of the bandage over the cut on my jaw. "You're very lucky. There are a lot of ways an injury that close to your neck could go really wrong, really fast." She turned to Nate. "Get some food in her, and make sure she gets some rest."

"I'm right here," I said.

"And were you planning on resting?" Adams asked.

"Well . . . I did have some plans to go over," I said.

"Exactly my point."

It was late in the evening when I was finally released, and I was starving. Jin left to report in to the rest of the team, and Nate offered to stop by the food court to grab something. I took the elevator up to my apartment and set the door to automatically open for Nate when he returned. I threw my clothes in the hamper and took a hot shower, cleaning the best I could around the bandage on my jaw. I threw on some yoga pants and a T-shirt and came back out to find Nate in the kitchen, dishing up the comfort food he'd brought up: macaroni and cheese, meatloaf, and lumpy mashed potatoes.

I walked up next to him, and he turned toward me. He dropped the spoon back into the mashed potatoes, grabbed the front of my T-shirt, and kissed me hard, being careful of my bruised cheek.

After we broke apart, Nate finished putting food on two plates.

"This was the first meal I ever ate here," I said.

"I know."

He set the plates on the kitchen island, where I had a pair of barstools. I grabbed a bottle of wine and poured us each a glass. We settled in next to each other.

"So," he said. "Let's hear what happened."

I told him everything, from the visit to the lawyer and the investigation of the upper floors of the Exponential Projects building to my fight with Catalyst and our low-speed car chase and escape downtown. I ended by telling him everything Cat had said to me, her guesses about who Doctor Oracle's mysterious new companion actually was. It was good I'd saved that part for last, because I got choked up and tears came to my eyes. It was the part I didn't want to think about but that I needed to worry about the most.

"But she said Alpha didn't believe her," he said.

"No, but she was *so* convinced," I said. "And she's working for them now. They may take her more seriously."

He blew out a breath. "Well, we'll figure something out."

"No, Nate, come on. You're always so calm about everything, sure that things will all work out." I pushed my plate away and stood up. "If word gets out that Sarah Valentine is working with Doctor Oracle, I won't be able to use my own name ever again. And I won't be able to show my real face anywhere but on this island. I won't be able to just be anonymous in a crowd anymore, because I'll always be worried that someone will spot me and know me. You have your secret identity, but I've completely lost mine." I walked over to the couch and flopped down on it.

"There are things we can do," he said.

"What, plastic surgery? Is that what it's going to take? If I want to show my face, I'll have to get a different one?"

"We'll come up with something."

I buried my face in my hands, trying not to cry, but not succeeding. Nate came over and sat down on the couch next to me, and gently rubbed my back.

"It's okay," he said. "It's going to be okay."

"That's *so* not what I want to hear," I said into my hands. "Reassuring platitudes suck."

"Fine. No platitudes. How about this: we get someone else to wear the blond wig and the silver outfit, just like the one you had on when you first met Cat. Jin's about your size; with the right makeup we could pull it off. She's seen with me, and we do something really audacious and public. Meanwhile, you're spotted in plain sight several states away."

I sniffed. "You really think that will work?"

"We might need to do it a few times, but sure, I think it will work. It'll be just like when Doctor Oracle comes here to the island on business and I'm seen elsewhere by a lot of people. And how about in the comic books? There's a running joke that you never see Superman and Clark Kent in the same place, and yet nobody figures it out. Well, if we can show that Sarah Valentine and this mysterious blonde villain are in different places at the same time, it'll be obvious that you aren't working with me."

"That's in the comics," I said. "Nobody's that dumb in real life."

"*Everyone's* that dumb in real life," he said. "If the easy answer is that you aren't working with me, because you're in a coffee shop a thousand miles away, people will believe it. They always believe the easy, obvious thing. That's part of what makes them human."

I sniffed and wiped my face. "Okay, we'll try it."

"Good," he said, putting his arm around me. I leaned into him, and we sat quietly for a few minutes.

"It's not that I'm *entirely* against plastic surgery," I said. "Especially if I got new boobs out of the deal."

"Your boobs are perfect as they are. Let's try the less extreme options first."

"Okay." I took a deep breath and let it out and wiped the remaining tears from my face.

"Not to change the subject . . ."

"Go for it," I said. "This has been all about me."

"I want to apologize if I was acting like an ass on the drive over, and in the hospital wing. But I have to admit, when you guys called in that you needed to visit the hospital, it hit me harder than I expected."

"What, that I got hurt? It was bound to happen. Everybody gets hurt."

"I'm not in love with everybody," he said. "The rest of the team, they're like my brothers and sisters. You're definitely *not* like my sister."

I sat up and moved away, turning toward him. "You aren't taking me off this project, are you?" That was the last thing I needed, to fail the mission when we'd just really started to get things rolling.

"No, no," he said, holding up his hands. "This is my problem to deal with, not yours. And yeah, everybody gets hurt. I just have to figure out how to handle these emotions when it's you."

"It's not like I couldn't get hurt in other ways," I said. "Yeah, we're in more dangerous situations than most people, but if we were out there in the real world, I could get hit by a bus tomorrow."

"I know. And I've thought a lot about all of the stupid sayings that people throw around. If you love someone, set them free. It's better to have loved and lost. All that stuff. I've been thinking about it for quite a while now, and I thought I had my emotions sorted. But obviously, that isn't the case."

"And here you wanted to get married in Vegas."

"I haven't changed my mind on that," he said. "I'm game if you are."

"I don't see a ring."

"Fine, I'll figure out a ring. Not stolen, right?"

"Right," I said. "And when you figure that out, I'll start taking you seriously."

He reached over and gently touched the bandage on my face. "I'm sorry this happened."

"Not your fault," I said. "Although . . . just a thought here, maybe this kind of thing wouldn't happen if you didn't date crazy women."

"Well, if you marry me, you can be the last crazy woman I date."

I didn't have much to say to that, so I kissed him instead.

NINETEEN

We had a breakfast meeting at Nate's the next morning to go over what we'd found out at Exponential Projects. I got lots of sympathetic hugs, in addition to congratulations for getting my first injuries on the job. Oscar insisted I describe my fight with Cat to everyone, since I'd already told him everything on the flight back. As I told it, I could see Nate squirming a little in his chair, but he didn't say anything.

Elliot seemed just as sympathetic and supportive as everyone else, but that wasn't entirely surprising. First off, everyone in the group was at least a somewhat decent actor, as we'd all had to take on roles as other people while on missions. But secondly, he'd never been unsupportive to my face. For all I knew, he actually *hoped* I'd succeed but had figured out statistics or math or something that predicted I wouldn't. Still, I didn't like thinking about that bet I'd overheard him make with Rupert, wagering a bottle of scotch that my first time as team leader would be a failure.

I filled the team in on everything Cat had said. Nate proposed his plan to be seen in public with Jin while she wore my blond wig and silver outfit, and Rupert said he'd start putting the makeup together right away. It was just a relief to know that the mission was going to go on as planned and that the possibility of the supers knowing my real identity wasn't going to get me kicked out.

"Security is high at the EP building now," Evie reported. "But there were no police reports filed about the fight or about anyone being injured."

"So they know that someone is poking around," I said. "And that someone might or might not be affiliated with Doctor Oracle. But they don't know what we're trying to find."

"And that's where we have the advantage," Evie said. "I've been digging around in as many dark corners as I can, and I've discovered that Exponential Projects is backing quite a few things, in quite a few places. Most of them are experimental, and have the potential to improve a lot of people's lives, which is great."

"If we've inspired them at all to be a little more community minded, instead of all about the fame and prestige, I'm all for it," Nate said.

"So they'll be watching and waiting," I said.

"They already have extra guards on site," Evie said. "And without a doubt, the key card you gave me won't work anymore, but I have a little work-around that may make it useful if we get inside."

"It's just a matter of getting inside," I said.

"I'm working on that," Jin said. "I have a couple of ideas and some messages out but haven't heard back from my sources yet."

"Keep working, everyone," I said. "Do you think we'll be able to meet up again tomorrow, same time, and have more information? We're less than two weeks out from Labor Day, and the clock is ticking."

"I should have some preliminary plans in place by then," Jin said.

"A little more tweaking on some things, and we'll know if my key card idea will work," Evie said.

"Oscar, I'll want you in the field, since you've been in the building already," I said. "Anyone else think they'll be helpful out on this job?"

"I, for one, will be more than happy to stay here," Evie said. "I've been to Arizona. What a ghastly place."

"You think so?"

"My dear, it's like a giant ashtray," she told me. "So dry and brown and dry. And hot, this time of year."

"I didn't mind it so much," I said.

"Perfect. Then I volunteer to stay behind here and do any monitoring necessary."

We broke up the meeting, agreeing to convene again for breakfast the next day. Everyone drifted out, leaving me and Nate behind. Since I had a bandage on my jaw and the bruise on my face was quickly turning a nice shade of bluish black, I didn't really want to go out and have too many of the minions on the island see me. I was able to brush my own hair over my cheek for the quick trips down the hall and back between Nate's apartment and mine, but other than that, I was going to stay in for the most part. Nate had promised Dr. Adams that he'd make sure I ate and rested, so we bummed around his apartment for much of the day, taking a well-needed day off. We read books, watched TV, played a variety of card games, and fooled around.

In the early afternoon, Evie pinged my ChatterBox, asking to come up to show me something. She showed up a few minutes later with a tablet in her hands.

"Since we're worried that the Ultimate Faction now knows who you are, I checked the security cameras we set up in your old apartment," she said.

My heart sank. If she was bringing something to show us, it meant the cameras had recorded something at my creaky old loft. "What happened?"

She propped the tablet up on the kitchen counter, and the three of us sat around it on the barstools. She scrolled forward through the recorded footage.

"Here," she said. "Time-stamped last night, a little after midnight."

The image on the tablet was split up into four separate feeds: three inside my apartment and one covering the street and front door outside. As we watched, a beat-up old car pulled up in front of the building. Someone wearing a hoodie got out; it was impossible to see their face in the shadows. However, the picture was clear enough and the streetlight bright enough that I could make out the person's shape. It looked like either a thin, short boy, or a woman.

The person approached the front door of my building and stood there for a minute, fiddling around. I figured the person didn't have a key and was picking the lock. Jin would have shaken her head sadly if she watched it; she could probably pick that old lock in ten or fifteen seconds. I wasn't the expert that Jin was, and even I could have had the door open in less than half the time of the person in the hoodie.

I felt a little less panic, since it appeared that the midnight visitor was something of an amateur.

Finally, the person moved in through the front door. We waited for another few minutes, watching the silent footage as the person climbed the stairs up to the third floor and, I presume, struggled again with picking the apartment's front-door lock.

Finally the door opened, and the person wearing the hoodie walked into my old apartment.

I wasn't too worried about the person finding anything, since I'd gone in and cleaned out any real personal items and valuables already. But I felt a vague sense of violation, seeing someone break into my apartment.

Then I realized that my job was now to break into places exactly the same way and that the people on the other end probably felt the same sense of being violated. We left the apartment set and monitored just to catch people breaking in; I guess I needed to put some thought into my new career and how, in some ways, it denied me the right to be hurt or offended by certain things.

The person in the hoodie skulked around, opening drawers and cabinets, but there wasn't much to see. Then they pushed their hood back, and I could see long hair and hints of the person's profile. It was a woman, but I couldn't make out a lot of detail, since the lights were off inside the apartment and she hadn't opted to turn them on. But the woman's hair was straight, and not as long as Catalyst's mass of red curls, so I knew it wasn't Cat.

She flipped over the cushions on the couch, feeling around underneath. Then she went into the bedroom and searched everywhere, including under the bed and between the mattress and box spring. We knew she wouldn't find anything, but it was fascinating to watch.

She pulled a number of books from the shelves and riffled through them, holding them upside down so that any paper tucked inside would fall out. So she couldn't pick a lock very fast, but she had received *some* training. A piece of paper fluttered out of one of the books onto the floor, and she bent over to pick it up. I thought from the size and shape that it was probably just a bookmark, a thought that was confirmed when she threw it back over her shoulder.

The mystery woman passed by the windows, and the streetlight outside finally gave me a look at the color of her hair. It was a bright, vibrant red, the kind that came from a box of Manic Panic. The hoodie was an equally vivid shade of red. I couldn't think of anyone I'd met, or anyone in the database, who wore head-to-toe red except for Catalyst.

"And now, here we go," Evie said.

"What?" I asked.

"Brace yourself," she said.

The woman turned around a few times, too fast to catch a solid look at her face. Then she grabbed one of the throw pillows from the couch and scratched at it with her fingernails. Even in the low light, I could see the pillow split open, its white stuffing spilling out.

I knew exactly who the girl was then. Her name was Bethany, one of a number of junior members of the Ultimate Faction. I'd met her during the two days a few months ago when I was in the Faction's custody, supposedly to keep me safe after rescuing me from Doctor Oracle. In fact, I'd given myself up as a distraction so that Nate could get away, so there was no actual rescuing involved. There was also no safekeeping involved, since I'd overheard Commander Alpha discuss using interrogation techniques on me that I'm sure wouldn't have been covered by the Geneva convention.

I'd gotten Bethany into trouble with Commander Alpha by convincing her to let me do a little roaming around the compound where they were keeping me. So I wasn't sure if she was there on official Faction business, or if she'd heard Catalyst's ravings about me being in cahoots with Doctor Oracle and decided to pay me a visit herself for a little bit of personal revenge.

As we watched, she used her superpower—fingernails that could grow into deadly foot-long claws—to shred almost every fabric-covered item in the apartment. Every throw pillow, the cheap IKEA couch, the lumpy mattress I should have replaced years ago. She dug through all the stuffing and filling and fluff and didn't find anything.

She didn't shatter any dishes from the kitchen cupboards, but I suspect that since the visit was at midnight, she was trying to be quiet. It made me think even more that this was a personal mission, not one the Ultimate Faction had sanctioned. For the most part, the Faction was allowed to do as much damage as they wanted, and all was forgiven because it was under the umbrella of fighting bad guys.

When everything was shredded and the apartment was a mess, every surface covered with so much white fluff that it looked like it had snowed inside, she finally realized that there was nothing to find. She put her hood back up and left, re-locking the front door on her way out. After a minute of everything being still, she came back out the front door of the building, hopped in the junker car, and drove off.

"Well," I said, trying to make light of the situation. "Glad I didn't really care too much for that furniture."

"This is that girl you told us about, right?" Nate asked. "The one who cut me that one time."

"Yeah, Bethany," I said. "Junior member of the Ultimates. I guess I'm not on her friends list."

"What do we think? Does the Faction believe that Sarah is working with us?" Evie asked.

"I'm not so sure yet," I said. "This almost felt like a secret mission. It looked like she was being very quiet about the whole thing, even though she made a huge mess."

"The Faction is usually more open about their operations than this," Nate agreed. "Especially if they believed that Sarah was working with Doctor Oracle. They'd be breaking down that apartment door in broad daylight, not sneaking in at midnight."

"But . . . oh," I said.

"What?" Nate asked.

"Her hair. The hoodie. When I met Bethany before, her color scheme was all purple, both the hair and the outfit."

"And now it's bright red," Nate said. "Like someone else we know."

"Exactly. If Bethany found out that Catalyst was going after me, because she thought the mystery blonde and Sarah Valentine were the same person, maybe Bethany joined up with her. I'm pretty sure I got her in trouble with Alpha when I was there, but I have no idea how *much* trouble."

"Enough so that she'd join up with Catalyst? Change her whole color scheme and become, what, a partner? A sidekick?" Evie asked.

"The theory fits," Nate said. "So Cat convinced one person about her ideas. And when one person can be convinced, others could be right behind."

"Yeah, so if you want to try this idea of being seen around town with a fake me, we should get on it," I said.

Nate nodded. "I've been thinking about it today. If Jin has her plan in place for how to get into Exponential Projects, she and I could take a quick jaunt out to Seattle sometime tomorrow. We'll zip you out in the jet, to a different city, and anonymously alert the locals there to keep an eye on you, since there's a chance that Doctor Oracle could be trying to find you to recapture you."

"Where do you think is far enough away?"

"Well, when you quit WonderPop, you let them know you were going into hiding. Where would the old Sarah Valentine have gone?"

I thought about it. "I've kind of always wanted to see Colorado."

"Done," he said. "Pick your place. Aspen, Boulder, Denver, wherever. I'll take the lead on project throw-them-off-Sarah's-trail while you keep working on the Lucy project."

"Speaking of Lucy, I should give her a quick call," I said. "Update her on our progress."

"I can get an encrypted voice over IP line for you whenever you like," Evie said. "Should be good for at least ten minutes before you have to worry about being traced."

"I'll give her a call tonight, then. Can I get it set up in my office around eight?"

"Absolutely, my darling," she said. I gave Evie a hug, and she packed up her tablet and left.

"Want me to go down and grab some dinner?" Nate asked.

"I have enough stuff to do sandwiches at my place, if you want."

"Sounds good." We gathered up the books we were reading and our tablet computers and went back down the hall to my apartment. Even though it had mostly the same layout as Nate's place, the color scheme was different, and I had a view of the ocean instead of his view of the jungle and hills at the center of the island. It was a nice change of scenery.

I pulled out what I had in my refrigerator, and we made sandwiches side by side.

"I just hope . . . ," I started, but I didn't finish the sentence. I realized I just didn't want to say the words. I was afraid just talking too much about something would make it come true.

"What?" Nate asked. I shook my head, but he clearly didn't want to accept a head shake as an answer. He pointed the nozzle of the mustard bottle at my face, a gentle yellow threat.

I sighed. "Fine. I was just going to say, I hope this disguise plan works. I'm still mostly convinced that my picture is going to appear on the front page of newspapers any day now, tying me in with Doctor Oracle."

"No way," he said. I opened my mouth to speak, but he held the mustard back up. "And that's not just me being an optimistic goober, I'll have you know. Seriously, if Commander Alpha believed Catalyst, it would be all over the papers already. She needs hard proof, and she doesn't have any. Any video footage of you at the Exponential building will show a blonde who looks nothing like Sarah Valentine. And this trip to your apartment was clearly an attempt to get that proof she needed, and they got nothing from it."

"You're probably right," I said, and took the mustard away from Nate so I could use it. "But you know me, I like to find weird things to worry about. You took away my opportunity to worry about whether you'd kick me off the island if our relationship tanked, with all that legal paperwork. I have to have *some* reason to worry about being kicked out of the club."

"That paperwork would also cover this situation," he said. "The lawyers are pretty thorough. It doesn't just have to be our relationship tanking, which I sincerely doubt will happen, especially if we get married."

"Oh my God," I said, aiming the mustard at him as he'd done to me. "Not again with the marriage. Do you have a ring?"

"Nope, just keeping it fresh in your mind." I put the mustard back in the fridge. "Anyway, that offer of a good reference and the cashing out of your profits is there for a ton of situations, not just relationship tankage. Hell, the profits are so good already, you could retire somewhere that doesn't extradite to the United States and live a long, comfortable life."

"Yeah, but how boring would that be?"

"Right? Best that you stay right here, we do this thing to trick the supers, and we keep stealing stuff, making stuff, and changing the world in awesome ways."

"All right. I hope we don't tank, because you can always talk me down from a ledge." I kissed him, we put everything else away in the fridge, and we took our sandwiches out to my deck to eat while watching the sun set.

"One interesting thing," he said. "You're way ahead of me."

"What do you mean?"

"Only a few months as a villain, and it looks like you already have not just one, but *two* nemeses."

TWENTY

Lucy didn't sound as upbeat as usual on our phone call and asked to meet with me in person as soon as possible. Nate had come down to my office with me, under the guise of keeping an eye on me. We consulted briefly while I covered the mouthpiece of the phone; then I agreed to meet her the next day in Phoenix.

The next morning, we had another breakfast meeting over at Nate's. We laid out the next steps in our plan for helping Lucy, and Nate's plans for getting the supers off my back. I would go with Oscar to Phoenix in the jet to meet up with Lucy in the morning; then we'd go up to Denver, where I'd be seen publicly shopping and sitting in a coffee shop. At the same time, Nate in his Doctor Oracle outfit, with Jin by his side dressed in the same style of outfit I'd worn when I first met Catalyst, would be up in Seattle raising a little hell. They didn't elaborate on what exactly they'd be doing but promised that we'd probably see it on the Internet before the day was through.

As far as helping Lucy, our plan was almost solid. Jin had an idea about how to get us into the Exponential Projects building and back out again without having to deal with the guards; she'd gotten in touch with some friends who were willing to help, for the right price. In addition, her tech-and-gadgets team was working on a device to help us out.

As the team leader, I listened to all the ideas, asked questions when things were unclear, and offered up suggestions.

It's what I'd seen Nate, Oscar, and Jin do when they were taking the lead. Nobody jumped up and accused me of being a fraud, so hopefully I was on the right track. Elliot seemed just as cheerful and interested as usual, but I couldn't help wondering if he having a good mental laugh at my ineptitude.

I stopped in at the hospital wing, where Dr. Adams pulled away the bandages on my jaw and gave me a mirror to take a look. Where there was a bloody mess before, now there was a new pink scar with six neat stitches in it. She put more nanogel just along the scar tissue and covered everything up with a small, flesh-colored bandage. From a distance, you could barely see that I had the bandage on. My stomach was a little sore, and my shin still hurt a bit, but overall, I'd really improved in a very short time.

Not only had the nanogel done a great job on the cut on my jaw, but it had also taken the bruise on my cheek through the blue-black stage and onward to the greenish-yellow stage in record time. It was still pretty visible, but I'd be wearing prosthetics and makeup over it for all my work that day. Dr. Adams requested another visit the next day and cleared me for light duty.

Oscar and I headed out early so I could go meet with Lucy. Rupert, who rarely went out into the field, came along since I'd need a disguise on to meet with Lucy; then I'd need to appear as a version of myself while being seen in Denver. He'd remove the disguise makeup, then cover up the bruise on my cheek with something more natural looking.

"I'll just stay in the jet while you two gallivant around," he said.

"You're sure?" I asked.

"Absolutely. I've done a few missions, and I even took the lead on a couple, but it always filled me more with dread than excitement. You all may enjoy the thrills and chills, but I'm more suited to my studio back home."

Oscar and I left Rupert behind at the airfield and drove to meet Lucy. I was wearing the same wig, glasses, and false face as the last time we'd met up in person. Oscar had upgraded from the mustache from our previous mission to a full beard, which made him look ten years older.

He looked at me as we got close to the meeting site. "You're sure you don't want me by your side?"

"Yes," I said. "I'm, like, ninety-nine percent sure she isn't going to lock me in a bathroom and hit me with a wrench."

"That leaves one percent, which isn't zero," he said. "I promised Nate I wouldn't let you get hurt this time out."

"Do you normally promise Nate to not let other members of the team get hurt?"

"Well, no, but—"

"No buts," I said. "You're my backup, not my bodyguard."

He shifted in his seat as he drove. "Ugh," he finally said. "I feel like a kid torn between my parents."

"First I'm like your sister, then I'm like your mother? See if I ever let you look down my blouse again."

"I didn't mean it that way," he said. "Sorry. Okay, how about this: You're like a total stranger to me, who I care nothing about." I knew the tone of his voice when he was being sarcastic, and he was laying it on thick.

"Good," I said. "I think."

We pulled up to a small outdoor shopping complex. I got out of the car first and strolled along the storefronts, looking into the windows. When I made it to the pet store near the end of the row of shops, I sat on a bench out front next to a woman in a large, floppy hat.

"You've stirred up quite a bees' nest," Lucy said. She didn't look at me, just stared at the parking lot from under the shadow of her gigantic hat. I couldn't see her eyes behind her big sunglasses.

"Really? What's the word?"

"I hear that the supers know that Doctor Oracle, or someone affiliated with him, might be interested in one of their pet projects. No word on which one, but they're on high alert."

"That's fine," I said. "We have a plan in place. We'll slip in right under their noses to get what we need."

"I hope so," she said, and her voice caught. She raised a gloved hand and dabbed at her face with a handkerchief.

I looked around and spotted Oscar nearby, watching our reflections in the window glass. I turned toward Lucy. "What's wrong?"

"I'm so sorry," she said. "I've been fighting with myself on whether I should tell you, but I just can't let you go on without knowing, so you can make decisions based on all the information."

"What information should we have?"

She sniffled. "I'm afraid I don't have anything to give you anymore as a reward."

"What do you mean?"

"My stash of data. It's gone."

"Gone? How? Did somebody steal it?"

"No, it's worse," she said. "My computer was at my mother's house. I even had everything backed up to a portable hard drive. But the night before last, my mother's house burned to the ground."

"What? Are you kidding?"

"I wish I was," she said. "Nobody was home, which was a relief. But everyone knows you in a small town, and I guess people heard that I was back, staying with her. I was harassed pretty badly in school, called a freak and a mutant and worse. I never would have thought that someone would try to hurt my family because I was staying with them, but—"

"But they did," I said. She nodded and hiccoughed, and wiped her eyes with the handkerchief again.

"They did."

"What did the police say?"

"They're doing their best, but they don't have many leads. It looks like someone broke in, smashed everything they could, then poured gasoline on the living room sofa and lit it on fire."

"Oh, God, that's terrible," I said.

She reached into a large purse sitting by her feet and pulled out a paper bag. "Here's the hard drive from the computer and the portable drive I backed everything up on. The backup was hidden under the floorboards of the living room, so while my computer itself was smashed and burned, the other drive just got the full brunt of burning gasoline. If you can get anything off of them, it's all yours." I looked inside the paper bag; there were a ton of blackened, twisted, wet computer parts in a large zip-top baggie. I had no idea if anything could be recovered from them.

"You didn't back anything up off-site? In the cloud?" I asked.

"I thought about it, and almost did it a couple of times. But both times, huge stories broke about people getting hacked. Like those movie stars with the naked pictures." Her shoulders slumped. "I just don't know how I didn't see this coming."

"You're not a psychic," I said. "Well, I mean . . ."

She made a combination sniffle and laugh sound. "But I am, though, aren't I? I should have seen it."

"Nobody can see everything. Or feel everything."

She reached back into her purse and pulled out a manila envelope. "I started making backups of some of the data on CDs and kept them in a safe-deposit box at the bank. I was doing it a little bit at a time, so it isn't anywhere near the entire collection of material I had for you, but I hope it's enough. If not, I understand if our deal is off, but I hope you and Doctor Oracle can find it in your hearts to keep going. Not for me, but for the millions of people who could be hurt or killed."

"I'll have to talk to him," I said, putting the envelope in my purse without looking in it.

"Yes, of course."

"But I'll be in touch as soon as possible to let you know either way."

"Thank you," she said. She removed one of her gloves, then reached out toward me. "May I?"

I held out my hand, and she took it. After a minute, she sighed and shook her head. I was itching to know what she'd felt from me, since at that moment there was at least a chance the job might not continue. I thought the prospect of saving people was more important than a hard drive full of data, and I was at least

90 percent sure that the rest of the team would feel the same way, but even though I was the team leader for this particular mission, it wasn't entirely my call to make.

"Lucy," I said.

"Nothing," she said, then sighed. "Or maybe everything, I don't know. I've always tried to keep my own emotions in check so I could let the feelings come through. Right now, I'm too clouded by my own stuff to be able to figure out anything else."

"I'm sorry," I said.

"Thank you."

"I'll be in touch. Soon."

"Thank you," she repeated.

I got up, the bag full of broken computer parts in my hand. I turned to walk away, then stopped and turned back.

"Sarah," I said. "My name is Sarah."

She tilted her head back so she could see me from under the brim of her huge hat and gave me a weak smile. "Sarah, whatever happens, it's been a pleasure to meet you." She put her glove back on, stood up, picked up her purse, and walked away.

I slowly walked back to the car, glancing in the shop windows and watching Oscar follow me. I got into the passenger side, and a minute later, he was in the driver's side, starting up the car. I told him about Lucy's sudden lack of a reward.

"That's terrible," he said. "But we're going through with this thing, right?"

"That's two votes out of eight," I said. "We'll have to see where everyone else stands when we get back."

We had one more stop to make before we could get back to the island. Neither of us wanted to call Nate and Jin yet, since they were busy preparing some sort of public appearance up in Seattle. We didn't want to distract them. We went back to the airfield and told Rupert about Lucy's misfortune, and our count went up to three votes to continue.

While we flew to Denver, Rupert removed my disguise and made me up into the old Sarah Valentine. He even had a wig styled like I used to wear my hair—a boring shoulder-length bob.

My opinion of the wig told me that I'd truly taken to my new, edgier hairstyle.

In Denver, Oscar and I took separate cars to the busy downtown area. While I got out and browsed around through the shops, I knew that Oscar was coordinating with Evie to contact the local authorities. They'd be notified that I'd been spotted in town and that there was a concern that I could be a target of the evil villain Doctor Oracle.

The supers wanted to capture Doctor Oracle, but every local police officer probably also wanted a crack at catching such a widely known criminal. I wandered through some shops, purchasing a pair of shoes in one and a paperback book in another, and when I left the bookstore I noticed two police officers nearby, staying back a respectful distance but keeping me in sight. I knew Oscar was also keeping an eye on me, but he was much better at hiding; I couldn't see him at all.

I found a little coffee shop and ordered an iced mocha; then I took a seat at one of the outdoor tables and cracked open the book I'd purchased. I pretended to read, turning the pages at a regular pace, but my thoughts were on Lucy. I didn't want my first leadership role to fizzle, not when we'd put so much work and planning into the job already. I hoped the others would feel the same way.

After a good half hour, I walked back to my car. By that time I was able to spot three police officers and two plainclothes guys who, if they weren't cops, at least watched and followed me like cops. I got a chance to practice some of the driving techniques Oscar had taught me when at least one car followed me through town, causing my little tracking device to flash red and beep.

Oscar himself, in his own car, drove alongside me for a moment and caught my eye, then merged in behind me to block the car following me. I drove through a yellow light while Oscar stopped, blocking my tail from making it through the signal. I took the opportunity to take a few quick turns through some side streets and lost my shadow without having to find a parking garage or anywhere else to hide.

We met up at the airfield and flew back to the island. It was early evening when we got home, with Nate and Jin scheduled to arrive less than a half hour behind us. We called the rest of the team to ask them to meet us up at Nate's so we could go over the developments of the day and vote on whether to continue.

By the time the eight of us assembled in Nate's apartment, I wasn't nervous so much as just ready to get an answer. I raised my issues first, explaining what had happened with Lucy. I gave Evie the bag with the two hard drives in it, and she promised to see if she could extract any data. She looked more pleased to receive the envelope with the data CDs in it.

"If Evie can't get anything off of those drives," I said, "then essentially there's very little in this for us. The reward is hugely diminished, only a fraction of what we thought we were going to get. Except that we can save potentially millions of lives, which I think is something. I know we need to take a vote on whether to continue on this mission. I want you all to know, I'm absolutely committed to seeing it through to the end, but I know it isn't just up to me."

"All in favor of continuing?" Nate asked.

Everyone raised their hands, and I relaxed more than I'd expected to. My sensible brain knew that everyone in the group would put lives ahead of the data, but the primitive lizard part of my brain was still wired to expect people to be jerks unless there was a reward to be had.

I was glad Elliot raised his hand along with the rest; even though I knew he was betting against me, at least he was willing to keep the mission going in order to save thousands of lives—if I succeeded. I wondered what I could possibly do to give him a little more faith in me. *Well now, hold on*, I thought. *Why do I have to do anything? His attitude is entirely his problem, not mine. The only thing I can do is just keep on doing the best job I can.*

"Unanimous, thank goodness," I said. "I'd hate to have to disown you all."

Nate laughed. "Was there any question that we'd go for it?"

"You never know," I said, looking around the room and trying not to stare at Elliot. "You guys might have been shielding me from your truly monstrous nature up until now."

"Well, at least for me, it's not entirely my charitable nature," Nate said. "We've beaten some of these groups separately before, but I'll find it *extra* satisfying to beat a bunch of them together."

"Plus," Jin said, "this is your first lead. Ending it halfway through would be demoralizing for you, and it would deprive the rest of us of the opportunity to see you succeed."

"Or wallow in my failure," I said, not looking at Elliot.

"That, too," Jin said. "But even if continuing the mission is a mistake, you have to make mistakes to learn from them."

"Wait," I said, squinting at Jin. Elliot making a bet was one thing; my second-in-command predicting I'd fail was something else entirely and needed to be addressed. "Does that mean you think it's a mistake to continue? Am I screwing up by seeing this through?"

"Hell no," Jin said.

"Jin, would you tell me if this was a mistake?"

Jin grinned. "Hell no."

I shook my head, but I could tell she said it with love. I still felt like she was supporting me: she wasn't making bets behind my back, but telling me right up front that if mistakes were going to be made, they'd be made, and we'd figure things out as we went along.

Since I'd promised to let Lucy know as soon as we had an answer, I dashed off a quick email on my tablet: "Still on, good to go."

"Okay, great," I said. "Next order of business: I was seen by a lot of people doing mundane things in Denver. What happened while I was out there?"

"Someone may or may not have robbed a jewelry store," Nate said.

"By crashing into the front of it with a really cool vehicle that may or may not have been kind of tanklike," Jin added.

"A jewelry store, huh?" I said. Nate smiled, shrugged, and pulled out the pockets of his shorts to show that he didn't have anything hidden in them.

We spent the next hour watching a surprisingly large number of Internet videos of Doctor Oracle, resplendent in his lab coat, goatee, and distinctive scar, wreak havoc on downtown Seattle with a blonde, silver-clad woman at his side.

TWENTY-ONE

Jin promised that she had people who could help, and she definitely came through.

Our field team, consisting of me, Jin, Nate, and Oscar, traveled to the outskirts of Albuquerque, a city name that always made me think of Bugs Bunny cartoons. There, we landed the jet at a small private airfield owned by two of Jin's old friends. They came out onto the tarmac to meet us, and I liked them right away: two short women who could have passed for sisters, but according to Jin, they weren't related. They'd met in the military years ago, become immediate friends, and were now in business for themselves, running the small airfield and offering airplane and helicopter tours of the area. They also did side jobs of questionable legality, which was why we were there.

Jin told us her friends had no love lost for the supers and were more than happy to help us out for the right price. We were under strict instructions to not mention the name Doctor Oracle around them; they didn't know who Jin was working with these days, and it was best to keep them as in the dark as possible.

"Hi there," one of the women said, sticking out her hand. "Shannon Miller. Jin's got us all up to speed."

I shook her hand. "A pleasure to meet you, Shannon. Glad to have you working with us." I handed her an envelope with 20 percent of our agreed-upon fee in cash, the rest to be paid electronically when we returned.

"We don't need to know your names, but if you have code names for this operation, that would be helpful," Shannon said.

Nate stepped forward and shook Shannon's hand. "You can call her the boss," he said, pointing at me. "You already know Jin. How about I'm number one, and he's number two?" Nate tilted his head toward Oscar.

"No way am I number two," Oscar said. "I'm way too dreamy for a name like that."

"How about we call you dreamboat, then," the other woman said. She shook my hand. "Lee Miller." I was glad the two had somewhat different hairstyles so I knew who was who. They both had bright eyes and wide smiles and didn't seem at all like the tough military type.

They led us toward one of the hangars, and I walked alongside Jin. "You said they aren't related, right?"

"Right," she said. "Same last name, though. Everyone refers to them as the Millers."

Shannon turned back toward us. "We know it can be confusing. Think of us like Duran Duran. Three of those guys had the same last name, but none of them were related either."

"Shannon and Lee are the ones who taught me to fly," Jin said. "They're the best pilots I've ever met. And excellent mechanics to boot."

"Thank you, my friend," Lee said. She unlocked and pushed open the door of a large hangar and led us inside. Shannon went over to flip on a light switch, and we looked at our ride for the job.

I knew enough to recognize it as a helicopter, but it was like no helicopter I'd ever seen. It was all matte black, with a body made up of straight, hard angles. The blades on the rotor, however, weren't straight—they had zigzagging angles in them and looked like whoever had assembled them was drunk at the time.

"You guys, she's beautiful," Jin said. I took her word for it.

"Thank you," Shannon said. She turned to the rest of us. "She's a heavily modified Sikorsky S-70, with all the latest developments in silent running and stealth technology. And a few of our own special modifications."

"Don't get to take her out much," Lee said. "So when Jin asked to borrow her, we jumped at the chance."

"I should mention," Shannon said as she saw me studying the blades, "she isn't *completely* silent. No chopper is. But she should be more than quiet enough for the situation you've laid out."

I had no idea how the angles of the blades would make the helicopter quieter, but I remembered back to Nate's biggest philosophy: as long as he had people around him who really, really knew their stuff, he didn't need to learn everything about everything. He depended on the rest of the team to make sure their parts of the plan worked, and I figured I'd do the same. If Jin trusted the Millers to do their part, I had to trust them, too.

We spent the evening carting our gear from the jet to the helicopter and making sure everything was in its place. Oscar showed off his culinary skills in the Millers' kitchen, earning even more adoration. As soon as it got dark, we changed into our full tactical suits: the usual impact-resistant black from head to toe, with hoods, goggles, and gloves. We strapped on extra safety harnesses, and Jin had an additional tool belt slung on her hips. With Shannon and Lee at the controls of the helicopter, we headed out on our mission.

I left my goggles off for the first part of our flight so I could watch the scenery. It was different from flying in the jet somehow, like we were more out in the open. The first leg of the journey was about an hour, from the Millers' airfield to another small private airfield in the outskirts of Phoenix where we could refill the chopper's gas tanks. As we waited for Shannon and Lee to finish fueling and get us back up in the air, we went over the plan again. We checked to make sure our ChatterBoxes were synchronized and their communication channels connected. Nate had a separate comm channel patched into the Millers' headsets so he could talk to them; when we left the helicopter, he'd stay behind and be our main point of contact between the two teams.

The Millers returned and we took off again, headed toward the Exponential Projects building. It wasn't as loud inside the helicopter as I thought it would be, but despite all the stealth technology involved, it wasn't exactly whisper quiet either. I was glad we'd made plans to account for the noise. Nate checked the time on his CB as we flew; since he was sticking with the Millers, he was in charge of our relatively tight time line. We figured we'd have around an hour's worth of helicopter fuel to get in and out of the building, but were shooting for forty-five minutes to be safe.

"Coming up on the right," Shannon called back to us.

The same problem that made the building hard to get into made it very easy to spot: it sat alone, twelve stories tall, right in the middle of a parking lot. Very few lights were on inside the offices, but there were a number of lights outside, shining both inward on all the main doors and out toward the parking lot. I grabbed a pair of binoculars and looked around the base of the building. It was hard to see anything clearly due to the motion of the helicopter, but it looked like there were several vehicles and guards.

"They're expecting us," Oscar said. "Or at least they're expecting *someone*."

"But not the way we're coming," Nate said.

The Millers steered the helicopter around so that we were hovering over the freeway that passed near the building. Since the chopper was all black with its running lights turned off, the plan was to let the reduced noise of the helicopter blend in with the freeway traffic. Anyone on the ground who was listening would just hear a background of vehicular white noise, all coming from the same direction.

We double-checked our safety harnesses while Nate unstrapped a large cylindrical object from where it had been tucked away. He unfolded the sturdy metal legs and set up the compressed-air launcher.

We all clipped our safety lines to the inside of the helicopter, pressed ourselves against the wall, and Oscar slid open the door on the side. We were probably four or five hundred yards away from the roof of the Exponential building and at least two hundred feet higher. Nate loaded the launcher with a giant grappling hook. The Millers steadied the helicopter the best they could, Nate took careful aim, and then he fired the launcher. The loops of reinforced cable made a sizzling sound on the floor of the helicopter as the line paid out.

I put my goggles on and switched them over to night-vision mode, but there wasn't much to see—the hook and line were both black, and it was night. The hook must have landed somewhere, because the line angled sideways out of the open door; if Nate had missed, the cable would be dangling straight downward.

The Millers drifted the helicopter gently away from the building, and I watched as the line grew taut. We were definitely connected to something. Nate checked the angle of the line and looked at the roof of the building through night-vision binoculars, while Oscar checked a video feed on his tablet.

"I think we're good," Nate said. "Looks like I got the railing around the very top."

"Confirmed," Oscar said. He turned his tablet around to show us the video feed coming from a tiny lipstick camera attached to the grappling hook. The lighting was terrible, but we could make out some concrete and what looked like an air-conditioner unit.

Oscar was the first to head over: he connected his harness to the line connecting the helicopter to the building. He also clipped on a rappelling brake: in case the grappling hook came loose, he'd be able to engage the brake to slow his slide enough so that he didn't go flying off the end of the line or get impaled on the hook.

The Millers adjusted their position to give the line a little bit of slack so they didn't tear the hook away from the building. As the rest of us watched, Oscar jumped out the side of the helicopter and zip-lined down. I lost sight of him less than halfway to the building, since his black tactical suit blended in with the darkness all around him.

After a minute, I heard him in my ear. "I'm down. Tightening up the connection here at the hook."

"How's the landing?" Nate asked.

"Good. There's another ledge on the outside of this railing, so I landed pretty clean. Didn't have to dangle against the side of the building this time."

"This time?" I said.

"Remind me later to tell you about Brazil," Oscar said. "Okay, we're secure down here. Next?"

"Boss, you're up," Jin said. We were trying to keep banter to a minimum to avoid the Millers overhearing who we were and what we were after. Hopefully when the mission was done, all they'd know was that they did a favor for some of Jin's friends for an obscene amount of money.

I connected my own safety harness and hand brake to the line, took a deep breath, and jumped out the side of the helicopter. For a moment, because of the curved angle of the line, it was like I was free-falling. Then I felt the tug as my harness settled onto the line, and I zipped along through the pitch dark toward a dark building. The wind howled in my face, it was the craziest thing I'd ever done in my life, and I felt like whooping with joy.

My slide slowed down, and I came to a stop a few feet short of where the hook connected to the building. I pulled myself along the line hand over hand until I was well over the lower ledge that Oscar had mentioned. I unclipped my harnesses and dropped onto the ledge, then hoisted myself up to the upper level of the roof and climbed over the railing our hook was connected to.

"I'm down," I said.

"On my way," Jin said in my ear. A minute later, she was dangling on the line in front of us. She unhooked and dropped down, then joined Oscar and me on the upper roof. "I'm down, we're all good."

"I don't know about you guys, but I *really* enjoyed that," I said.

"You'll never be able to go on a normal daytime zip line again," Oscar said.

We walked over to the roof access door. Jin pulled a scanner out of her tool belt and ran it around the door, searching for electronic signals or any evidence of an alarm system on the door.

"Nothing, just a normal locking door. They must not be expecting anyone to arrive from above."

I looked around at the roof, which was littered with ventilation units, antennae, and plenty of other crap. "Nowhere to land a helicopter, so they probably don't see it as a threat." I looked back out into the sky where we'd come from but couldn't see the helicopter out there. The only thing I could see was our dark-colored line stretching out into the sky, then disappearing. I listened, but whatever sound those crazy rotor blades were making blended in beautifully with the traffic from the freeway down below.

Jin picked the lock on the access door, and we slipped inside. She pulled out a roll of black duct tape and put several pieces over the latch in case we needed to make a quick exit.

We were in the same stairwell that Oscar and I had used the other day. It was just as gray and gloomy, only a little bit darker.

"Starting the timer," Nate said in our ears. "You have forty-five minutes."

"Forty-five, check," I repeated back. "Let's move."

TWENTY-TWO

We headed down the stairwell, passing by the twelfth-floor landing in order to get to the eleventh floor, where the records room was located. When we got to the door, Jin used her scanner but, once again, didn't find any evidence of an alarm. Jin looked through the little window in the door to make sure the coast was clear, picked the lock twice as fast as I had, and slowly pushed the door open.

There were no alarms, flashing lights, or anything else, so we hustled out into the hallway. The lights were off in the offices on either side of the hall, but the hall itself was dimly lit, just enough to see where we were going. We made our way down to the door marked "RECORDS" at the end of the hall.

I checked the little window in the door; the room beyond was dark. Jin opened up one of the pockets on her tool belt and pulled out a device she and Evie had put together. It looked like a smartphone connected to a key card, which was exactly what it was. Jin launched a program on the phone, then slid the key card through the slot next to the records-room door.

The light on the card reader stayed red, but numbers began scrolling across the screen of the phone. The card was a clone of Catalyst's, so the Exponential people must have already removed its access from the system and given her a new one. Or fired her, for all I knew. I didn't much care what had happened to her, as long as I didn't have to meet up with her in an enclosed space again.

"About three minutes," Jin said. The numbers continued to flash on the screen of the phone, too fast for me to follow. To kill the time, I borrowed Jin's security scanner, checked the door to one of the offices, then picked the lock and went inside. I walked over to the windows and looked out.

I could see the freeway across the way, bustling with cars in both directions. I leaned my forehead against the glass and looked down; there were cars parked around the building, with a small floodlight shining on the side entrance below me. I could see people walking around down there, and nobody seemed to be in any kind of panic or hurry. We were pretty good so far.

I looked off into the sky above the freeway, but there was nothing to see. It was hard to believe that the helicopter was up there, tethered to the building by our very thin, very strong line. I pressed my ear against the glass but couldn't hear much of anything. At least nobody inside the building would see or hear our ride.

On my way out of the office, I browsed around the desk and a set of bookshelves. There was a picture of a middle-aged couple with two kids on the desk; none of them looked like a super, but you never know. My suspicion was that Exponential was run by ordinary people for the most part, with a few supers on-site to keep an eye on things.

I re-locked the door and joined the others. "Can't see a thing out there."

"Good," Oscar said.

Jin's smartphone beeped and the screen flashed. She went back to the key-card reader and swiped the card again. This time, the reader's indicator light turned green, and the door popped open with a beep and a click.

"The lock is open, we're going in," I said, updating Nate on our progress.

We moved into the room, splitting up. Jin went for the computers and turned one of them on. Oscar and I turned on flashlights, being careful to not point them toward the windows, and headed for the filing cabinets. It wasn't as huge an array as

I'd seen at the Planning and Development office downtown, but there were at least forty large cabinets. Each one was labeled with a number and nothing else. I started with the nearest one, and Oscar went down to the end of the row to start there. Hopefully when Jin got the computer up and running, she'd find a guide to how things were filed.

My first filing cabinet had a ton of paperwork stuffed into it but nothing pertinent to our mission. I moved on to the next, flipping through files as quickly as I could.

"The computer is password protected," Jin said. "This might take a few minutes." She pulled a thumb drive out of her tool belt and plugged it into one of the USB ports. The screen flickered; then the computer restarted itself. The gadget was one of Evie's, and all I knew about it was to plug it into a computer, and there was a good chance it would get you access.

I moved to the next filing cabinet, scanning for anything that might relate to the digging project. I was looking for words like *digging, drilling, water, power, steam*, or anything else that sounded likely. I checked the contents of the folders, but nothing jumped out at me.

On my fourth filing cabinet, I hit pay dirt.

"I have something," I said. Oscar came over to join me while Jin kept working on the computer. The files I'd found were labeled "Goldwater Dig," and they took up at least one whole drawer. We both pulled folders out and looked at the information inside.

"Bingo," Oscar said. "This looks like it." There were tons of memos, invoices, and legal documents in the files. In flipping through, I discovered that the dig was happening on government land: a site owned by the air force, flanking Interstate 8 for over a hundred miles near the southern edge of Arizona. I flipped through the rest of the files, but it was all letter-sized sheets of paper.

"We're at thirty minutes to go," Nate said in my ear. It was hard to believe we'd only landed on the roof fifteen minutes ago.

"Thank you, thirty," I acknowledged. I looked down at the drawer in front of me. "No plans, no maps." I stopped and looked around and spotted another grouping of filing cabinets, the kind with the big flat drawers used for larger documents. I left Oscar searching for anything useful in the memos and went over to the larger cabinets. They were all locked. I knew I could pick the locks if I had enough time, but it would be easier if I had a key. I thought about the offices I'd worked in and where a key would be hidden so the employees would have easy access to it.

I went over to Jin, who was shaking her head at the computer. "This thing isn't cooperating," she said. "Either Evie's gadget is busted, or whoever has access to this thing uses a really complicated password."

I went through the drawers of the desk the computer was sitting on. One was full of snacks, another held a pair of shoes. The third drawer had a key ring with a dozen or so small keys on it. I grabbed the ring and slid the door shut, but Jin opened it back up again.

"What's up?" I asked.

She pulled a piece of paper out of the drawer. "It can't be this easy." I read the piece of paper:

> *admin1*
> *The rain in Spain stays mainly on the plain*

Jin hit the power button on the second computer, since the first one was busy with Evie's program. I went back over and tried the keys on the big file cabinets. I lucked out and opened the first cabinet with the third key I tried. There was nothing about the Goldwater Dig, so I moved on to the next set of drawers. I spun the keys around on the ring and tried the next key on the next lock; it popped right open.

"I have computer access," Jin said. I looked over, and she was shaking her head and grinning, holding up the slip of paper. She put it back in the drawer, unplugged Evie's device from the first computer, and shut that one down.

"We're looking for Goldwater Dig," I told her. She went to work looking through the computer files.

I found what I was looking for in the fourth cabinet over, just like the masses of paperwork had been in the fourth cabinet. I felt like smacking myself in the head for not starting on number four. I found all sorts of treasures in there, including a full map of the Barry M. Goldwater Air Force Range, a plan of the dig site, and sheets of blueprints for the digging equipment itself. It was a thief's Christmas.

I took multiple pictures of everything, alternating between my smartphone's camera flash and the light from my flashlight to make sure every detail was accounted for. We each plugged away, Oscar and I taking pictures and putting things back exactly as we found them, Jin copying any files that looked useful onto a portable drive.

I was flipping through a set of maps when Jin said, "Everybody down."

I'd been trained pretty thoroughly in certain phrases, and that was one that triggered an immediate response. I slammed the drawer shut and dropped into a crouch, shutting of my flashlight.

I heard another filing cabinet drawer shut, then Oscar's voice whispering over the comms, "Status?"

"There's someone with a flashlight out in the hall," Jin whispered. "I just shut off the computer monitor, and I'm making my way back to you." I looked at the head of the aisle I was in but couldn't see anything. If there was someone outside the main door, I knew the best place to be was as far from that door as I could get. I stayed hunched over and walked as quickly and silently as I could down to the far end of the row of cabinets.

I rounded the end of the row and squatted down, pressing my back against the side of the file cabinet. Straight ahead of me was a floor-to-ceiling window, an unexpected bonus. Since it was so dark outside, the window would hopefully provide at least a little reflection of what was going on in the room behind me.

Jin and Oscar both appeared a moment later out of two other aisles and took up similar positions to the one I was in.

Nate asked, "Status?"

"Not sure," I whispered. "We're hidden, waiting to see."

"Roger, listening for an update." I felt bad for him, out in the helicopter separated from the rest of the team. On the other hand, if someone was coming in, he was the safest one of us.

We heard the beep and the click of the door unlocking, then footsteps.

"So I told her, no, I really *don't* want to go to your mother's house," a man's voice said.

"And she still *went*?" Another man. I looked for reflections in the window but couldn't make out much. I looked up at the ceiling instead and figured from the way someone was waving a flashlight across the room that they were just looking around in general, not looking for us specifically.

"Yeah, can you believe it? Then she says to me—" A tinny crackling sound interrupted the first guy.

"Unit two," the second guy said. More crackling sounds, which I realized was a voice on a cheap walkie-talkie. I couldn't make out what the person on the other end was saying.

I looked at Jin and Oscar, and they looked back at me. My legs were starting to cramp from the squatting position. Oscar had his silenced tranquilizer pistol in hand, looking as comfortable and at ease in his squat as anyone else would look while lying on a pillow-soft bed.

"You got it, sir," the second guy said. "We'll be down in a minute." More crackling, then silence.

"God, I hate that guy," the first guy said.

"Seriously. You'd think one inspirational speech a day would be enough. I guess we can kiss the next half hour of our lives good-bye."

"Like, the only really *super* thing about him is his ability to talk your ear off." The men laughed, one of them swept the flashlight around the room one last time, and I heard the door open and shut.

"Checking to see if we're clear," Oscar whispered. He held his gun at the ready and went down one of the aisles back to the front of the room. In less than a minute, he reported that he'd watched through the small window in the door as the two men got into the elevator.

"Let's get back to it," I said. "Sounds like we have a half-hour speech about to start downstairs."

"We're at about fifteen minutes," Nate said in my ear. "Glad you're all okay over there."

"Thank you, fifteen," I said. "We're glad, too. Any idea who the super is?"

"Nobody's driven up on this side of the building. Either he's been inside the whole time, or he arrived on the other side," Nate said.

I finished up with the drawer I was working on, opened the next, and found documents for a different project. I'd found everything I was going to find on the Goldwater Dig. I locked all the cabinets and put the keys back in the drawer where I'd found them.

"Almost done here," Jin said. I looked at the computer screen and saw a progress bar at 95 percent. Above the bar it read "34,050 out of 35,842 files copied."

"Good lord," I said. "What are you copying?"

"Everything it has," she said. "Got the Goldwater stuff first, then figured I'd grab the rest. Hopefully there will be something useful in there. At least it's a newer computer, so it has the latest and fastest USB ports."

"Good call." I went back over to Oscar, who was just finishing up with his file cabinet.

"I skipped a lot of stuff like invoices," he said. "Found a number of things worth keeping, but overall there isn't much here. Since these drawers are unlocked, I don't think anything here is confidential."

"No worries," I said. "Jin and I found plenty of stuff." We finished the cabinet and set everything back in its place. When we made it back to the front of the room, Jin was powering down the computer.

We checked over everything to make sure we were leaving nothing behind. Unless they tracked key-card usage, Exponential

Projects would have no idea we'd been there. And even if they did track key-card usage, they would have no idea which one of their many projects we were investigating in their records room.

We secured the door behind us and hustled down the hallway to the stairwell, keeping an eye out in case the disgruntled guards decided to come back. Jin re-locked the door behind us. We went up to the twelfth-floor landing and paused there.

"Time check, number one?" I said.

"Eleven minutes," Nate said.

"Should we check out the big offices on the twelfth floor, since we're ahead of schedule? And since the guards are apparently being lectured downstairs?"

"Your call, boss," came the reply in my ear. I looked to Jin and Oscar, who both nodded. Jin scanned the door and quickly picked the lock; then we split up. Jin and I picked the locks on the offices nearest to the stairwell, and Oscar went into the first one. He'd readily admitted that he wasn't good with locks or other "little fiddly stuff."

I searched several offices but didn't find anything of note. They truly appeared to be staffed mostly by civilians, and nothing important was kept in their offices overnight.

I made it to the last office at the end of the hall and popped the lock. It was a corner office at least twice the size of the other offices on the twelfth floor, with amazing views: the city on one side and distant rolling hills on the other.

As with most of the other offices I'd looked at, there was a framed picture of a happy family sitting on the desk. I glanced at it, looked away, then looked back. The man in the picture caught my eye, because he was unusually large compared to everyone else. He made the normal-sized woman and children in the photo look freakishly small. I'd met my fair share of tall people, but something about the sheer bulk of him struck me as odd.

I took a picture of the family photo, searched through the desk drawers, then went to the bookcases off to the side. Just as in the other offices, it was a variety of both business and law books, most of them leather-bound with gold-stamped titles. I scanned the rows and noticed that a few books stuck out a little bit farther than the others. It only jumped out at me because so many of the books were the same size.

I pulled the books forward and pointed my flashlight behind them. Tucked up against the wall was a thin notebook, much smaller than the rest, with no title on the front, just a decorative border stamped in gold.

"Five minutes," Nate said.

"Thank you, five," I said. "Let's get moving back upstairs." I grabbed the small notebook and stuffed it into one of my cargo pockets, then pushed the larger books back where I'd found them, just slightly out of kilter with their neighbors. I re-locked the office door on my way out and met up with Jin and Oscar at the stairwell.

We climbed back up to the roof, where Jin pulled the tape away from the lock and shut the door behind us. She stuffed the used tape in one of the pockets on her tool belt, since we didn't want to leave behind a shred of physical evidence that we'd been there.

"We're on the roof," I said. Jin and I climbed over the railing of the upper roof and stood on the wide ledge just below. The line attached to the grappling hook was right next to us, stretching off into the darkness. I thought I heard the slightest change in the hum of traffic noise coming from the direction of the freeway, and the line slowly went from sloping down toward us to sloping down away from us. The Millers were carefully lowering the helicopter.

"We're in position, come on back," Nate said.

Jin hooked her safety harness and hand brake to the line, then stepped off the edge of the building. She slowly slid along the line off into the darkness.

"I'm in," Jin said after a minute or so. "Next up."

I clipped my harness to the line, put my own hand brake on but left it wide open, made a conscious decision to not look down along the side of the building, then stepped off the edge. For some reason, it was easier for me to step out of the side of a helicopter and launch myself toward a building than it was to step off the side of that same building and launch myself toward darkness.

The angle of the zip line wasn't as acute as on our approach, so it wasn't as terrifying or as exhilarating a ride on the way back. Not only did the Millers need to keep the helicopter far enough above the freeway to avoid being spotted, but dipping too far down would put the cable too close to the rotors. I stopped sliding just short of the chopper's open door. Nate reached out, grabbed one of the straps of my harness, and pulled me in. I switched my safety lines over to the inside of the helicopter and stepped off to the side.

"I'm in," I said. "Get ready down there."

"Ladies, if you would be so kind," Nate said to the Millers. Whichever one was flying the helicopter slowly steered us upward and toward the building, keeping the line just slack enough to avoid trouble. I leaned out the open door just enough so that I could watch Oscar, far down below on the roof of the building.

"We're in position," one of the Millers shouted back at us.

"All right, dreamboat," I said. "Tarzan time."

I could barely see Oscar moving around at the edge of the roof, but because I knew the plan, I knew what he was doing. He attached his safety harness to the line, put his hand brake on and fully clamped it down, then disconnected the grappling hook from the railing of the building and stepped into the curve of the hook. The helicopter dipped slightly with his sudden weight on the end of the line, and where it stuck out the open door of the helicopter, the line went from slightly off to the side to hanging straight down.

"I'm good to go," Oscar said. We gave the thumbs-up to the Millers, who gained altitude and turned the helicopter back to the small airfield on the outskirts of Phoenix so we could fuel up again before heading back to Albuquerque.

Nate started up a winch, which slowly pulled the line up as we flew. After a few minutes, Oscar's head appeared in the open doorway. He clambered up the side and just held on to a railing, standing on part of the chopper's wheel strut. It would be too dangerous to transfer his safety lines while we were in the air, and during the planning stages, he'd expressed his lifelong desire to cling to the side of a helicopter while it was in flight.

At the fuel stop he finally climbed back in with the rest of us, and we were able to shut the side door. "Man, that was amazing. I'll have to cross it off my bucket list."

"Only you would have riding on the outside of a helicopter on your bucket list," Nate said.

"Some of us have ballsier buckets than others," Oscar said.

We made it back to Albuquerque without incident, and with a few taps on his tablet, Nate paid the Millers the remainder of their fee. We moved everything from the helicopter back to the jet, shook hands again, turned down the offer of a drink before we hit the road, and headed back to the island.

"Well, that went well, I think," Nate said.

"It certainly did," I said. We flipped through some of the images on my smartphone, but most were hard to make out on the tiny screen. "I got a lot of plans, Oscar got some stuff, and Jin copied just about everything from their computer system."

"It never hurts to be thorough," Jin said.

"That's for sure," I said. "Because being successful on this first lead is on *my* bucket list."

Oscar shook his head. "Bo-ring."

TWENTY-THREE

Over the next two days, we went over all the information we'd collected. Thanks to the maps I'd photographed, we knew where the dig site was. Thanks to the files Jin copied, we knew how to disassemble the drill and take the battery out. And thanks to some of the invoices Oscar found, we knew what make and model of security system they had installed at the dig site.

The project was in the far eastern corner of the Barry M. Goldwater Air Force Range. I'd assumed when I first saw the full name of the place that it was just a base, but it turned out the range was a huge, barren wasteland of desert where both the air force and the marine corps practiced bombing things. In general, it didn't sound like the safest place to break into.

From the documents, it looked like the corner of the range where the dig was happening was off-limits to the bombing traffic, for good reason. No sense in blowing up your pet project.

On the far eastern edge of the range there was a small airfield, the Sonora Flats Air Force Auxiliary Field. Most of the planes that went to Goldwater to test their bombs actually flew out of other military airfields in the area; it looked like Sonora Flats was mostly used for emergency landings and refueling stops but was close enough to the dig site that they probably used it as their main airfield for supplies.

We studied the maps, plans, schematics, and documents and refined our plan. It was less than a week until Labor Day, which was when we were going to make our move. We knew from the records Jin had copied that the facility would be at its most deserted on a national holiday: most of the staff would have the holiday itself off, and the crew living on-site would be given the entire three-day weekend to visit their families.

Jin and I took some trips out to Arizona that week, scouting the area around the range and the tiny airfield next to it. I got a lot of good practice time in the Cessna and learned all about how when you fly a private plane near military areas, there are very strict regulations about where you can fly and at what altitude.

It also gave us a chance to talk. Not just about the job, but about relationships.

"I just don't get how it's different," I told her. "I understand that Nate could get hurt. I've seen him bloody and stitched back up. Why would it be so weird for him to see me the same way?"

"Mark had a hard time dealing with it, too," Jin said. "Even though I was working in the field before he and I were dating. I think it doesn't matter how tough of a woman you are, they still want to protect us. And when we get hurt, that means in a way that they've failed."

"But does that mean Nate feels guilty when *you* get hurt?"

"Probably. But I'm sure he doesn't feel as guilty about me as he does about you."

"It shouldn't make a difference," I said.

"It shouldn't, but it does. I mean, I'm sure Nate feels responsible for everyone on his team coming back in one piece. But he's going to hold you up and above the rest of us, and it's just something both you and he have to figure out how to deal with."

"Ugh," I said. "Maybe I should talk to Scar to try and get inside his head."

"I think Nate was going to do the same thing."

"Oy," I said. "Now we even go for romantic advice to the same people. Promise me that if we ever start finishing each other's sentences, you'll punch me."

"It's a promise."

Later that evening, I invited Scar out for a drink at one of the island's little bars. It was run on a sort of drink-ticket system, and I had plenty of credits available. When I'd first come to the island, I was suspicious that a system like that could work, but Nate had it right: when people didn't feel the need to relax or unwind after a day at a job they hated, they didn't feel the need to have a drink or two every single night. I was doing work I loved, and my wine consumption had overall gone way down.

I got us each a beer, and we found a table in a quiet corner of the bar.

"How's that cut on your jaw healing up?" Scar asked. I turned and tilted my head so he could see. I'd visited Dr. Adams earlier that day so she could finally remove the stitches from the barely visible wound. She put a thin layer of nanogel over the small scar and predicted that in less than a week I wouldn't be able to see anything except for fresh pink skin.

"I can't see a thing," he said. "Amazing."

"Kind of a shame I don't get a souvenir scar from my first big fight, but oh well," I said.

"You'll always have your memories," he said, smiling. We each sipped our beers.

"So, you probably know what I want to talk about," I said.

"I've been prepped by Jin, yes. And I had a talk yesterday with Nate."

"How do you do it? How do you not worry about Jin getting hurt or killed when she's out in the field?"

"I don't," he said. "I'll always worry. But I've learned to live with it, because the Jin who goes out in the field and risks her neck, and sometimes comes home with a broken bone or two, is the Jin I love. I know she'd be miserable if she couldn't go out and help get things done."

"That makes sense to me," I said. "I can't imagine Nate not out there. He already goes stir-crazy when he isn't elbow deep in a job, like when his broken foot was healing up a while back. He was so depressed when he couldn't go out into the field with the rest of us."

"You're two of a kind," he said. "And I honestly couldn't tell you if that's a good thing or a bad thing in the long run. I think

Jin and I balance each other out, because she's an adventurer, and I'm the homebody who doesn't like to leave the island if I don't have to."

"But you love what you do here," I said. "If I had to know everyone's name, and something about them, and do all of the managing and paperwork and everything else you do, I'd quit in no time."

"I come from a long line of butlers, valets, and manservants. It's in my blood."

"So, see, you and Jin are two of a kind. You've both found your passion and are fully enjoying it."

"I suppose that's true," he said.

I took a sip of my beer. "Did you tell all this to Nate?"

"Somewhat. I worded things a bit differently."

"How so?"

"Well," he said, "I'm not about to tell you to get your act in gear, man up, put on your big-boy pants, and just *deal* with it, because things are the way they are, and you wouldn't want to change them even if you could."

"Wow, yeah," I said. "Thanks for not laying that on me."

"As far as I can see, you have your big-girl pants on pretty securely."

I laughed. "I'll have to tell your wife you told me that."

"Good," he said. "She thinks the same thing. Listen: I've known Nate for almost all of our lives. And for the most part, he's easygoing, mellow, a real cool customer. But now and then, very rarely, he finds something that gets him fired up, and that's when he really comes to life. He's fired up about battling the corruption throughout the government and the supers. He's fired up about helping the world become a better place, in any way he can. And now, he's fired up about you."

"Great," I said. "Now I'm up there with world peace and ending hunger."

"You're more right than you know," he said. "Nate has always had this protective streak in him. So like it or not, you're going to be on the receiving end of that. But he knows, like it or not, that he has to let *you* follow whatever *your* passion is."

"And put on his big-boy pants," I said.

"Precisely."

* * *

The next day, Jin and I took another flight out to Arizona and talked through more of our plan. We were pretty well set on the when and the where, but there were a few pieces left to put in place. We tossed some ideas back and forth, but nothing was really sparking.

"Did I tell you? I heard from Evie about the rest of the computer files I stole," she said.

"Anything good?"

"*Loads* of stuff. Like we thought, the supers are financing a lot more projects. Some of them are probably doomed to failure, but some of them are brilliant."

"Helpful projects?" I asked.

"Most of it," she said. "It warms the heart that finally, we aren't so different after all."

"Until they start crowing for all the glory," I said. "That's one of the things I love most about what we do. There's no shouting 'look at me'; there's just getting things done."

"Time will tell."

"Oh," I said, "remember that book I found in one of the offices?"

"The one full of writing that made no sense?" After our visit to the Exponential Projects building, I'd pulled the small leather-bound notebook out of my cargo pocket and leafed through it. It was all letters and numbers and a few symbols, but I couldn't figure any of it out.

"That's the one. Rupert asked to take a crack at it."

"Does he think he can decode it?" Jin asked.

"I have no idea," I said. "But Evie ran it through every program she could find, and none of them could make heads or tails of it."

"It doesn't surprise me," Jin said. "Rupert has yet to meet a puzzle he didn't like. Crosswords, cryptics, sudoku, and even those locked-room smartphone games—they're all right up his alley."

"Well, I think he's passing a few small selections out to some puzzle-loving minions," I said. "We'll see if they come up with anything."

We flew as close as possible to the air force range, staying strictly within the distance and altitude guidelines. We could just barely make out the cluster of buildings in the far distance, in the middle of a barren stretch of desert, where the Goldwater Dig was taking place. We each took a turn checking things out through high-powered binoculars while the other one was at the yoke. Whichever one of us was flying the plane would do some traditional student maneuvers: a few ninety-degree turns, and ascending and descending in hundred-foot intervals.

Jin tried to make her flying a little rougher to match mine, though overall, I was getting better every day.

On our way back home, over the wastelands between Arizona and California, Jin reached out and rested her hand on the throttle. I knew what was coming, so I checked the area for any other traffic, but it was a clear sky with nobody else around.

"Your engine has just conked out," she said, pulling back the throttle far enough so the engine coughed and sputtered. "Next steps?"

I glanced around at the ground below us and checked the instrument panel. "First, look for any nearby traffic. Then check for possible landing spots. Keep my nose up, but not too high to keep me from gliding smoothly." I pointed at the instrument panel. "Try to restart the engine."

"No go," she said. "The engine won't restart."

"I have a lot of flat-looking desert off to the right, and there's a pretty wide, deserted road on the left."

"Up to you, you're the pilot."

I went into a series of gently banking turns to line myself up with the road. Satisfied, Jin pushed the throttle in, and the engine roared back to life. I climbed back to our cruising altitude and thought about the test.

"Jin," I said, "could you make the plane have engine failure on purpose but have it be a quick and easy fix?"

She pursed her lips and squinted at me. "Yeah, there might be a thing or two I could do."

"Good. Keep them in mind."

TWENTY-FOUR

The plan came together with time to spare, but there were some elements we still needed to complete. Jin and her team were at work on an important piece, so I took Nate with me to Arizona in the jet. I was already looking forward to the day I'd be able to fly places with passengers without needing my instructor.

I could have taken Oscar, but we were going to meet Lucy, and Nate had met her face to face already. I'd discussed it with the team, and everyone had signed off on inviting her to take part in the final mission at the dig site. Not only would it give her the opportunity to make sure it was done right, but I thought we could really make good use of her skills, too.

Now it was just a matter of convincing her to join us.

We met at another great hole-in-the-wall restaurant; Lucy knew all the most delicious places to eat in the state of Arizona. We didn't wear masks, but Nate and I wore the same false faces as when we'd met her before. Giving her my common first name was one thing; showing her my actual face was a step I wasn't willing to take just yet.

"It's so good to see you," she said, and then she hugged me. "And thank you again."

"You're more than welcome," I said.

She hugged Nate; then we sat down to look at the menu. The restaurant was Greek, which seemed like a strange choice for Arizona. But it smelled amazing, and Lucy swore it was great food. Our server came over and took our orders, then quickly returned to drop off drinks. She was efficient but not in our faces, which I appreciated.

"So," I said, "I want to make sure you aren't worried about the data you were going to give us. It turns out that one of our stops along the way afforded us a great deal of information, which more than made up for it."

"That's wonderful," she said. "Though I feel guilty."

"It wasn't you that burned your mother's house down," I said.

"True, but I should have been more diligent about backing things up somewhere else."

"There is something else you can do to make it up to us," I said.

"What's that?"

"Join us on this final part, when we go in and get the leaking battery out of the drill."

She went alarmingly pale, and one of her hands fluttered in front of her mouth. "Oh, no, I don't know."

"Your skills would help immensely," I said. "Plus, you'd be absolutely sure that we did what we said we would."

"Oh." She tapped her fingers on the table. "Let me think about it, please?"

"Please do," I said. "Only don't take too long."

"Labor Day is two days away," Nate said. "That's when we're going in, since it should be pretty quiet."

Our food arrived, and I proceeded to eat one of the best gyro sandwiches I'd ever had in my life. It was accompanied by some incredible fresh hand-cut french fries. I hoped that we'd remain on good terms with Lucy when the whole thing was over, because she truly did know about all the best restaurants.

As we ate, we went over the broad strokes of the plan, not only to let her know what we'd be doing but also to try and convince her to take part. I tried to stress how helpful her power could be while explaining how she could use it during the mission.

"Nobody ever wanted to take me into the field this way before." She tapped her fingers against her water glass. "With every other group, they just wanted another body, more muscle along for the ride."

"But you admit, nobody ever really knew how to use your powers," I said.

"True. I've always used them behind a desk, with a book or newspaper in my hands."

"Well, this would be a chance for you to take them for a test-drive in the field, maybe the way they were meant to be used. Surrounded by a team of professionals who won't push you into anything you don't want to do. We won't let anything happen to you."

She dipped one of her french fries into the side of *tzatziki* sauce she'd ordered, and I could see her mulling it over.

"The one thing I worry about is getting caught," she said. "If the hero community found out I was working with you, it would be terrible. I don't really want to work for another of the super groups, but I've made some friends through the years. I'd hate to lose them."

"We can disguise you," I said. "I mean, do you think these are our real faces?"

"I suspected they weren't," she said. She leaned over and stared at me for a moment. "But it's amazing work."

"If the plan goes as we hope it will," Nate said, "especially with you on the team, nobody will know we were ever there. And even if you do get spotted, you'll be wearing the same black suit as the rest of us."

"How soon do you need my answer?"

"By the end of the day," I said. "If you don't come along, we'll have to spend a lot of tomorrow making adjustments to our plan."

"All right," she said. "I'll let you know by then."

"Just know," I said, "even though nobody else has seen it, I think you'll be amazing in the field. Not as hired muscle or an extra body, but doing exactly what you do best."

"I do like your plan," she said. She shook her head. "I just . . . I worry. About being caught, about freezing up, about everything. You'd think being able to feel the future would keep me from worrying, but I think it makes me worry more. I worry about everything I *can't* feel. Or the feelings I can't make sense of."

I reached out my hand. "I'm happy to let you see whatever you can from me."

Nate held his hand across the table, too. "Same here. You should absolutely know what feelings you're getting from us when you make this decision."

Lucy smiled and pulled off both gloves. Being careful to not touch the table, she rested her hands gently on each of ours. She bowed her head as if praying, so we couldn't see what emotions she felt. After a minute, she let go of our hands. She raised her head and put her gloves back on, smiling.

"You two are so well matched," she said.

"Oh, brother," I said.

"Do tell," Nate said with a grin.

✳ ✳ ✳

We hugged Lucy good-bye and headed back to the island, because there was work to be done. And as project leader, I had to make sure that everything was in its place. I visited all the team members, and as usual they each impressed me with their thorough and impeccable work. Rupert had even put together a custom tactical suit for Lucy, since if she'd worn one of Jin's or my suits, it would have been too short.

Jin was my last visit. I checked in the workshop, but it was deserted. I found her in her office, working on some paperwork. There was a small box on the corner of her desk.

"Is that it?" I asked.

"Sure is," she said. "Take a look."

I lifted the lid and looked inside. From my layman's viewpoint, it was a perfect replica of the plutonium-strontium battery. "Wow, great job."

"Thank you. It even has a battery of its own inside, sealed tightly enough to be earthquake proof, so it'll power things just enough for them to test the thing before they go back to digging for the day."

"Am I wrong in thinking that it's kind of pretty?"

"Not at all," she said. "I kind of like it. The chrome highlights are pretty cool, but heaven knows why they designed it that way. Probably just to be showy." She opened a folder on her desk and showed me all the source material they'd worked with, from schematics to actual photographs of the battery. Some had come from the Exponential computers, others from the Italian team that had developed the battery to begin with.

"It seems like a shame to put your beautiful replica in the drill if it's just going to get wrecked by that earthquake."

"An impermanent object in an imperfect world," she said.

"That's so Zen, I could barf."

"I hope you don't. It'll make a mess on my beautiful chrome."

I put the lid back on the box and sat across from Jin. "I hope everything goes all right."

"First-mission nerves," she said. "Even worse when it's your first lead. Remember how scared you were when we broke into the Green Lady's mansion to steal her diamond?"

"I do," I said. "But really, wasn't my first mission going to a supervillain nightclub, where I ended the evening in the custody of the supers?"

"I guess so, if you want to get technical. But you weren't stealing anything that time."

"True."

"So, you didn't tell me," she said, "how did the meet with Lucy go? Is she in?"

"She's thinking about it. I gave her until the end of the day."

"I hope she does it. It'll make things easier on all of us. And also, I really liked her."

"I should see if she's written," I said. "Can I use a computer?"

"Be my guest."

I went into the workshop and logged onto one of the computers. As I waited for the email program to launch, I looked around at the vaguely organized clutter of pieces and parts of various machines. Jin's team hadn't packed everything away yet, so a lot of parts scattered on the workbench next to me looked like they could be a part of the battery.

A metal box on a shelf caught my eye: it was labeled "MANOS MACHINE," so I figured it held the parts we'd taken back with us. I hoped the box was made of lead; then I hoped that lead was the thing that protected you from radiation, because I wasn't 100 percent sure.

The computer made its gentle chime to let me know that I had new messages. I fired up the generic doctor@doctororacle.com mailbox, where I'd set a filter to send Lucy's emails to the top of the list so I didn't have to cull through all the crap sent to us. There it was, one unread email at the very top of the box.

I breathed deep and double-clicked. It was a really short message: "I'm in. Tell me what to do."

I ducked my head into Jin's office. "She's in."

"Oh, thank goodness." Jin visibly relaxed, leaning back in her chair and smiling.

I went back to the computer and sent Lucy an email detailing when and where we would meet her and thanked her profusely for taking part. As I was logging off, I looked over the workbench again, covered in fake battery parts. Then I looked at the (hopefully) lead box on the shelf. I went back to Jin's office.

"There are a lot of parts left out there," I said.

"Yeah. I'll have the team clean everything up tomorrow."

"I wonder," I said. "Do you think you have enough parts to make a second fake battery?"

She leaned forward in her chair. "Maybe. Probably. What are you thinking?"

I explained the idea I'd just had. Jin's response was to stand up, grab the box with her first fake battery in it, and take it out to the workbench, where she picked up and arranged several of the extra parts.

"I love it. I'll have the guys get on it first thing in the morning."

TWENTY-FIVE

The day before Labor Day was a Sunday, and the weather was beautiful in Arizona. The weather forecast was over a hundred degrees, but I was almost getting used to the heat, I'd spent so much time there. Jin and I were up in the Cessna, ready to start the first part of our breach of the Goldwater Dig site.

Before we left the island that morning, Jin had set her team the task of creating a second dummy battery with some very specific changes. We got a packed lunch from the food court; then we were off. We made a stop at our rented hangar at the Eagle Point Municipal Airport to top off the fuel tanks; then Jin monkeyed around under the cowl a bit, doing something to the engine that I couldn't see. It made me nervous that she was rigging the plane to have problems, but I figured if anyone could do it safely, it was Jin. Hopefully.

"Perfect," she said as we climbed in. "I'll be able to trigger it from the cabin."

"Trigger what, exactly?"

"I disconnected . . . You know what? I shouldn't tell you."

I stopped my preflight checklist and stared at her.

"You know, so you can be totally innocent."

I kept staring.

"It'll be fine. We'll be fine. I promise."

"Cross your heart?" I asked.

She drew an X over her heart with her finger. I sighed, then went back to the checklist. When everything was ready and we were buckled in, I opened up the pilot's-side window and shouted, "Clear!" I fired the engine up. Everything felt and sounded normal.

"I swear, we're good to go. Nothing will happen until I trigger it," she said.

I called the tower to report our plans for takeoff, steered the plane to the end of the runway, and pushed in the throttle. Everything felt totally normal, so I let myself relax a little. After takeoff, I performed a series of training maneuvers that slowly took us toward the Sonora Flats field. We got as close as possible to the military zone, then checked each other over. Our disguises were in place, and I had my shirt unbuttoned a little farther down than necessary. Jin wore a clingy tank top. We were ready to meet some military men.

She opened an access hatch underneath the control panel, reached inside, and wiggled something around. Nothing happened for a few seconds; then the engine sputtered and coughed. The little I'd let myself relax went away, and I tensed up.

"We'll be fine," she said. "You've trained for this, and I've landed cold plenty of times. Make the call."

I picked up the radio and dialed into the emergency frequency. "Mayday, mayday. This is passenger aircraft November five three zero nine, experiencing engine trouble. Any station, please respond." I'd planned on putting on a higher-pitched panicky voice; I didn't really have to fake it that much. Jin, as the more experienced pilot, probably should have used the radio, but she somehow knew that I'd get the nervous tone just right. Plus, if you aren't going to practice emergencies, then you only have yourself to blame when bad things happen and plans go sour.

The radio was silent for a moment; then a deep male voice crackled on the other end. "Roger, November five three zero nine. What is your location?"

I checked the GPS receiver. "Approximately thirty-two degrees and fifty-two minutes north, one hundred twelve degrees and forty-two minutes west." I checked the skies around for traffic and wiped my sweaty palms on my shorts.

"Roger that, November. Is your engine functioning?"

In a moment of perfect timing, the engine finally stopped its wheezing, sputtered, and died. "Negative," I said. "My engine has just failed. Altitude just under ten thousand feet. Is there a landing strip within . . ." I did a quick calculation in my head from the numbers Jin had taught me. "Fifteen miles?"

I already knew that Sonora Flats was around four miles away, while the next public airport was around twenty, which was why I'd kept our altitude low. Now that we were gliding, however, it felt like we were heading back down to earth at a remarkably fast rate.

There was more silence on the radio, and then finally: "November five three zero nine, we have you on our radar, and you are cleared for an emergency landing. Please turn northwest to three hundred and twenty-one degrees; the landing strip is four miles ahead."

"Roger that," I said. "November five three zero nine, changing course to three hundred twenty-one degrees. Thank you." I changed our course and continued to glide. We had enough altitude that I wouldn't have to fly straight in to the runway; I'd be able to fly alongside, take my turns, and line myself up well.

We flew in silence until the Sonora Flats airstrip came into view in the distance. I checked my cleavage again, then said to Jin, "I don't know if I'll want to try the old engine-trouble ruse again anytime soon."

"You're doing great," she said. "And I'm here to take over if you need me to."

The radio crackled back to life. "We have you in visual range, November. Change course to zero degrees, and prepare for landing pattern to runway one seven."

"Roger," I said. "November to zero degrees, coming around to runway one seven."

The voice on the radio guided me through the landing pattern, first flying alongside the runway and passing it by, then taking two ninety-degree turns to the left to line the plane up with the runway. We could see the giant number seventeen painted on the end of the runway, so we were definitely headed to the right place.

I glided the plane in for a landing, keeping an eye on my altitude and angle. When we passed over the top of the giant seventeen, I pushed in the flaps to both slow the plane down and make it lose altitude. Thank goodness it wasn't a windy day; my first no-power emergency landing was relatively smooth, if you ignore the fact that I was kind of having a little panic attack through the entire thing.

The tires touched down, and I pressed on the brake pedals. I slowed the plane down but didn't bring it to a complete stop; I could see a person up ahead on the side of the runway wearing a bright-orange safety vest, standing in the bed of a white truck. He held up a pair of lighted batons and waved me toward him. I let the plane roll down the runway toward him. As he slowly raised his arms up above his head, I gently pressed on the brake. When he crossed the batons in an X shape over his head, I brought the plane to a halt.

He set down the portable radio he'd been using to talk to us, jumped out of the bed of the truck, and walked over to our plane. Jin opened the window on her side so we could talk to him. He grabbed hold of the strut under the wing and stepped over the rear wheel on Jin's side, so his head was even with ours. "Howdy there, ladies. Any idea what's wrong?"

"No clue," Jin said. "But maybe we can take a look under the hood and figure it out."

"Let's get you off the runway," he said. "Hold tight and keep your foot on the brake, and I'll hook up the truck."

He ran over to his truck and backed it toward our plane with the ease of someone who's done the same move thousands of times. He pulled a tow bar out of the bed of the truck, attached it to the back, and hooked up the other end to the front wheel of our plane. Instead of towing us right away, he hopped back out and came over to my side of the plane, stepping up again.

"If you ladies want, you can come ride in the cab of the truck. It's a mighty hot one out here, and I have air-conditioning."

"That's awfully kind of you," I said. We unbuckled ourselves, and out of the corner of my eye I saw Jin pat the cargo pocket on her shorts. We both climbed out and joined the man in the cab of the truck. He slowly drove up the runway, then gently turned us and the plane onto a side access road.

"Roger," he said.

I looked at him. "Um . . . okay?"

He laughed. "No, my name is Roger. I know, I know, I've heard all the jokes about the movie *Airplane*."

We introduced ourselves as Ellen and Sue, names we'd used before in Phoenix. We explained the sounds the engine made as it was dying to Roger as he drove us toward a small hangar.

"It was kind of a grumble, then a cough-cough," I said. "Then sputtering, then nothing."

"Hmm," Roger said. "Sounds like maybe something lost pressure? We'll take a look and see what we can see."

"Thank you so much," I said. "May I ask where we are?"

"Air force emergency airfield," he said.

"Oh my gosh," I said. "I hope it isn't a problem that we landed here!"

"No problem at all. If I didn't help damsels in distress, I wouldn't be much of a military man, would I?"

"I suppose not," Jin said.

"So where are you ladies flying out of?"

"Phoenix," I said. "I'm a pretty new pilot. I've run some emergency drills before, but I was hoping I wouldn't have to put that know-how into practice quite so soon."

"Probably a one in a million thing," Roger said. "I've flown tons of hours in all kinds of planes and feel safer in them than I do driving on the freeway. Anyway, I watched you come in, and you did a great job landing." I was delighted to hear that, and I hoped Jin felt pride, too, since she'd taught me everything.

He pulled the truck around, then deftly backed the plane into the hangar. We all climbed out, and Roger opened up the cowl that covered the engine. He went and grabbed a light on a long cord and a little two-step ladder. He propped the light over the cowl, climbed up the ladder, and looked at the engine.

"I'm so sorry, Roger," Jin said, "but I wonder if you have a restroom I could use?"

"Sure thing," he said. He pointed to a door off to the left. "First door once you get inside; it's impossible to miss. Be warned, the air-conditioning isn't so great in there. We're having kind of a toasty day."

"I'll be fine," she said, and headed to the door. As soon as she was through, I turned back to Roger.

"So," I said, "I'm learning about how the insides all work. Would it be okay if I watched what you do?"

"Sure!" He went back to the workbench at the side of the hangar, grabbed a second ladder, and brought it over and set it up next to the first. He even offered me his hand as I climbed up. I didn't think it was the cleavage—Roger acted like a genuine gentleman.

I kept up a steady stream of chatter as he poked around inside the engine. He pointed out several parts, and I realized Jin was right: my ignorance of what she'd done was a huge advantage, because I could react genuinely to everything he told me.

"Now here's something that isn't right," he said, tapping a finger on a weird blocky-looking thing. "It looks like your air intake got disconnected from the air box."

"Wow," I said. "Um . . ."

He looked at me and smiled. "Do you know what either of these things are?"

"No," I said. "I've been meaning to learn more about this stuff but haven't had a chance yet."

"Well, then, you should probably have your instructor give you a guided tour of some of the parts of this engine."

"I definitely will," I said.

"Did you notice a drop in the manifold pressure before the engine died?"

"I didn't see any of the dials or gauges do anything funny, I don't think," I said.

"Well, that's something else to check out. You may have a broken gauge. But overall, this plane looks really well taken care of." He proceeded to explain about how the engine needed both fuel and air to run, and not getting enough air was just as bad as not getting enough fuel. I knew about that already but nodded and smiled at him anyway. Then he grabbed a screwdriver, reconnected a huge hose to the blocky-looking thing, and then put some duct tape on it for good measure.

"Not a permanent solution," he said, "but it'll get you back to a bigger airfield, where someone can take a closer look at everything."

Jin came back into the hangar and walked up to us. "Did you figure it out?"

"Something about air," I said. "The plane wasn't sucking hard enough."

Roger laughed. "That's not exactly how I explained it, but it gets the point across. You ladies should be good to go to get back to Phoenix, but you should definitely have a mechanic look things over there, to make sure there aren't any other problems."

I swapped places with Jin so she could see his repairs. She pretended to not know much about the engine so that he would point out what had gone wrong and how he'd fixed it. She climbed down from the stepladder and thanked him, so I guess his work was up to her standards.

He put the cowl back down over the engine, set aside his ladders and tools, and got back in his truck to pull the plane outside the hangar. He unhooked the tow bar and moved the truck well away from the airplane. With our permission, he hopped up into the cockpit to see if the plane would start. Jin and I both stood well off to the side.

"He isn't going to see whatever you did in there to trigger whatever it was, will he?" I asked.

"Not a chance," Jin said.

"Do you think he's looking around in there?" I had my own student pilot's license safely stowed in my pocket; we'd left a fully qualified pilot's license in Ellen's name out in plain view, clipped to the dashboard so it couldn't be missed.

"He'd be an idiot not to," she said. "And I don't think he's an idiot."

Roger leaned his head out through the open side window and shouted, "Clear!" He cranked the engine, which coughed and gasped a few times, then roared to life. He pulled the plane out a little farther so it was pointed back down the access road, then set the brakes and hopped out. We walked over and met him at the tail of the plane.

"Fantastic," I said, shaking his hand. "Thank you so much, Roger!"

"It was my pleasure," he said. "This was the most excitement I've had out here for weeks. Now you should be good to get back to Phoenix, but don't forget to have someone look at the engine right away."

"I know the perfect person," I said. "Knows engines inside and out."

"Great," he said. "Hop on in and give me a minute to get back inside so I can make sure there isn't any traffic out there to bother you." Jin shook his hand, and we climbed back into the plane and buckled ourselves in.

"Good?" I asked Jin.

"Good," she said.

We put our headsets on and waited for Roger to come back on the line. After a minute, his voice crackled in my headset. "November five three zero nine, you are cleared to taxi to runway one seven."

"Roger, taxi to runway one seven," I said. I released the brakes and pushed in the throttle, and the engine purred as we moved forward, as if Jin had never sabotaged it. I steered the plane down the access road, stopped for a moment to check both ways when I got to the runway, then headed down to the far end. It was a tight turn to get us pointing the right direction, but the plane was small and nimble enough that we made it.

"November five three zero nine, ready for takeoff on runway one seven," I said.

"Roger, November. Cleared for takeoff on runway one seven. Be safe out there."

"Roger, Roger," I said.

"I promise, I've heard that one before," he said. "You ladies have a great day."

I adjusted the flaps, pushed in the throttle, and we took off from Sonora Flats. We'd taken off pointing toward Mexico, so I took two ninety-degree turns to get us headed back north. I climbed up to our cruising altitude for the short flight back to the Eagle Point airfield.

"So everything's in its place?" I asked.

"All set for tomorrow." She pulled off one side of her headset and listened to the engine. "Like a kitten. I take it the fix was easy once he spotted the problem?"

"Sure was. All it took was a screwdriver. Oh, and don't forget the duct tape," I said.

"A little extra caution never hurts. Good old duct tape, handy for a thousand and one uses."

TWENTY-SIX

The first Monday in September, Labor Day in the United States, dawned warm and clear. Five of us were packing up the equipment we needed so we could all head over to Arizona. We could have done the mission with four, but Nate insisted that he wanted to come along inside the building this time, instead of staying outside the operation, monitoring and serving as our eyes and ears on the ground.

I have no idea how he convinced Evie to come along and be our monitor, especially because she was complaining about how much she hated Arizona as soon as we started loading the planes. At least he'd checked in with me to see if I was okay with him swapping assigned jobs, and he made sure to let everyone know that I was okay with it. It was my operation, though hopefully within twenty-four hours it would finally be done. I was ready to go back to being a follower instead of a leader, at least for a while.

On our way back from our emergency landing the day before, Jin and I had flown past the Exponential Projects building. It delighted me that they were still on high alert, patrolling the outside of the building as if they expected someone to break in at any time. Either they had no idea that we'd already broken in and taken what we needed, or they were keeping up a ruse to fool us. I was pretty sure it was the first option.

As we loaded equipment onto the jet, Oscar sneezed.

"All right, buddy?" Nate asked.

"Eh, a little stuffy this morning," Oscar said. "Nothing to worry about."

Nate went up into the jet and brought out a container of orange juice. Oscar thanked him and guzzled it down. I looked him up and down, since I wanted to make sure my team was at peak readiness. He looked a little tired, but otherwise normal.

"Try to catch a nap on the flight," I said. "You look tired."

"Yes, ma'am," he said, and saluted me with a smile.

We were taking both planes over, since the Cessna was only built for four people, but we'd need it for the job. Jin and I would fly the smaller plane, while everyone else was welcome to either stuff themselves in our backseat or ride in the comfort of the jet. Since it was a fairly short flight, Nate opted to fly with us, while Oscar and Evie went with the jet.

We took off and headed out. The jet was faster than our little Cessna, but on such a short flight, it wouldn't make all that much difference. It just meant that Oscar and Evie could get a head start on unloading the jet before we got there. Maybe that was one of the reasons Nate opted to ride with us.

I sat in the pilot's seat and did all the flying. I was glad to have Jin sitting at my side, but I was more confident every day behind the yoke, especially since I'd handled an unpowered emergency landing the day before. Nate stayed fairly quiet until we reached our cruising altitude.

"That takeoff was great," he said. "You're really getting good."

"Thanks," I said. "I know I'm technically ready to take my exams, but I feel like there's so much more to learn."

"So humble," Jin said. She twisted in her seat to see Nate in the back. "She'll be better than I am before long."

"Oh, whatever," I said.

"So," Nate said, "I hope you haven't had to make any sweeping changes to the plan since I'm now coming along inside."

I reached back and patted his knee. "Nah, it's good. We'll just consider you a spare, in case we need you. Maybe you can do some heavy lifting if the opportunity presents itself."

"Wow, you're really letting this team-leader thing go to your head."

"I learned from the best. Doctor Oracle himself."

"Jeez, you two," Jin said. "Get a room."

I glanced back at Nate. "How did you convince Evie to come along to the awful barren desert? Especially in the part where she's alone for most of the job?"

"What, you don't think I just asked politely, and she succumbed to my charm?"

"Not really, no."

"Well, first I appealed to her kinder nature. I told her that while I got bored and lonely when I had a solo role, she was always looking for a new book to read, or something new to study and learn. So it'd be perfect for her."

"Really? I'm not buying it," I said.

"Fine," he said. "I told her I'd help her expand her winemaking operation into brewing beer as well. We're going to try planting a half acre of hops, and some specialty grains, and I'll get all the equipment she needs."

"And you don't benefit at all from that," Jin said.

"Hey, I never said I wouldn't end up with a nice cold beer at the end of the whole thing."

"Well, she does a phenomenal job with her wine," I said. "Now I'm already looking forward to her beer."

"See? Win-win."

I was glad to have a topic to discuss that wasn't the upcoming job; it helped take my mind off the mission. I'd already gone over the plan, the emergency backup plans, and the backups to the backups many times in my head. I needed to stop thinking about it, or I'd be tempted to make a thousand small, pointless changes. We moved on to rounds of twenty questions, which lasted us until we got to the Eagle Point airfield.

Sure enough, the jet was already parked in our rented hangar, and Oscar and Evie were unloading the equipment. As soon as I pulled up, Nate jumped out to help them while Jin and I got the plane settled in, which looked tiny and quaint next to the fancy, sleek jet. Some of the equipment got transferred to the small cargo area in the Cessna, and our suitcases went into the back of the SUV.

Jin took the wheel and drove us to our base of operations, a small motel near the intersection of an interstate and a highway in a little town called Buckeye, in the outskirts of Phoenix. It was close enough to Eagle Point for the job but far enough from the city center to keep a low profile. We checked in under the guise of a family on one last leg of our vacation before the summer was over.

Nate had made the motel arrangements, and I had no problems with the quality. It wasn't anything fancy, but the place was clean and tidy. He and I were sharing a room, as were Oscar and Jin. Evie got one of her own, to hopefully make her feel a little kinder toward the entire state of Arizona. We weren't planning on staying the night—it was just a handy place to store things, change clothes, and take a nap before our nighttime excursion.

I noticed that Nate checked us in as Mr. and Mrs. Horatio Barker. As soon as we got into our room, I called him on it.

"We just *had* to be married, didn't we?"

"I blame you," he said.

"Why on earth would you?" I asked.

"Back in Vegas, you made the comment, and I'm paraphrasing here, 'Who on earth wants a fake marriage?'"

"So since I said it's something I *didn't* want, you decided to give it to me?"

"Well, I figured a fake marriage would make you realize that a real one wouldn't be so bad."

"Oh my God," I said. "That makes no sense at all."

"Or does it make *too much sense*?"

"No, I think I had it right the first time."

"Maybe that isn't the reason at all," Nate said. "Maybe I'm just messing with you."

I tossed one of the pillows at him. "Why did I even let you come along on this?"

"Because I'm great in the field. And you love having me around."

"Ugh," I said.

"Plus," he added, "you aren't stressing out and overthinking things when you're busy being all eye-rolly with me."

"This is true," I said. "I guess I need you around for every time I lead so you can irritate me just the right amount."

He smiled wide. "So you might want to take the lead again after this? That's great!"

"We'll see, after this thing is through."

"Yeah, you will," he said. "You like to plot and plan. And fret and worry, but if you fret the right amount, that's a good thing."

I was about to respond, when there was a knock at the door connecting our room to the one next door. I opened it to find Evie on the other side; I pushed the door open wide and let her in.

"This awful place," she said, "is like being in a convection oven. Thank goodness I didn't have to go outside to get to your room. Why did I agree to come here, again?"

"Think of the beer," Nate said.

"Ah, yes." She closed her eyes. "Lovely, lovely beer."

"What brings you by?" I asked.

"Just wanted to let you know that I've checked over my monitoring equipment, and we're all aces."

"Good," I said. I looked at the black ChatterBox unit on my wrist, which was currently only serving the function of a watch. "It's about lunchtime. We should find some grub, then get to work."

"Any idea where to go?" Nate asked.

"As a matter of fact, I already asked Lucy where the best place in town is," I said.

*** * *** * ***

After what were probably the best sandwiches to be had in the state of Arizona, or possibly the entire Southwest, we got to work.

Jin and Oscar headed out in the SUV, leaving Nate, Evie, and me at the motel to check over the rest of the equipment and all our tactical suits. We finished inspecting the suits just as Jin and Oscar returned, this time in two cars instead of one, since we'd be splitting up to go two different ways.

I'd actually scheduled a nap time in the early afternoon. Everyone was allowed to do whatever they wanted during that time, but I'd found that it was always helpful to have a rest period before jumping into action, even if that rest was just closing your eyes for a little while. I set an alarm on my ChatterBox, and Nate and I flopped down next to each other on one of the beds.

It felt like I'd barely closed my eyes for a minute, then my alarm went off, letting me know I'd slept for an hour. After slapping some water on my face, I felt refreshed and ready to go.

Everyone knew the time line, and in a few minutes, they had all convened in our room. Jin and Oscar were sharing the room on the other side of us, so we left all the connecting doors open to make it a three-room suite of sorts. We went over the plan and discussed some small changes. Oscar sneezed again, and I glanced over at him. He looked tired.

"You're sure you're all right?" I asked.

"Maybe it's allergies," he said. "I'm just all stuffy."

"Because if you're coming down with something, we do have Nate here as a spare." I poked at Nate's side, and he swatted my hand away.

"Nah, I'm good. Even if I'm getting sick, I can work through it." He sniffed and looked at me. "If it's okay with you, that is."

I looked at Nate, who just raised his eyebrows at me. The decision was all mine.

"Fine, but if you give me a cold, I'm going to be *pissed*," I said. "And I expect you to let us know if you feel like your performance will be impacted in any way."

He pulled a black bandana out of his pocket and tied it around his face. "I promise to keep my germs to myself."

We broke up the meeting, and I went with Jin to her room to help her put on a disguise. My work wasn't anywhere near as good as Rupert's, but the pieces of latex he'd supplied us with were mostly foolproof. When we had Jin's false face in place, she drove off in the SUV for the next part of the mission. I rejoined Nate, who helped me with my own disguise. He and Oscar were easier, since they didn't need to do anything with their hair—they both just put on baseball caps. On the one hand, I cursed having to wear wigs. But on the other hand, I loved being able to throw on an entirely different look. We all had bits of latex on our faces, and I applied some makeup.

Evie helped where she could. She wasn't putting on a disguise, because the plan didn't actually require her to meet Lucy or go anywhere near where people could see her.

"You're good to go with the lonely role?" I asked her.

"Never a problem," she said. "I actually picked up a wonderful book the other day, and I'm about halfway through. And you know me, usually happier in a cozy corner than with a rollicking crowd."

Over her shoulder, I saw Nate smirk at me. He'd joked that she'd be happier with the solo role, but I hadn't really believed him.

As soon as Jin pulled up outside, Evie went through the connecting door to her room. She was on her own for the rest of the evening, though we'd be in contact with our ChatterBoxes.

Nate answered the knock on our door, and Jin and Lucy walked in. Lucy looked a little bit pale and a little bit shaky, almost like Oscar. She wasn't wearing a mask, but I had no idea if she had on a disguise. Her face was the same as the last times I'd seen her, so maybe all this time she'd been showing us her real face.

"Hi, Lucy," I said. "Everything all right?"

"Just a little nervous, is all," she said. She came over and hugged me, which was a surprise. "It's good to see you, Sarah."

"Good to see you, too," I said. I'd already let everyone know that I'd given Lucy my real name, so it wasn't a surprise for them to hear it. "And thank you for agreeing to be a part of this. Don't hesitate to let us know if you need anything or want to take extra time on something."

Lucy nodded and looked around. "So I've met Sue already, and here's Ethan," she said, using the fake names Jin and Nate had used when meeting her before. "So there's just one stranger. I don't suppose you're Doctor Oracle?"

Oscar stepped forward. "Nope, Oscar," he said, reaching out to shake her hand. I was surprised that he gave her his real name, but then again, I'd done the same thing. There was just something about her I trusted. "Doc's busy with something else and sent us out on this one, but don't worry. You're in good hands."

She shook his hand. "Are you playing the part of the train robber, Oscar?"

"What? Oh, this." He touched the bandana he'd rewrapped around his nose and mouth after his makeup and prosthetics were done. "Feeling a touch under the weather, and the boss has warned me to not get her sick."

"Oh, no," Lucy said. "I hope you'll be all right."

"I'm sure I'll be right as rain before long."

She looked at him, then raised one of her gloved hands. She tugged at one of the fingers, indicating that she wanted to take the glove off. "May I . . . touch you?"

"Sure, why not?" Oscar held out his hand. Lucy took her glove off and grasped Oscar's hand again, then closed her eyes. She breathed deep for about a minute, then opened her eyes again. I'd seen her smile before, and it was beautiful, but this time it was the broadest, most glowing smile I'd seen yet.

"Oh, yes," she said. "You'll be just fine. It's absolutely my pleasure to meet you, Oscar."

There was an awkward silence for a moment as she put her glove back on.

Finally, Jin cleared her throat. "Well, how about we go try on your outfit to make sure everything fits?" She led Lucy into the connecting room and shut the door.

I looked at Oscar. "Wow, that was weird. What was that all about?"

He looked just as lost as the rest of us. "I have no idea."

TWENTY-SEVEN

We planned everything around the sunset. Fortunately, there wasn't a cloud in the sky to force us to change our timing. There was plenty of time for Nate to drive out and grab some pizza; he delivered one to Evie's room, then came back to our room with the rest. It wasn't the healthiest dinner before a job, but it was good enough. The pizza place was Lucy's pick, and as usual, it was excellent.

"How do you know where all the great restaurants are?" I asked.

"I've lived in this area my whole life, so I've probably eaten just about everywhere. The ones that stick around the longest are usually the good ones. My mom used to be an Avon lady, and she'd take me along a lot. So we hit every small town from Vegas to Tucson."

"If it means eating this well," Oscar said, "I'm more than happy to team up with you again."

He had to take his bandana off to eat, but he'd courteously moved to the far side of the room, away from the rest of us. I noticed Lucy glancing at him frequently. For all I knew, she was smitten, even though he was kind of snotty and wearing a disguise. Oscar just had that magnetic way about him.

"How you feeling over there?" I asked.

"Pizza cures all ills," he said. "I'm like a new man."

We finished our food, suited up in our tactical outfits, loaded some equipment in the back of the SUV, then headed back to the airfield. Oscar took the passenger seat so that he wouldn't be crammed in the back, spreading his germs around. That meant I was in the middle of the backseat between Nate and Lucy. I was glad that none of us was particularly large.

Jin pulled into the airfield and took us to our hangar. Lucy stepped out and looked at the jet, then at the Cessna. "Let me guess, we're taking the small one."

"It's much more nimble," I said.

"Maybe now is when I should tell you I've only been up in a plane once, and that was when I was five."

I looked Lucy in the eye. "Are you going to be okay?"

"I hope so," she said. "I took half a Xanax before you picked me up. It won't dull my abilities, but it puts a tighter lid on my anxiety. Just promise me you have barf bags in this thing, just in case."

"We're fully stocked," Jin said. "But, you know, it'd be best if you didn't barf."

"I'll see what I can do."

We loaded the cargo hold of the plane carefully, strapping things down in specific predetermined spots. Jin and I ran through our inspection and preflight checklist; then Jin checked how full the fuel tanks were.

"We're good," she said. "Coming in slightly underweight, I think."

"Wait," Oscar said, "is there a concern that we would be *overweight*?"

"Count the seats, Oscar," Jin said. "This thing is only meant to hold four people. With fuel and equipment, we have just about nine hundred pounds left over for people. We are, collectively, just under eight hundred pounds, so everything should be fine."

Oscar coughed into his bandana. "If there are only four seats, where's the fifth person going to sit?"

"There's room enough for someone in the cargo area," she said. "Oh, did I fail to mention that? I think it'd be the perfect quarantine zone for someone hacking his germs everywhere."

"Great," Oscar grumbled.

"It isn't too late to back out," I said. "We have a spare; we'd be fine. You could go back to the motel and get some rest."

"It's like you don't know me at all," he said. "As if I'd quit!"

"He won't quit," Lucy said. We all turned to look at her.

"See?" Oscar said. "We just met, and she has more faith in me than you guys have."

"It isn't that," she said. "I just . . . felt that you'd be going along."

We all stood there for a moment. If everyone else was like me, they were wondering just what Lucy had felt when she'd touched Oscar earlier and what she wasn't telling us about it now.

"All right," I said. "If we're going to do this, let's do this."

We all put our ChatterBox earpieces in, and we showed Lucy how to link up to the rest of us. Nate tapped some buttons on the front of his ChatterBox; to give him something to do, I'd assigned him to be head of communications.

"All connected," he said. He turned the microphones on so Lucy could experience having our voices in her ear.

"You get used to it," I said. She flinched a tiny bit when I spoke, and I totally understood. My previous experience with sound in my ear was either through cheap earbud headphones or a Bluetooth headset connected to my phone. The tinny sound out of those things couldn't hold a candle to the sharp, clear sound from the CB earpiece; it was almost like having someone talk inside your head.

Nate switched our microphones back off. "We'll try to keep chatter to a minimum."

We climbed into the plane, Oscar grumbling but taking up his spot in the cargo hold. He managed to find a position to lie down that didn't look completely uncomfortable. Jin and I took the front seats, and Nate and Lucy sat in the back. I finished my checklist, started up the plane, and taxied down the runway.

"Remember," Jin said, "this is a much heavier load than you're used to."

"Who are you calling a heavy load?" Oscar shouted from the far back of the plane.

We ignored him, and Jin continued. "The plane will feel different, but the fundamentals are all the same."

I glanced back at Lucy, who looked really nervous—she had her hand up against her chest, almost as if she were clutching her pearls. "You haven't flown like this before?"

"I'm still learning," I said. "But we have an expert pilot and instructor up here, who will take over at the drop of a hat."

"Could I just . . ." Lucy was wringing her hands in their black gloves. I figured out what she wanted, took off my own glove, and held my hand back to her. She whipped off her glove and grabbed my hand. After a moment, she nodded. "Okay. I can't promise not to throw up, but that helped." She let go, and I got back to the business of taking off in an almost-overloaded plane with a probably illegal number of passengers.

It was kind of nice, in a way, that Lucy felt better about our upcoming flight. I felt less nervous myself; I figured if something was going to go wrong, after touching my hand she would have jumped out of the airplane.

Jin was right: the plane felt different, like when you offer to help someone move and then your normally empty car is filled with someone else's crazy-heavy furniture. It was more sluggish and slow to gain altitude, but once it was in the air, I got the feel for how to handle it.

Nate dialed up Evie on his ChatterBox. "We're in the air, base. On our way." It was easier to just call her "base" instead of a fake name. I couldn't hear Evie's response.

"All good on her end?" I asked.

"All good. She's on her way."

"Excellent." I flew a roundabout path from the airfield down to the area where the Goldwater Dig was housed. As we flew, the sun finally disappeared below the horizon, and the sky turned from orange to dark blue. I heard Nate and Lucy talking in the seat behind me, though I couldn't make out most of the words over the sound of the engine. I knew he was explaining our plan in detail from start to finish so there wouldn't be any surprises about what we would do. I hoped it would ease her anxiety.

I flew around the outside of the air force range, over a green area on my map that designated a national forest. Unlike the lush, green forests I grew up with in Washington, this one contained a lot of cactuses and Joshua trees. By the time I'd gone past the southern end of the range and was turning the plane to come back around headed north, it was full dark.

"We're closing in," Nate said in the back. "Get ready."

I checked our location on the GPS, then turned toward Nate. "We're in position, ready to go."

"That's a go, base," he said. He listened to Evie in his ear for a moment. "Okay, she's set off the first bomb."

"And the bomb was for what, again?" Lucy asked.

"Smoke bomb," Jin said. "I planted them yesterday at the nearby air force landing strip."

"A handy distraction," I said. I pulled back on the throttle, and we began to lose altitude. I could see a few lights far off in the distance; according to my compass, that was the dig site. There were no other lights anywhere nearby. I flipped a switch on the instrument panel, and all the running lights on the outside of the plane went dark. The faint glow from the instrument panel was the only thing to see as we headed toward the distant buildings in the middle of a flat, dusty plain.

"Okay, good," Nate said. He'd been listening to Evie's report as she watched the inside of Roger's little control room thanks to the camera Jin had planted the day before during her excursion to the bathroom. "They're evacuating the area; the control room is currently empty."

I flew straight and true toward the distant lights, using the flaps to help lose a lot of altitude in a small amount of time. I tried to keep it smooth so that Lucy wouldn't feel sick, but I had to concentrate on flying and couldn't look back to check on her. We all got very quiet. I dropped us down until the altimeter read thirty feet. Thanks to the distance from Sonora Flats and the curvature of the earth, we were literally flying under their radar.

Jin gently rested her hands on the controls, ready to take over the landing. Finally, she said, "I've got it." I felt her put pressure on the controls, so I could take my hands off and wipe my sweaty palms on my legs.

"Thank goodness," I said.

"You did great," she said. But we both knew that landing on a flat stretch of unfamiliar desert in the dark was a task better done by a professional. She kept an eye on the GPS, made small adjustments to her course, and took us even lower. The lights of the buildings where the drilling operation was taking place weren't very far away anymore.

I turned toward the back of the plane. I couldn't see Lucy or Nate's faces clearly in the dark. I called toward the cargo hold, "Oscar, brace yourself back there!"

"Aye, Captain," he shouted.

Jin was staring straight ahead, concentrating on the ground that she couldn't quite see. "In three . . . two . . . one . . ."

The plane touched down, bounced back up, then settled down to earth. Jin and I both pressed on the brake pedals, and she put the flaps all the way down to slow our speed. After a minute, the plane came to a halt.

I took a deep breath and let it out. We were in the middle of a flat expanse of desert; the plane was pointed north for a quick exit; we'd made it in one piece, and according to Nate's reports from Evie, nobody had seen us come in.

We unbuckled ourselves and got out. Nate went around to the cargo hold to help Oscar out, and they unloaded some backpacks and Jin's tool belt. Jin handed out goggles to everyone, and I showed Lucy how to switch them over to night vision.

"You all right?" I asked her. "Not feeling too sick? Do you need a minute?"

As soon as I switched over to night vision, I could see her face glowing green. She was smiling broadly.

"That was *awesome*," she said.

TWENTY-EIGHT

We shouldered our backpacks, Jin strapped on her tool belt, and Nate took the job of marking the location of the plane using a smartphone with a GPS-based parking-spot-finder app. Otherwise, there was the chance of heading out into the desert in a slightly wrong direction and ending up way off course.

We walked in a single-file line toward the largest building to keep ourselves as hard to see as possible. Oscar was in the lead, with me right behind. He was the perfect choice for point man, since he was nimble and our best fighter. Lucy was in the middle so we could protect her if need be. Jin and Nate followed up in the rear. Our comm channel was open, but since there were likely a few guards around, we stayed quiet.

Oscar led us on a curved route toward the building so that we would come at it on the side that wasn't very well lit. There were a few scrub bushes and trees on that side—someone's depressing idea of landscaping. We made it to the building without incident and pressed ourselves against the wall.

I nodded at Lucy, and she took one of her gloves off. To avoid leaving fingerprints anywhere, she pressed the back side of her hand against the building. After a moment, she nodded at Jin, indicating that she felt good about our location.

Our plan A was to get in and out without being seen, and Lucy was a major key in that plan. Through touching the walls, floors, or whatever else was around us, she could feel whether we were going the right way or if we needed to wait a moment to let someone pass by. In a way, it was like playing a video game when there's a little mini-map up in the corner that identifies where all the enemies are located.

Plan B would mean subduing anyone who happened to see us, but we hoped to avoid that in order to play out the final part of the plan the following morning. The guys had their tranquilizer pistols out and ready, but I hoped that they wouldn't be necessary.

Jin crept off toward the right side of the building, which wasn't as large as I thought it would be: the blueprints of the facility showed that most of the building, including where the digging was taking place, was underground. The lights on the outside of the building were mounted on the roof and pointed out into the desert, so Jin quickly disappeared into the dark shadows alongside the building.

While she was heading around to disable the alarm system, Nate shrugged his backpack to the side, unzipped it, and pulled out a small electronic device. He nestled it in a shrub that looked like a tumbleweed attached to the ground. For all I knew, that's exactly what it was—tumbleweeds had to come from somewhere. Nate pressed a switch on the side of the device, and a dim green light glowed on the side.

"Found the electrical panel," Jin whispered in my ear. Lucy jumped a little bit at the sound. As we waited, I knew that Jin was opening the enclosure and either disarming or temporarily disabling the security system. Thanks to Oscar's eagle eye in spotting the invoice for the security system, she'd been able to bring exactly the tools she needed to work around it. Of course, she brought a wide assortment of additional tools—that was just good heist etiquette.

"Good to go," she whispered. After a minute, she appeared out of the darkness and rejoined us. Lucy rested her hand against the wall, then nodded toward the left side of the building. We crept around that way in our single-file line. The wall wasn't straight; it was dotted with nooks and bump-outs, architectural features that felt like they were from the fifties. We could see several smaller buildings up ahead; according to the plans, they were dormitories for the on-site workers. Since the crew had all been allowed the three-day weekend off to visit their families, the buildings were completely dark and deserted.

"Wait," Lucy whispered as we were almost to the corner of the building. We all froze. After a moment, she whispered, "Go."

We took the corner and saw a guard far up ahead, walking away from us. We walked toward him as quietly as possible, while Lucy kept her hand in contact with the wall.

"Nook here," Oscar whispered.

"Take it," Lucy said. Oscar turned toward a shadowy part of the building and went into it. I realized that both the nooks and bump-outs were shaped like half-hexagons, probably the designer's idea of a futuristic look. The space barely fit the five of us.

Jin pulled a tiny dentist's mirror out of her tool belt and held it just outside the nook so she could see around the corner and watch the guard. I'd done much the same thing a few months back with a shiny metal cafeteria tray, so I knew how handy a mirror could be for checking around corners.

"He's turned, coming back this way," she whispered. "Looks like the doorway is about fifty feet further along."

We waited as the guard ambled back toward us; he walked a long, slow path along the side of the building but, according to Jin, stopped just short of the main doorway and turned back around.

As soon as he was on his way away from us again, Lucy whispered, "Good."

"Good," Jin whispered at almost the same time, looking at her mirror.

Oscar took the lead again, and we covered the fifty feet to the doorway as quickly and quietly as we could. Fortunately, the doorway was indented into the wall, so we could all crowd in there and stay hidden if the guard made his way to the end of the building and turned back toward us.

Jin quickly pulled out her lock-picking kit, and as fast as it took for us all to switch our goggles from night vision to regular vision, she had the door open for us. We all piled through and shut the door behind us. No alarms sounded, so Jin's work was successful, and we'd managed to elude the slowpoke guard.

The area just inside the door was done up like a reception area: a giant wooden desk, a few older-looking chairs, and several doors around the room. Lucy went around to touch each of the doors.

Nate shifted his backpack around to the side again, opened it, and pulled out a tiny white cube. He handed it to Oscar, who climbed nimbly up on the massive desk. He stuck the cube up in a corner where two walls met the ceiling; it was so small and inconspicuous, I only knew it was there because I was looking for it. He squeezed it gently, then stepped off the desk.

Suddenly, Evie's voice was in my ear. "There you all are, my dears. Camera one is active here at base."

We'd initially planned on hacking the facility's own camera feeds so that we could use them, but our research showed that the facility actually didn't have cameras. They depended on guards on foot and alarms on the doors and windows. It puzzled the rest of us, but Lucy filled us in. The head of the Southwest Storm, a guy who just went by Eminence, had once told her about why he didn't put cameras on secret projects: too easy for the wrong people to see what you're doing. Plus, if things went south, that was a possible visual record.

We wanted to observe the facility the next day, when the earthquake happened, so we had to plant a few of our own cameras. It wasn't a necessity for the job; we were all just curious and wanted to watch how everything went down. Plus, it was a good test run of some new tech: the tiny cameras and the signal-boosting device Nate had hidden in the bushes behind the building. Thanks to the combination of gadgets, Evie was able to see our camera feeds from her position, parked miles away along the perimeter road outside of the air force range. One of her tasks was to plant a relay there before she left so that the feeds from the cameras would be watchable the next morning when we were back home.

Nate pulled a tablet out of his backpack and tapped on it, bringing up the plans of the facility. "Looks like either door number two or door number three will get us there."

"Three," Lucy said after touching both doors. "Definitely." So that was the way we went.

Door number three opened onto a short hallway lined with a few more doors. We stopped just shy of a corner to wait for Lucy to nod her head; then we turned the corner. It was another short hall, with one door at the end marked "STAIRWELL." We went down almost to the stairwell, where the hall we were in joined another one that branched off to the left. According to Nate's map, that hallway connected back with door number two.

We stopped before turning the corner, and Jin took out her little mirror again, crouching down to keep it from being directly in anyone's eye-line. I leaned over her shoulder so I could see in the mirror. There was another guard up ahead, walking away from us. If he took a circular route through these hallways and then through the reception area, door two would have brought us face-to-face with him. Sure enough, he made it to the far end of the hall, opened the door, and went into the reception area.

"Now," Lucy said. She hadn't been watching the guard in the mirror; she'd only been pressing the back side of her hand to the wall. It was creepy and awesome at the same time.

We hustled across the hallway and into the stairwell. There was a little sliver of a window in the stairwell door, so we went down a flight before we stopped to check our location in case the guard made his way back around and took a peek.

"Three more flights down," Nate said as he tapped on his tablet. "We're headed for level D." I looked at the wall next to the door we'd come in through; there was a giant letter *A* stenciled in white.

I put my hand on Lucy's arm. "Are you doing all right? Need to take a break or anything?"

"I'm good," she said. Her eyes looked extra-large, but it might just have been the goggles. Or fear, or anxiety, or excitement. Or all of those, really.

"Good," I said. "Because you have *no* idea how helpful it is to have you along."

"I don't know," Oscar said. "Maybe it kind of takes the fun out of it, not having the chance for a good boo-scare going around every corner. And if this thing goes off smoothly, I won't get to shoot anyone with a dart." He sniffed, then coughed.

"How are *you* doing?" I asked. I pulled off my own glove and pressed the back of my hand against his forehead. He was flushed and warm.

"Good to go," he said. He rubbed at his nose through the black bandana. "I just hate mouth-breathing."

"I'm going to make the offer, even though you won't take me up on it," I said. "You could hang out here while we go downstairs, deal with the drill, then come pick you up on the way back."

"No way. I'm good."

"Have it your way," I said.

"Always," he said. We continued down the stairs past levels B and C. Level D wasn't the bottom floor, but I could see that there was only one more flight of stairs to the bottom. I went down and peeked through the thin window in the bottom-floor door: it looked like mostly storage and machinery. I spotted a metal cage with some sort of engine inside it. I beckoned Jin to come down and join me and pointed the cage out. "What's that?"

"Elevator motor," she said.

We'd missed the elevator entirely, because it was down the hall behind door number two. We hadn't planned on taking it anyway, since there were very few safe exits, and the noise of it running might have given us away. Now that I knew what I was looking at, it was obvious. I'd read the building plans and knew approximately where the elevator was located in relation to the stairwell.

We went back up to level D and waited for Lucy's signal, then headed out into the hallway beyond. If we'd exited the stairwell on the top floor, our hallway choices would have been to the right and straight ahead. This floor had both of those options and an additional long hallway to the left, which was where we wanted to go.

We pressed our backs on either side of the left-hand hallway as Lucy kept her knuckles against the wall. Jin squatted with her dentist's mirror, and I looked over her shoulder again. The hallway stretched away for maybe a hundred yards, with no doorways along the sides, just a pair of intersecting hallways along the way. It ended with a set of double doors. Everything looked clear, so I looked at Lucy. She shook her head, so we waited. Then, as I watched her, her eyes grew even wider behind her goggles. She glanced around at all of us, then fixed her gaze on Oscar, who was on the opposite side of the mouth of the hallway. I looked over at Oscar, who was staring off at one of the overhead lights, one of his eyes squinting and watering a little bit.

He bent over at the waist, clapping both hands against his face as tightly as he could, and let out a sneeze. The sound was muffled behind his hands and handkerchief but still seemed incredibly loud in that quiet building.

We all stood like statues for a moment. I glanced down toward Jin's tiny mirror and saw movement in it. There was a person about halfway down the hallway, crossing from one side of an intersecting hall to the other. That person had stopped in the middle of the hallway intersection.

We stood and waited, Jin and I both watching the little mirror, the others watching us. Nate slowly and quietly drew his tranquilizer pistol. I looked back at Lucy behind me, who had her hand on the wall. She blinked a few times, then let out a breath and nodded. I checked in the mirror, and the guard was moving down the side hallway, out of sight.

When Lucy gave us the signal, we hustled down the long hallway as quickly as we could. The double doors at the end were locked, but Jin once again picked the lock with surprising speed. As she was doing that, Nate got out another tiny white cube camera and put it in a corner at the top of the doorway, looking down the long hallway we'd just come from.

Lucy gave us the all clear, and we rushed through the door. Jin quickly locked it behind us. Fortunately, the door looked thick and well soundproofed, so we didn't have to worry about whispering once we were inside.

"Bless you," Nate said to Oscar.

"Thanks, man," Oscar said. "That one was intense."

"Guys," Jin said. We all turned to look at her, then followed her gaze to take in the room. The place was enormous, more like a giant cave than a room in a building. Which I guess it was, since we were several stories underground. The ceiling was surprisingly high; it felt like it surely had to go almost to the surface.

There was machinery of all shapes and sizes throughout the space. I glanced at Jin, who was looking around with a smile on her face like a kid in a candy store. We walked toward the center of the room, obviously the focal point of the whole operation. There was a giant machine there, with a thousand parts I'd never understand, next to a deep, dark pit in the ground. I was glad for the safety railing around the pit.

The part of the machine I recognized was a cylinder hanging over the pit on a winch. From the pictures we'd looked at, I recognized it as the plasma cutter they were using to dig down through the rock. It was the part that held the plutonium-strontium battery we were there to take.

Nate tapped on his ChatterBox. "I'm cutting out the feeds between us for now, since we're all here in the same room. But we're all still patched in to base."

Jin had turned her back to the crater at the center of the room and was looking around at all the machinery.

"Focus," I whispered.

"I know," she said. "Man, though, it's all beautiful. Some amazing stuff down here."

"Battery first, then you can look for a souvenir."

"Guys," Lucy said, "I'm feeling like we shouldn't dawdle."

"You heard the lady," I said. "Let's get a move on."

TWENTY-NINE

Nate handed me his backpack, then went over to the plasma cutter to figure out the easiest way to get to the cutting head that contained the battery. The top of the pit was surprisingly wide, probably thirty feet across. It sloped down in a graceful curve until it looked to be maybe three feet across way down below, at least twenty feet farther down than where we were standing. From that point, it was just a terrifying inky-black void straight into the earth. The whole thing was shaped exactly like a giant funnel.

I stayed away from the edge, even though there was a safety railing. I unzipped Nate's backpack and pulled out more of the little white cube cameras. I walked around the pit, keeping my distance and looking at how the dig was set up. The arm that held the plasma cutter connected to a large machine; I found some control panels that looked like they had important buttons and switches and put cameras in hidden spots pointing toward those panels. I aimed another toward the double doors we'd come in through and one more at the pit itself.

I tucked a signal-booster device in an out of the way corner so that the feeds from the cameras could be received outside the concrete building. I switched it on and stepped back. "Cameras are live, base. Are you getting a signal?"

Evie whistled in my ear. "Now that's an impressive hole. Have I told you lot lately how happy I am to be out here and not in there?"

Lucy was wandering around the room, pressing the back of her hand against various machines. Every now and then she'd also touch the floor and walls of the room we were in. I counted on her to let us know if there was anything we needed to worry about or if something was about to go wrong.

Jin was off in a corner, breaking into a machine that wasn't connected to the drill. I figured as long as anything she stole wasn't discovered immediately, it was all good. She could take away as much as she could carry.

Nate and Oscar, after some discussion, came up with a plan to get the cutter over to the edge of the pit without starting up the machine, since despite the soundproofed door, the machinery would still be loud enough that the guard in the hallway would come to investigate. The cutting head dangled low in the pit, mere feet above the three-foot-wide hole at the very bottom.

Oscar took a coil of thin, ultrastrong rope out of his backpack. Nate took the loose end, while Oscar held the coil, feeding it out. They stood next to each other right next to the safety rail on the side of the pit, then walked in opposite directions around the outside of the railings. As they walked around, the rope lengthened in a straight line between them. When they were finally on opposite sides of the pit, they had the rope stretched straight across, gently touching the cable holding the plasma cutter.

They continued walking along until they were next to each other again, each with one end of the rope that stretched out and looped around the cable holding the plasma cutter. They each tried pulling on the rope, and just barely got it to budge—the cutting head was incredibly heavy. I was glad they both had protective gloves on.

Jin came over and dropped her full backpack on the floor. She joined Oscar, and I went to help Nate. Each of the guys looped their rope around a section of the safety railing, and with two of us on each end of the rope, we slowly and steadily pulled until the plasma cutter was just about even with the top of the safety rail, resting maybe a foot inside the pit. Nate and Oscar tied off their ropes in matching knots.

Jin got out her tools, but I stopped her before she could step over to the cutter. I got a second rope out of Oscar's backpack and looped it around her waist, then tied it to a heavy-looking machine against the far wall.

"Better safe than sorry," I said. "I'd hate to lose you down into a giant well. There's no Lassie here to get you out."

"Good call," she said. "I'm not exactly enthusiastic about the idea of going for a slide." She stepped back up to the cutter, got out some tools from her belt, and opened up the hatch on the side.

I went over to where Lucy was feeling one of the machines. "Doing all right?"

"Good right now," she said. "This one makes me happy."

I looked at the machine. Like many of the others in the room, it was a big bulky mess of dials, levers, wires, and metal. "I wonder what it does."

"I don't know, but I hope someday I get to find out."

"So . . . how are you feeling in general? About this mission?"

She wrinkled her brow. "It's coming and going, like things could go either way right now. We should all be careful, because nothing is ever certain until it's in the past."

"You sound like a fortune cookie," I said.

"Feel free to add 'in bed' to the end of what I just said."

"Classic," I said. "All right, let us know if you feel anything bad."

"Hey," she said. "You know, you're being pretty heroic here, saving millions of lives."

"And you're being pretty villainous here, stealing this battery from the heroes and possibly destroying a billion-dollar project," I said. "Makes you think about how similar we really are."

"That it does," she said, and smiled.

I went back over to check on Jin and the guys. Oscar and Nate were each on high alert, with one hand resting on the knot holding the rope to the safety railing, and one hand out toward Jin, in case she lost her balance. Jin was working slowly and being extra cautious, since any wrong move would send a tool or even the battery itself down the hole at the center of the pit.

I shrugged out of my own backpack, opened it up, and pulled out the box that contained the fake battery Jin's team had constructed. I placed it on the ground behind her, a safe distance from the edge of the pit. Then I got into Nate's backpack and pulled out a large photographer's film bag. The original purpose of the bag was to protect photographic film from X-rays while going through airport security; we were going to use it to hold the battery until we could get it into a safer container. The lead lining would be just as useful at keeping the battery's radiation inside as it would be at keeping film safe from X-rays on the outside.

I shook out the bag and opened up the mouth as wide as possible so it would be ready when Jin got the battery free. I watched as she slowly disconnected some wires, put all her tools safely back in her belt, then reached in with both hands and pulled out the shiny gold battery.

She slowly stepped back from the edge of the hole and turned. I came up to meet her, holding the bag open. She gently put the battery inside, and I sealed the top of the bag.

"Halfway there," she said. I set the lead-lined bag on the ground and opened up the box that contained the fake battery. I pulled it out and handed it to her, and she spun it around in her hands until it was in the same position as the original had been. She stepped back over to the edge and carefully put the fake battery inside the plasma cutter. Tools in hand, she attached the wires back onto our replica.

I got a second larger lead-lined bag out of my backpack and put the first lead-lined bag inside it. Someone was going to have to carry a leaking radioactive battery out of this place on their back, and we'd all have to be near it on our plane ride out. I wanted as much lead as possible between it and the members of our team.

I looked up at the plasma cutter, where Jin was just putting the last screws in place. In a minute or so, we'd be done, and we could slowly lower the cutter back into place.

As I was setting the double-bagged battery down on the ground, I heard Lucy call my name. I glanced over at her and knew immediately that something was wrong. She was down on her knees on the floor, one hand pressed against the concrete, the other one tapping against her breastbone. She was looking around the room as if she was trying to find something, and it looked like she was muttering under her breath. I left the battery where it was and hurried over to her.

"Lucy, what's wrong? What is it?"

"I don't know!" She kept looking around, and I started doing the same, trying to figure out what was triggering her. "No, no, no. Something . . . I feel it, but I can't tell—"

She stopped abruptly and gasped. I saw her looking over at Nate. I looked at him, but he seemed fine. Then I looked at the safety railing he was standing next to and saw what Lucy had seen. Nate glanced over at us, and I saw his smile turn to concern as he saw us staring at him. He slowly started to turn toward us, and his hip brushed the safety railing. It was like everything was suddenly in slow motion.

Lucy shouted, "The bolts!"

I shouted, "No!"

The nudge from Nate's hip was the last straw for the safety rail. It pulled its bolts free from the concrete floor and went tumbling back into the pit. And Nate, who was holding onto a rope tied to that railing, got yanked into the pit.

Jin and Oscar both reacted fast, reaching out for him, but their gloved hands closed on nothing but air.

My brain wanted me to get up and run to the pit, but my legs suddenly felt watery with fear, and didn't want to work at all. I felt queasy and light-headed, so I half-crawled, half-dragged myself as fast as I could the fifteen feet or so over to the edge of the pit and looked down.

Nate was still in the upper part of the funnel. My entire body went limp with relief when I saw him.

He slid to a stop as I got to the edge. He had his arms out wide, and his legs spread as well, to make it as difficult as possible to go down the black hole at the bottom of the pit. He was flat on his back, and as he stopped, his rear end was dangerously close to certain, unrecoverable death. He kept his legs spread apart and propped his feet up against the far side of the funnel.

The broken section of railing was next to him, slightly too wide to fall down the hole. The plasma cutter, now free of the rope that had pulled it all the way to the side, was doing exactly what a pendulum does in a pit: it was swinging freely from side to side, skimming just a couple of feet above the sides of the funnel, which meant it was clearing Nate by mere inches. He lay as flat as he could against the side of the pit, because to sit up meant he'd be hit by the incredibly heavy cutting head.

"Are you all right?" My legs still didn't want to get me up, so I stayed lying on the cold concrete floor, with my head over the edge of the pit so I could see him.

He turned his head to the side and upward so he could see us. At least he was awake and aware. The clenched feeling in my gut eased up a little bit. He groaned and looked at the ChatterBox on his wrist. I immediately tapped on my own CB, opening our comm channel back up.

"Hey," I said. "Status?"

Nate groaned quietly in my ear. "That really hurt."

"Anything broken?" Oscar asked, peering over the edge of the pit.

We all watched as Nate slowly wiggled both arms and both legs, testing himself out, without raising anything up high enough to get hit by the swinging plasma cutter. "I don't think so, but I hurt like hell. It feels like I pulled about a hundred muscles."

"We can get another rope and pull the cutter out of the way again, so we can get you out," Jin said.

Nate groaned again. "Maybe not enough time. My legs *really* feel like they're going to give out."

"Okay," she said, and I was incredibly glad she'd taken over the lead for the moment. "It's too steep for you to climb out anyway. We'll have to drag you. Can you reach the section of railing down there with you?"

He moved his arm and shifted his body to the side a little bit, but the broken section of railing was still slightly too far away from his hand. The cutter swung back by his head again, as if it was rubbing in our faces that it wouldn't let him just sit up and reach over.

"Nope," he gasped, and I worried about how much time we had before his legs gave up or he passed out.

"All right, no problem. We've got this," Jin said.

She looked down at me with an expression on her face that somehow combined her concern for Nate, her pity for what I must be feeling, and a laser-like message of *Now would be a good time to get up, Sarah.*

I climbed to my feet, though my legs were still shaky. *Not as shaky as Nate's,* I thought. *Suck it up and deal, because being weepy and weak doesn't get the job done.*

Jin untied the rope I'd put around her waist, and Lucy ran to the other end to untie it from the machine where I'd anchored her. Jin looped that rope around the first rope, which led from Oscar's safety railing down into the pit, where it was still tied on to the one resting near Nate.

As we worked, Nate said, "Hey, Lucy?"

"Yes?" She was working just as hard as the rest of us and seemed just as concerned as everyone else.

"Call me Nate."

"All right," she said. "Nate. We're going to get you out."

Just as we'd used the first rope to pull the cutter into place, we now took the second rope around to the side of the pit and pulled, using it to scoot the first rope, and the section of broken railing, over toward Nate. We went as fast as we could while still keeping it slow enough that we didn't hit Nate with the railing.

He reached out and grabbed the metal bar on the top of the rail. Oscar pulled up on the rope attached to the rail, and the broken railing slowly slid up over Nate's head. Nate moved his other arm up along the side of the pit and grabbed hold. He had both arms stretched above his head, holding on to a broken piece of safety railing, which he couldn't even see because he was on his back.

Oscar handed me the second rope. "Tie yourself off somewhere."

"What?"

I couldn't see his mouth behind the bandana, but his eyes were intense. He pulled his CB out of his ear so Nate couldn't hear him. "I need to pull up the rope, so you'll have to be ready to jump after him if he can't hold on. So tie yourself off somewhere, just in case."

"Can't I tie off somewhere and climb down in after him?"

"And what, lift him up? That would be impossible, and the rest of us would have to pull two of you up out of there, instead of one." I had to admit, he made a lot of sense, so I did as he told me. I probably should have known what needed to be done, and in any other case, I probably would have been able to do it without being asked. But it was Nate trapped down in the pit, all my training appeared to have gone out the window, and I was *this close* to freaking out.

I tied the rope around my waist, glad at least that I could still tie strong knots. I tied the other end to the giant base of the plasma-cutter machine, figuring that if it was heavy enough to stay upright with the weight of the cutter coming off it, it'd be strong enough to hold my weight.

"Let us know when you're ready for us to pull, Nate," Oscar said. He, Jin, and Lucy all grabbed the rope that was attached to the broken piece of railing.

"Do it," Nate said, sounding exhausted. "Fast as you can."

The plasma cutter was still swinging, but it was slowing down, not reaching as high up the walls of the pit as it had been. I put my trust in the rope holding me and slid my upper body out over the pit, holding myself up by pressing my hands against the steep wall of the pit. I wanted to be as close to Nate as I could, to grab him as quickly as possible.

The other three started pulling on the rope, and Nate slowly started sliding up the side of the pit, just under the swinging head of the cutter. As soon as he didn't have to prop his weight up with his feet anymore, I saw Nate's legs spasm and straighten out. He was like a high-diver, ramrod straight, but pointed in the wrong direction. My guts clenched again; I knew that if he couldn't hold on, he probably wouldn't be able to stop himself from shooting straight down the deep, deadly hole.

I kept a close eye on Nate's grip on the railing as he slid slowly up toward me. "Hold on, Nate," I said. "You can do it. Just a few more feet."

"Damn it, Nate, hold on," Evie said in my ear. Terrifying though this was, I was suddenly glad I was in the room with Nate and not miles away watching on a monitor. I thought about how I'd react, watching everything unfold on a screen, unable to do anything about it. Then my brain gave me a flash of a world without Nate, which filled me with dread. I tried to push the negative thoughts away and concentrate on getting him through this.

The broken railing made a soft clanging sound as it hit the concrete at the edge of the pit. We'd pulled Nate up as high as we could. I reached down but was still inches shy of being able to grab his hand.

"Guys, any time now," Nate groaned.

"Almost there," I said. I scooted a little farther out over the pit and reached again, but I was still a little bit short. I felt something tugging at my waist and looked over my shoulder. Oscar was there, grabbing on to my belt and clutching part of the cutting machine's base with the other hand. With him holding on to me, I was able to move farther out over the pit and grab a handful of Nate's sleeve as tightly as I could.

He flopped his head to the side and looked up at me, giving me a weak smile.

"Hey," he said.

"Hey," I said. "I've got you."

"I knew you would." He sighed and wiggled his shoulders, then tightened his grip on the railing. He started to pull himself up.

"Dude," Oscar said, "no need to show off." Oscar lowered me a little more so I could grab Nate's hand with my free hand. I still had a tight grip on his other sleeve. Oscar slowly pulled me up by my belt until my center of gravity was back over the concrete floor, then reached over with his longer arms and got a grip on Nate's jacket. Together we pulled him up, being careful so that his head didn't hit the edge of the pit like the railing had.

As soon as we had Nate's upper body over the edge, Jin and Lucy grabbed hold of his jacket, and we slid him up and out of the pit. We all sat next to him for a minute as he lay on the concrete floor.

"I'm just gonna take a minute, okay?" Nate said.

I tried to keep my tears in. "Whatever you need." I held his hand tightly as he lay there.

"Nathan," Evie said in my ear, "don't you *ever* do that to us again."

"Yes, ma'am," he said, and squeezed my hand.

While Nate gathered his strength, and I sat with him; the rest of the team got back to work. I could tell they all wanted to stay with Nate, the way they kept looking back over at him, but we had to get out safely first. Oscar pulled the broken section of railing up out of the pit, and Jin inspected the metal plates on the bottom where it had been bolted to the floor. The original bolts were nowhere to be found and were likely at the bottom of the hole. Jin got up and wandered off to the far side of the cavernous room.

"I think we're even on worrying," Nate said to me, his breathing starting to even out. "Seems like a near-death tumble into a bottomless pit is equal to a bathroom fistfight."

"No way," I said, wiping his sweat-soaked hair off his forehead. "You're totally back in the lead."

"Fine," he sighed. "You know, if you married me, maybe I wouldn't do so many dangerous things."

"Nate, I swear. If you refer to the circle of safety railings as your ring, I'm going to throw you back down the hole."

He grinned, a little bit of color coming back to his pale, sweaty face. "See? You can even predict my terrible jokes. We're perfect."

I shook my head and grinned, just happy to have him alive and in once piece, stupid jokes and all. I looked over at the ring of safety rails, incomplete now. "So much for getting in and out undetected," I said. "They're probably going to notice the missing railing."

"Oh, ye of little faith," Jin said. She'd found additional bolts somewhere and was fitting them into the plates on the bottom of the railing.

"Seriously? Can you fix it?" I asked.

"*Can I fix it?*" She shook her head. "I'll let you choose whether you compare this to what a bear does in the woods, or what kind of hat the pope wears."

"I take that as a yes, then."

She didn't answer, just got what looked like a small tube of toothpaste out of her backpack. She put the railing and the new bolts into place, opened up the tube, and squeezed out a milky-brown sludge that most definitely was *not* toothpaste. She spread the stuff around the underside of the metal plates where the railing bolted to the floor, and along the length of the new bolts, then pulled the railing back to where it should be.

"Industrial epoxy, one of our own special blends," she said, holding the railing in place. "Give it a minute or so to start firming up. By tomorrow morning, it'll be nice and solid."

"I wouldn't want to lean against it," Nate said, pushing himself up onto his elbows.

"Besides the fact that you already *did* lean against it, you dweeb," Jin said. "This should actually be stronger than it was before."

"Oh, good. Then maybe I will lean on it."

"Not a chance," I said. I helped Nate up to his feet. He was a little shaky, and I could tell that he was in a lot of pain, but he could move.

"You know," Nate said, "that fun little ride gave me an idea." He limped over and rummaged around in the bottom of his backpack. There were some of the tiny cube cameras left inside, and he pulled one out. He carefully reached under one of the railings, set the camera down, and let it slide down the curved incline of the pit until it fell through the small central hole. I saw him shudder a little bit as it disappeared.

"What on earth happened there?" Evie asked in my ear. "That one went all black."

"Who knows if we'll get something on that or not," Nate said. "But it might be cool."

I shook my head. "Who knows if it'll even broadcast. That well could be a thousand feet deep."

"Deeper," Jin said. "I studied the plans. They're going at least a half mile down, maybe more. The whole point is to find a place where the groundwater is really hard to reach, because that's the water they could never hope to tap otherwise." She gently and lovingly poked Nate in the arm. "A very good reason to *not* fall in the pit."

"I'll keep that in mind," Nate said, shuffling back to me. "I guess we'll see if we see anything."

I looked at the plasma cutter. It had almost stopped swinging back and forth; by the time someone came in the next morning, everything would look completely normal. I took a deep breath, closed my eyes for a moment, then got back in the right frame of mind—the job wasn't done quite yet, so we needed to get moving.

We made sure to gather up everything we'd brought, with the exception of the cameras and the signal booster. Jin tried to clean as much of the dust and grit off the broken railing as she could. We double-checked everything, then put our backpacks back on. Nate carried the double-wrapped battery in his. I tried to argue that with him, to give his bag to one of the rest of us to carry, but he refused.

Jin unlocked the door, and Lucy pressed her hand against it. On her signal, we went out and Jin quietly shut and locked the door behind us. We walked as quickly as we could down the long hallway, with Nate holding on to Oscar for support. I looked down the side hallway as we passed: the guard was walking away from us toward the far end.

We gathered near the door to the stairwell so Nate could rest, and waited for Lucy to indicate when to go. On her signals, we went back up to the first floor, avoided the guard making a loop around the hallways, the guard walking back and forth outside the building, and two more that we'd completely missed on our way in. It was a much slower trip out than in, with Nate sore and limping. Oscar managed to stifle another sneeze, and we made it back around to the rear of the building without incident.

Jin crept back over to the electrical cabinet and reconnected the security system, while Nate pulled a smartphone out of his backpack and fired up the GPS tracker so we could get back to the plane. He held up the phone, and I could see a green arrow on it, pointing out into the darkness. I squinted in the direction it pointed but couldn't see anything at all, much less our little airplane.

Jin rejoined us, and with our goggles switched to night-vision mode, we made our way back out to the plane. The wind had picked up while we were underground, and I was very glad that Jin would be handling the takeoff. I'd practiced taking off in side winds before, but never in pitch darkness in the open desert.

We loaded everything into the plane, and Oscar started to climb into the cargo hold. Nate grabbed Oscar's shoulder and shook his head. "I'm going to take the luxury suite for this trip."

"Seriously?" Oscar asked. "After everything you've been through?"

"*Because* of what I've been through," Nate said. "All I want to do right now is curl up in the fetal position. Seems easier back there than in one of the seats."

"You both look like hell," Jin said. "Even in night vision." I had to agree.

Oscar helped Nate climb into the cargo hold; then Oscar and Lucy got into the rear seats. Jin and I did a vastly shortened preflight inspection, since we'd just left the plane an hour or so before. We looked over the propeller with an infrared flashlight and night-vision goggles, since we couldn't risk the outdoor guards seeing normal flashlight beams off in the distance.

With all our outside checks done, we got into the cockpit and proceeded to our interior checklist. While Jin tested some system, I called in to Evie. "Base, we're prepping for takeoff now."

"Blast," she said. "And I was just getting to the sexy part of my book."

"You could read it out loud to us," Oscar chimed in.

"I think not, young man," she said. "It might melt your ears with how hot it is."

Jin finished her checks, and we were ready to take off. "All right, base, we're good to go when you are," I told Evie.

"Firing off the second set of smoke bombs," she said.

We waited patiently. I pictured the scene in my head, even though I hadn't seen the inside of the Sonora Flats control room. Guys sitting around, having a cup of coffee. One of them notices a trail of smoke. "Not again," one of them shouts. Then a guy slams his hand down on a giant red button marked "EVACUATE."

Probably it was a lot more mundane than that, but it sure looked cool in my head.

"There was just one fellow watching the radar," Evie said. "Looks like he's shouting on a telephone. Ah, he's hung up the phone, and he's just run out of the control room. You are a go!"

Jin cranked the engine without the usual call of "clear" to make sure nobody was standing near the propeller; it was pretty much a given that if someone had been standing near the propeller, they would have made themselves known. She lowered the flaps and pushed in the throttle, and the plane rolled forward.

"This is going to be bumpy, and probably pretty windy," she said. "Everyone hold on tight."

"All right in the hold?" I asked.

"As good as I'm going to be," Nate said. "I'm curled up snug as a bug."

I looked back at Lucy as Jin stared straight ahead, the plane picking up speed rolling across the desert. "You good?"

"I'm fine," Lucy said, and she seemed surprised to be able to say it. "I think Oscar's fallen asleep."

I craned my head to see Oscar behind me, and sure enough he was out cold, with his head tilted back and his mouth wide open. I heard a snort in my ear. Before I could say anything, Nate chimed in from the cargo hold. "Muting his microphone and earpiece." Still on the job, even after what he'd been through.

"Here we go," Jin said. I turned forward and rested my hands lightly on the steering yoke both in case she needed some extra strength and so I could get a feel for how she was taking off. Jin pulled back on her own yoke; the plane bumped and shifted sideways, and then we were airborne. The plane felt less heavy and sluggish, since we'd lost some of the plane's weight in spent fuel on the way.

Jin gained enough altitude to avoid trees and power lines, then turned us sharply to the right in order to get us out of the military's airspace. I watched our progress on GPS and felt relief when the little dot that was our plane was over the green mass of the national park instead of the gray mass that was the air force range.

"All good out there at base?" I asked.

"Looks good here," Evie said. "Nobody's come back into the control room yet. You're in the safe zone?"

"We're clear," I said. "Thank you, my friend. We'll meet you back at the motel."

"I'll be reading this torrid book when you get back," she said. She was quiet for a moment, then came back on the line. "My goodness, is Oscar all right? I was expecting a clever comeback."

"He's asleep, so we've turned off his ChatterBox," I said.

"Oh, bother," she said. "I'll have to have another go at him in the morning. Nate, you're all right?"

"Ready for a nap," Nate said from the cargo hold. "And as many aspirin as I can get."

We signed off. Jin offered to let me take the controls, but I was feeling tired and overwhelmed myself, so I asked if she could get us back to the airfield.

"No problem, boss," she said with a smile.

I pulled my goggles down and slung them around my neck and just looked out the window. It was nice to be able to sightsee, or just let my mind drift, and not have to keep rotating my focus between the instrument panel and the sky outside.

Jin took us on a roundabout path back to the airfield. When the lights of the city were finally below us, I was feeling the crash after the adrenaline of the mission and Nate's slide down the pit. I looked at Lucy in the backseat; she was as conked out as Oscar was, with her head leaned against the window, a smile on her face. She had one hand curled up in her lap. I looked closer and noticed that the hand in her lap held an extra glove.

I twisted around to see the backseat better. Oscar was still out like a light. I was startled to see Oscar's glove on the seat next to him; Lucy must have taken it off his hand while he slept, and she now held Oscar's bare hand in her own. I looked back at her, wondering what on earth she felt when she held his hand.

Then I looked beyond their heads at the heap of black objects in the cargo hold—a bunch of backpacks, with poor Nate curled up somewhere in the middle of the pile—and I figured I might have some idea.

THIRTY

We landed well after midnight. We woke everyone from their naps, unloaded the bags from the back of the Cessna, and packed most of the stuff away into the jet. We were going to let our well-rested pilot take us all back to the island so that we could all sleep in our own beds, and we'd come back to our hangar to pick up the Cessna later. A limping Nate and a sneezing Oscar both promised to get tucked away in the jet, while Jin and I dropped Lucy off and went back to the motel to pick up the few things we'd left behind. We'd also pick Evie up there, return the extra car, and get back to the hangar as quickly as possible so we could all get home.

Before we left, Lucy and Oscar had an extensive handshake. With bare hands. Lucy was smiling; I couldn't see what Oscar's face was doing underneath his bandana, but his eyebrows looked pretty cheerful.

Finally, Nate nudged Oscar toward the stairs into the jet, and we women got into the SUV. Jin drove, and I sat in the back with Lucy.

"So," I said, "I know you want to stay on the *good* side of things, but it was great having you along. I don't know if we could have done it without you."

"I'm sure you could have," she said. "But I'm glad I got to be a part of it, even with everything that happened. Fieldwork with you guys was far easier than I expected it would be."

"Have we changed your mind about adventuring?"

"Maybe a little bit," she said. "But on the other hand, maybe it wouldn't be the same without all of you."

"No way to know until you try, I guess," I said.

"I suppose not."

"You have everything you need for tomorrow?"

She pointed at one of the black backpacks, stuffed full, resting at her feet. "I'm good."

We sat quietly for a while as Jin drove. Finally, I just had to ask. "I know it isn't any of my business—"

"Oscar," she said, smiling.

"Yeah."

"I don't even know how to explain it," she said. "I've spent my entire life keeping a catalog of my feelings so I can refer back to them. I guess there are some emotions I still need to figure out."

"It's good, though?"

Her smile grew even brighter. "It's very good."

"Then I'm happy for you."

Jin pulled into a supermarket parking lot and stopped next to a cute little compact car. There were only a few other cars in the lot, and none parked as far away from the store as the little one.

"This is me," Lucy said. "Thank you again, for everything."

"Thank *you*," I said. "We'll be keeping an eye out tomorrow. Good luck."

We awkwardly hugged in the backseat of the SUV; then she hopped out and got into the compact car. I got out of the backseat and moved up to the passenger seat next to Jin. We drove off in one direction, and Lucy in the other.

"Nice kid," Jin said.

"She sure is," I said.

"Of course, if she breaks Oscar's heart, she's toast."

"She sure is."

✱ ✱ ✱

We all tried to nap on the jet flight back to the island, some of us more successfully than others. As soon as we landed, we took Nate and Oscar straight to Dr. Adams, who insisted that both of them spend the night in the hospital wing. She shooed me out, telling me that Nate would be fine but needed some uninterrupted rest. Jin and I went back to our apartments and collapsed for a few short hours of sleep before we regrouped in Nate's office the next morning, since he had the convenient wall of TV screens that could all be tuned to separate channels. Evie had patched in the video feeds from our little cameras on the top two rows, including the pitch-black one that Nate had slid down into the pit. On the lower screens, she tuned in the major Phoenix TV stations, which were currently showing national morning shows, and a pair of twenty-four-hour news channels.

Nate was there, moving slow but otherwise appearing whole. I went straight to him and kissed him.

"How are you feeling?"

"Like I was run over by a bus, then beat up by the bus driver," he said. "And I'll tell you right now, if you think the nanogel is terrible for a cut, wait until you have to taste the drinkable form she's developed for strained muscles."

"I think I'll pass." I poured a strong cup of coffee and grabbed a doughnut from the display Scar had set up on a side table. I needed the coffee—I was feeling more than a little exhausted, and it felt like I barely got any sleep before my alarm went off that morning. We were all sleep deprived, and Nate and Oscar were undoubtedly worn out, but none of us wanted to miss how the rest of the plan played out.

The Goldwater Dig had given all shifts the weekend off for Labor Day, but according to their schedule, some of the crew got a little more weekend than others. The morning crew clocked in around six o'clock, ready to get back to digging. I'd arrived in Nate's office around six thirty, expecting them to take a lot of time to start the machinery back up and run safety checks on everything. If anything exciting happened earlier, I knew that Scar would let us all know.

"Perfect timing, by the way," Nate said as I sat down next to him in my own desk chair, which Scar must have rolled down the hall from my office. Bless that man and his organization skills. "They're just about to test the cutter."

As we watched, a man in white coveralls on one of the screens hit a series of buttons. On another screen, I could see the big cylindrical head of the plasma cutter light up briefly with an eerie purple fire. The man pressed more buttons, and the fire stopped. The guy didn't seem alarmed at all: he picked up a clipboard and made a single motion with a pen, probably a check mark.

"Nice job, Jin," I said.

She nodded and gave me a thumbs-up, since her mouth was full of doughnut.

"And the resolution on these cameras is fantastic," I said. "Really impressive."

Jin swallowed and took a drink of coffee. "I'll pass that along to my team. And I'll tell them that Doctor Oracle said it."

"Oh, jeez," I said.

Nate laughed. "That's what happens when you're the team leader. You get to be the figurehead."

"That's maybe a little too much responsibility for me," I said.

"Well, it all worked out pretty well so far. Except for your fistfight. And my little spill." He shook his head. "Okay, so it wasn't perfect. Few jobs are. At any rate, whenever you find another project you want to take the lead on, just say the word."

I touched the side of my jaw, where I had a patch of new pink skin. "We'll see."

"On the note of your fistfight, by the way, I think I have a way we can repeat our fake-out. You can head to Colorado, or wherever else you've always wanted to visit, and Jin can put on the blonde-in-silver costume so we can go make another public appearance."

"Sounds good, but only if you're feeling up to it."

"Hey, guys," Oscar said, shuffling into the room. He had a fresh black bandana wrapped around his face, and he sounded even more stuffed up than he had the night before.

"What's the verdict?" Nate asked. Adams had cleared Nate to limp his way back to the party but kept Oscar behind to go over a variety of test results and swabs with him.

"Adams says it's just a cold, and then read me the riot act because I waited too long for her to be able to do anything. She says she has that stuff that the rest of you can take."

I looked at Nate. "Don't tell me you've developed the cure to the common cold here."

"Nope," he said. "But she does have a mix of vitamins, immune boosters, and antivirals that can knock a cold down pretty well if you take it early enough. It's all stuff that's readily available, just a unique combination. You could still get sick, but at least it won't be as bad. Most people, including Oscar, don't get treatment until they've felt terrible for a couple of days; for this stuff to be effective, you have to take it before you're showing symptoms."

"So why don't more people take it?"

"You have to be a pessimist," he said. "People see a friend or coworker who's sick, and optimistically think they won't catch it. Then, several days later, they're showing symptoms and it's too late to do anything. Fortunately, Dr. Adams *is* a pessimist, and sometimes forces her pessimism on the rest of us for our own good."

"They're lowering the cutter," Jin said. We turned our attention back to the screens. All the safety checks had gone fine, so they were ready to get back to work.

"How long will that battery of yours run?" I asked.

"Depends on the power drain. Fifteen minutes? Maybe a half hour, tops."

"Will that be enough?"

"I hope so," she said. "Lucy said this was going to happen pretty early in the morning, and it'll take a while before they get the cutter all the way to the bottom of the hole."

We waited and watched. They lowered the plasma cutter slowly, which made sense, since it was a delicate and expensive piece of machinery. I looked around at the other screens. There were people watching monitors, people operating machines, and several people standing around the rim of the crater.

Two men were standing next to the railing we'd glued back in place, and I had a tiny heart attack when one of them rested a hand on it. But Jin's epoxy was solid, and the railing didn't move. Not only did the railing not wiggle at all, but it didn't break free and send a scientist plunging down a pit to his death either. So it was win-win.

Oscar went over to the loveseat in the corner of Nate's office and threw himself down on it, kicking his feet up on the armrest. "Digging is *really* exciting."

"Good to know how you feel about it," Nate said. "Next time we have a project that involves digging a giant hole, I know who to call."

The guys in coveralls picked up the pace of their button pressing, and I hoped that meant that the drill was nearing the bottom of the shaft. More things were checked off on clipboards, guys rotated around so that others took places at new controls, and finally, the actual work was about to start.

More activity on the main screens; then suddenly, the one black screen flared to life with a bright purple glow. I wasn't the only one who jumped a little bit. The purple glow sharpened into what looked like purple and orange flames for a moment; then the screen went dark again.

"I think our little camera just melted," Jin said.

"Yeah, but . . ." Evie went to Nate's desk and tapped on the surface of it, activating the computer interface integrated into the glossy surface of the desk. The image on the screen went into reverse, showing the purple and orange flames again. She scrolled forward, froze the display on a frame, and with a few more taps, expanded the image so that it filled up the wall of screens.

"What did you see?" Nate asked.

"Look," Evie said, getting up and pointing at some spots. "I think those are bubbles."

Nate squinted at the screens. "I think you're right."

"So, what," Oscar said, "the thing is underwater?"

"I think so," Jin said. "Wow, okay. So they've already reached the deep groundwater and are going even deeper down. If that battery was in there, it'd leak plutonium and strontium straight into the water supply as soon as that earthquake happens."

Evie tapped on the desk again, and the screens went back to showing different images on each one. We watched the team at work for a few more minutes, but now that the drill was in place and cutting, nothing very exciting was happening in the control room.

My tablet chimed, and I grabbed it from Nate's desk where I'd left it. I poked at the envelope icon and opened a message from Lucy. The only words in the message were "Here we go." They were followed by a series of numbers.

"It's Lucy," I said. "She's starting." I pushed the tablet over to Evie so she could type the numbers onto Nate's desk. The lower-right screen on Nate's wall lit up, showing a live video feed with a news reporter brushing dust off his sport coat. It looked like he was standing in an empty expanse of desert. The numbers Lucy had given us were the transmission frequency of the remote news crew's uplink feed, so we could watch and record everything before it was edited to go on air.

The camera pulled back, and we could see Lucy standing next to the news reporter, fully costumed. Her sleeveless bodysuit was mostly coral colored, with highlights of white. She wore coral elbow gloves and a matching coral mask. Her hair was loose, long and straight and black, blowing slightly in a breeze.

I looked at Oscar, who was watching the screen intently. I looked back at Lucy and felt a momentary pang of jealousy at how model perfect she looked in the bodysuit. Then Nate grabbed my hand, and the pang passed.

Evie raised the volume for that feed, and we watched as the reporter interviewed Lucy, laughing at some of her responses. The news stations we had tuned in to were all showing commercials: nobody had broken in with an emergency update yet. Though given what Lucy said in the interview, I wouldn't have broadcast it live either. Her predictions would sound crazy to someone who hadn't seen her in action.

Everyone was on the edge of their seat. I didn't know which screen I wanted to look at, since things were about to happen on several of them. Down in the corner, the news camera kept filming as Lucy stopped speaking. The reporter spoke to someone offscreen, then rolled up the cord attached to his microphone. Lucy looked off into the distance and stood there quietly for a minute; then the picture began to shake. The reporter's eyes widened, and his jaw dropped open. He quickly regained his composure, unrolled the microphone cord, and started talking at whoever was behind the camera.

On the top row of screens, the feeds were also shaking. Men in coveralls were grabbing on to things to hold steady, and one them fell onto his butt. Fortunately, nobody fell over a railing down into the pit.

The quake was over in less than a minute. At the Goldwater Dig, everyone was furiously at work, reeling the plasma cutter back up to the surface. Lucy stood serenely in the desert while the reporter next to her talked on a cell phone. He'd stuffed his microphone into the pocket of his blazer, so we couldn't hear his side of the call.

On one of the local TV channels, a commercial abruptly ended halfway through, and a bold "Breaking News" logo filled the screen. It cut to a man behind a desk, letting the city know about the earthquake they'd just experienced, as if anyone awake and watching the Phoenix morning news hadn't felt it happening.

After a minute, the other TV channels did much the same thing. One of the anchors looked like she'd been grabbed while halfway through hair and makeup and thrust in front of the camera. We paid close attention to the station with a reporter out in the field with Lucy. Evie changed the audio over to that station's broadcast.

"Again, we have just experienced one of the strongest earthquakes this city has seen in quite some time," the woman behind the desk said. She touched her finger to her ear for a moment. "I'm told we have Jim Pressman out in the field with one of our local superheroes, who may have *known* this was going to happen. Jim?"

The broadcast switched over to a live feed of Jim Pressman standing with Lucy. It was weird to be seeing the footage live on one screen, and delayed by a few seconds as it went out over the airwaves, presumably with enough time to give someone a chance to press a bleep button if anybody swore.

Pressman stayed silent for a moment, looking offscreen. Then he pressed his hand against his ear, put his microphone in front of his face, and looked at the camera. "Yes, Jessica, I'm here with Lucky Starr, one of our local heroes with a very unique ability." He turned to Lucy. "Miss Starr, would you tell us about your ability?"

The camera zoomed in on Lucy, and the name "Lucky Star" appeared on the screen. I suspected they'd get the spelling right soon enough.

"I am empathetically prescient," she said, and smiled.

Pressman blinked and frowned. She'd described her abilities using different words earlier; I wondered if he even understood what she'd just said. "And could you tell our viewers what that means?"

"That means that I can sense the future through my emotions," she said.

Pressman moved the microphone back over to himself. "Jessica, I was out here with Miss Starr just a few minutes ago, and when she told me we were about to have an earthquake, I'll admit, I didn't take her seriously." He looked offscreen again and nodded. "I'm told we have that footage ready to show you."

The image skipped, and then it was the interview we'd already seen. Lucy had timed it perfectly; they'd had just enough time to get the footage ready to roll, without enough time to edit out Pressman's reactions.

"So you go by Lucky Starr?" Pressman asked.

"Yes, with two *R*s," she said.

"And you've asked us to meet you out here in the desert this morning because you have a warning?"

"Yes, Jim," she said. "We're about to have an earthquake. A serious one."

"How do you know? Is your power the ability to create earthquakes?"

"No, no it isn't. I've seen that it's going to happen. My ability is a limited form of precognition."

"What exactly does that mean, 'a limited form of precognition'?"

"I can sense future events, but only through my own emotional reactions."

He laughed. "So, what, you get feelings about the future?"

"Yes, Jim."

He laughed even harder. "So what makes you different from any other woman?"

She stayed calm and serene. "I don't think you understand how my powers work."

"And I don't know if you really have powers. But I will say, I really like your outfit."

"Just wait, Jim. The earthquake will happen shortly."

"Because you had a *feeling* about it."

"Precisely."

Pressman looked off camera. "I think we're done here." We could hear the muffled sound of a response; then he rolled up his microphone cord. Lucy gazed off into the distance and stood there, quiet and serene.

"Nice guy," I said.

"A real class act," Nate said.

Then the camera shook, Jim Pressman's eyes bugged out, and he started unrolling the microphone cord. He looked at whoever was behind the camera. His voice was muddy and distant now that he wasn't holding the microphone to his mouth. "Holy crap. Lou, get the station on the line. Make sure they know we're out here and ready."

The recorded footage ended, and the picture cut to a split screen of Jessica behind the news desk and the live feed of Jim and Lucy out in the desert. Someone had fixed the spelling of Lucky Starr's last name.

"Amazing," Jessica said. She raised an eyebrow. "Jim, do you now *feel* like Ms. Starr's powers are something to laugh at?"

"Ouch," Oscar said. I suspected that Jim Pressman wasn't popular with his female coworkers.

"I'm thoroughly convinced," Pressman said, "that Miss Starr has a genuine ability."

Lucy reached out and lightly grabbed his microphone. "Then perhaps you'd like to hear about the other thing I foresaw?"

"Yes, we'd love to hear it," Pressman said, and thrust the microphone at her.

"There's a project going on in the desert behind me, in which two deep wells are being dug. One will go down to an untapped source of groundwater, while the other will be dug to reach a pocket of magma. When these two elements are combined, the water meeting the hot rock will create steam. That steam can be used to create power here on the surface, and the steam can be condensed back into drinkable water for the region."

"That sounds like a great project," Pressman said.

"It is," Lucy said. "Except that the drill they're currently using is powered by a nuclear battery in its head. That drill head is underground right now, in our groundwater, and has likely been damaged by the earthquake."

"Wait." Jim Pressman thought about what Lucy had just said. "Do you mean that a nuclear power source has just broken in Arizona's groundwater? Will it leak radiation?"

I glanced up at the screens that showed the activity inside the Goldwater Dig. The head of the drill was just coming up out of the pit. The people at the control panel were still in white coveralls, but a pair of workers had put on heavy green radiation suits and were standing near the railing, ready to grab the drill head as it swung around.

"The nuclear power source *was* there, but it isn't there today," Lucy said.

The green-suited men gently lowered the drill head to the ground. Even from our angle, I could see that it had a huge crack through the middle of the cylinder, and the hatch where Jin had accessed the battery was hanging half-open.

"What do you mean?" Pressman asked.

"The other thing I foresaw was someone evil taking that nuclear battery from the digging project," Lucy said.

The men wrenched the hatch the rest of the way open while everyone else stood as far back as they could. A third man in a green radiation suit came forward with a bright-yellow Geiger counter in his hands. He ran the sensor over the open hatch, shook his head, and pulled off his hood. He shouted something at the men in coveralls cowering in the corner.

"So you're saying the nuclear battery *isn't* in the drill right now?"

"No, it isn't," Lucy said. "Because I have it here." She reached down to the ground, and the cameraman widened the shot to show her pulling a clear glass box out of a backpack. Inside was the plutonium-strontium battery, gleaming gold and chrome in the sunlight.

Jim Pressman stepped back from Lucy. "*You* stole it?"

Lucy laughed. "No, Jim. I'm one of the good guys, remember? No, I took it away from the real thief: Doctor Oracle."

"*Oracle* stole this? How did you get it from him?"

"Not without a fight," Lucy said. "He got away, but I managed to get this as a souvenir." She reached into the backpack again and brought up one of Nate's signature white doctor's coats, with the Doctor Oracle logo embroidered on the front. We'd torn it in a few places and rubbed it in the dirt to give the appearance of a fight.

"You took on Doctor Oracle single-handed and managed to get back what he'd stolen?"

The scientists at the dig site had the fake battery pulled out of the drill, hanging by a wire. One of them was shouting at the rest. A man brought up a toolbox, and they started to disassemble the gold and chrome housing.

"Yes, Jim," Lucy said. "I did."

"Wow." Pressman took a nervous half step back from Lucy, then turned and faced the camera. "A real American hero, Lucky Starr. She not only saved stolen goods from the nefarious Doctor Oracle, but she saved us from radioactive groundwater at the same time. We owe this young lady a huge debt of thanks. Back to you, Jessica."

The team at the dig cracked open the gold housing of the battery, and one pulled out the smaller battery Jin had placed inside to power the drill for a short period of time. It was white with black markings on it. I couldn't quite see what the markings were on screen, but I already knew it was the Doctor Oracle logo.

"So Doctor Oracle doesn't get the credit for saving the Southwest from radioactive groundwater?" I asked. "After all, according to this story, he's the one who removed that battery from the drill."

"We all know, that isn't how it works," Nate said.

"Yeah, yeah. It still stinks."

"Other than a lack of credit for saving the world once again," Nate said, "I'd say that part of the plan went well. Lucy did a great job."

"She certainly did," I said. "I hope she can keep up with all the attention she's about to get."

"You know," Oscar said, "she might need a bodyguard. Just for a few days."

We all looked at each other. I turned to Nate. "Is this still technically my project?"

"We haven't officially closed the books on it," he said.

"Well, we *do* need to go back to Phoenix to pick up the Cessna," I said. "And I've heard that the desert climate can be good for the common cold."

THIRTY-ONE

Slowly but surely, Lucy appeared on the other news stations throughout the day. She identified Exponential Projects by name and gave the location of the Goldwater Dig. She stressed that the project had great merit but probably needed some oversight to ensure that they didn't use any more stolen or deadly parts.

We all took naps, had lunch, then got moving in the afternoon; the mission was almost done, but not quite. Nate, Jin, Oscar, Elliot and I flew out to Phoenix. Nate and Jin were headed into the city to make a public scene and threaten to get revenge on that wily Lucky Starr, while making it clear that Doctor Oracle was impressed with her moxie. And he actually planned on using the word *moxie*. I made him promise to not do anything too strenuous, and he was all too willing to agree. Jin was wearing the blonde costume again, so we could kill two birds with one stone.

On the flight over, I wrote a post for the Doctor Oracle blog saying much the same thing; I sent it off to Rupert to refine it with a bit more drama so I could put it on the blog that night. I also included a bit about how maybe they needed to check the stability of their safety railing if they wanted to continue their dig. No sense in having anyone lean on Jin's patch job and go for a slide like Nate had.

I put together a few high-resolution screenshots of the cracked drill housing I'd taken from the video this morning, as proof that had the battery been in place, it would have irradiated Arizona's water supply. Those pictures would be leaked onto the

Internet separately, since Doctor Oracle would have had no way of knowing that the destruction would happen. We'd make it seem like someone on-site at the dig had taken the pictures.

Oscar tagged along with Nate and Jin, who would drop him off at an arranged location to meet up with Lucy. He was stuffed up and wearing his bandana, but I assumed he'd let Lucy see his real face sooner rather than later. We sent him along with a dose of Dr. Adams's antiviral cocktail, so Lucy could hopefully avoid catching his cold.

After leaving three of them in Phoenix, Elliot and I continued on in the jet. This time we were headed to Austin, another city I'd always wanted to visit. Elliot was going to be my spotter, since Oscar wasn't available. I looked over at him, but he didn't seem interested in chatting. He'd brought what looked like a school textbook, as well as his tablet; he was probably doing more research on Lucy's weird DNA.

We sat in silence for a while; then I decided, *What the hell.* I'd zip-lined from a helicopter, done a highly illegal and dangerous dead-stick landing in the Cessna, broken into a government facility, helped save millions of people's lives, and most importantly, I'd almost lost the man I loved. Life was too damned short for grudges.

"So, you lost your bet," I said.

Elliot looked up from the thick book he was reading. "What?"

"You lost your bet."

He blinked several times, looking confused. "What do you mean?"

"I overheard you and Rupert talking. Making a bet that I wouldn't succeed." I was starting to get a little frustrated—I'd spent quite a bit of time thinking about that bet, and the lack of confidence behind it, and he was acting like he didn't remember.

"A bet that you . . ." He squinted at me, then looked down at his book, furrowing his brow. After a minute, he looked back up at me and started laughing.

His reaction confused me. I'd expected shame, guilt, remorse, boastful pride—anything but a laughing fit. "What the hell, Elliot?"

He got his laughter under control and took a deep breath. "That bet I made with Rupert wasn't about *you*, Sarah!"

"Really? What else could it have been about? Seems like I was the only woman around who was doing something new and could potentially fail at it." I couldn't believe he was going to try to play this off.

I think he saw how serious I was. "No, truly, Sarah, it wasn't about you at all. I'm so sorry that you thought it was. The bet Rupert and I made was about Evie. She'd borrowed some books and done some research and was trying to come up with a new hybrid yeast for her winemaking. I told her that her calculations were off and that the stuff she'd come up with would just make a bitter mess, but she was doing a test run anyway."

"Wait, so . . . you made a bet that *Evie* would fail? With some *wine*?" I thought back to the conversation I'd overheard, and sure enough, neither of them had ever mentioned me by name. They'd just referred to "she."

"Yeah. God, I'm so sorry you thought that was about you! You must have thought I was a grade-A jerk!"

"Well, now *I'm* the one who feels like a grade-A jerk." I felt my cheeks burning.

"Oh, no," he said, and unbuckled his seat belt so he could come over and sit beside me. He gave me an awkward sideways airplane-seat hug. "No, I wish you'd said something. I'm sorry. I wanted you to succeed. We all did."

"Ugh," I said. "I'm sorry, too." I sat there with his arm around me and sniffed, making sure I wasn't about to cry.

"On the plus side, I did win that bet," Elliot said. "Evie's test wine was bitter and undrinkable."

I laughed. "Okay, good. At least something positive came of it."

He squeezed my shoulders one more time. "We're cool?"

"I'm cool if you're cool," I said.

"Good. After seeing you in action these last few months, the last thing I want is for you to be mad at me."

"Oh, come on," I said. "Now you're pushing it with the compliments."

He went back to his seat and buckled in, since we were starting our descent into Austin. "Well, the last thing I want is for you to be unhappy today because of me."

I looked at him, since it was kind of a weird way to phrase things. "Why's that?"

He squinted, then smiled. "Well, since we're supposed to be having a nice day out in Austin, right? I guess I wouldn't want you mad or upset when you're supposed to be seen out and about having a lovely Austin day. Plus, you've been through a lot the last few days. I'm sorry I added at all to that."

"Okay," I said, but it still felt strange. We'd said we were cool, but I still wasn't totally sure. Since we were about to land, I decided to table the discussion and come back to it later.

Austin felt like a hotter version of Portland, Oregon. I did most of the same stuff I'd done in Denver: browsed shops, stopped for a coffee, and wandered around the downtown area wearing my Old Sarah Valentine disguise while a few cops—and Elliot, who was much more discreet about the whole thing—trailed me. Once again we'd let the authorities know in advance where I'd be, and once again they didn't disappoint.

I made sure to stay visible well past the time when Doctor Oracle was scheduled to make his dramatic disappearance from downtown Phoenix, then ducked into a busy outdoor market so I could lose the police on my tail. I made my way back to the car, picked Elliot up two blocks away, and drove a very roundabout route back to the little airfield on the outskirts of town.

"Another successful appearance," Elliot said.

"I wonder how many more of these I'll have to do before I feel like I'm no longer under suspicion," I said.

"As many as it takes, I guess. It would help if we had some way of knowing what Catalyst was telling people about you."

"I know, right?"

"Plus, you could always change your appearance a little bit. Nothing as drastic as plastic surgery, but even a small change can make people not recognize you. Ever thought of coloring your hair?"

I thought about it. "You know, I was a redhead for a while in college. I kind of liked it, but couldn't afford to keep it up." I thought about it even more and liked the idea. An edgy haircut like the one I was now wearing would pair well with an edgy color.

We took a detour on the way back to the airfield so I could grab a box of hair color at a drugstore. We had a hairdresser on the island, but there was just something about hanging out in your own bathroom, towel slung around your neck, glass of wine in hand, doing your own hair. I browsed through all the boxes and ended up grabbing a vivid shade of coppery orange-red, practically the color of fire. Go big or go home, I figured.

If it turned out awful, I could always have our hairdresser put brown back over the top. Or I could become another of Catalyst's sidekicks. The shade I chose was different enough from her deep red that it wouldn't make me think of her when I looked in the mirror, but it was close enough that it would infuriate her if she ever saw it. The thought of that delighted me.

On my way out of the drugstore, I glanced at the little coin-op toy machines next to the front door. One of them caught my eye—it had a number of small toys and figurines and a variety of kid-sized plastic jewelry. I went back into the store and changed a dollar for four quarters, then came back out and stood in front of the machine.

It's like a fortune cookie, I told myself. The whole mission had been about predicting the future, so I figured I'd finish the whole thing off with one final prediction. Whatever came out of the machine, be it a bouncy ball or a toy animal or a plastic gemstone in an adjustable ring, it might give me an idea about my future.

I put two quarters in the machine and turned the knob on the front. A round red plastic container popped out. Remembering back to my childhood, I squeezed the bottom of the container to pop the top off. I looked at the plastic-wrapped prize inside for what felt like an eternity, then plucked it out and put it in my pocket. I threw the container in the trash and rejoined Elliot at the car. He didn't ask about what kept me so long, which was a relief.

Elliot and I went back to the airfield and took the jet to our last stop: we were set to rendezvous with Nate and Jin up in North Dakota. We landed at the same small airfield outside Fargo and pulled up outside our hangar. The Cessna was already there waiting for us. Elliot and I hopped out of the jet and joined Nate and Jin in the smaller plane. Jin had left the pilot's seat open for me.

We'd taken a car out to the Vault the last time, since we'd all been riding in the jet. It needed way too much runway to be able to fly straight to the Vault itself. Since we had the Cessna along on this trip, with its much shorter runway requirements, we could cut our travel time by over half and land the little plane on one of the deserted stretches of road inside the perimeter fence.

It was less than an hour by air out to the Vault; we spent it catching each other up on our adventures. Nate, in full Doctor Oracle costume, with Jin by his side in the silver and blue outfit and blond wig, had made a nice public appearance in Phoenix, both cursing and praising Lucky Starr for having gotten the better of them.

I brought up Elliot's idea of coloring my hair, and Jin instantly offered to help. "I tried bleaching my hair once, and it turned an awful shade of green." She touched her jet-black hair. "It'd be nice to see how it's actually supposed to work." We decided to make a girls' party of it, and invite Evie along if she wanted to bring some of her homemade wine and laugh at us.

"A redhead," Nate said. "I can't wait to see it."

"I can always go back to brown if it's horrible."

"I doubt your hair could ever look horrible," he said. "It's on you."

"Come on, guys," Elliot said. "We're *right here*."

"Seriously," Jin said. "Sarah pulls a guy out of a deadly bottomless pit, and he's a total compliment machine."

It was a clear evening, and even though it was getting late, there was still some daylight out. One of the benefits of doing business up north in late summer. The air was relatively calm, so with Jin's guidance, I landed the plane on the stretch of straight roadway nearest to the Vault.

Nate got a backpack out of the cargo hold and we headed to the entrance. The guys fell behind as we walked, talking with each other quietly about something. Nate was still a little slower than usual, but already seemed to be feeling much better, thanks to whatever gross-tasting stuff Dr. Adams had given him. When we arrived at the little concrete building, Jin used a flashlight to tap out the pattern that turned off the security system. We went inside, and I unlocked the room again by putting my palm on the cracked concrete block. The hatch in the floor slid open, and down we went.

At the bottom of the silo, we all stepped off the elevator. Elliot excused himself to go check on some of his items, leaving me, Nate, and Jin to put our treasure away. We went to the center of the room; then Nate got out his trusty tablet to look up where we were headed.

"Section F, box four," he said, and led the way over.

"We put the electromagnet in section B," I remembered. "Box seventeen, I think."

"Good memory," Nate said. "Over time, you'll probably put enough things down here that you'll forget where exactly each one is."

"Everything in section F is lead lined," Jin said. Instead of the section being a part of the main silo, we went to a small door stenciled with a large letter *F*. "This door takes both a palm scan and an eye scan. Sarah, want to do it?"

I pressed my hand against the panel next to the door, then looked into a little scanner. I saw a brief blue pulse; then a green light went on over the top of the door, and it made a clunking sound. I reached out to pull the door open, but my first try didn't budge it at all.

"It's pretty solid," Jin said. "You gotta put some muscle into it."

I pulled harder at the door, and it slowly opened. The lights inside flickered on as we entered. It was a small room, with a number of vaults tucked into the walls. Each vault was separated from the next by at least three feet.

"The boxes are all heavily lead lined," Jin said. "And embedded deep in the concrete. Then the room itself acts as a second lead-lined chamber, so we're double protected." She opened up box number four. As advertised, it had a thick concrete door with a heavy slab of lead on the inside.

"Triple protected, really," Nate said. He set down the backpack he was carrying, unzipped it, and pulled out a large photographer's film bag with something heavy in it. He grabbed a pair of gloves from a hook on the wall, opened the bag, pulled out another smaller bag from inside, then opened that bag and removed the plutonium-strontium battery.

Next to where the heavy gloves had been hanging was a Geiger counter, which made sense here in section F. Jin picked it up and scanned the battery. The counter clicked, but not furiously.

"Slow leak," she said. "Not deadly now, but it sure could have been."

"I'm glad you made that second fake battery," Nate told Jin. "I think it'll really help Lucy out."

"It was Sarah's idea to use parts from Manos's machine," Jin said. "So Lucy's fake would have the right radiation signature."

"Aw, shucks," I said.

Nate put the battery back in the smaller bag, which he then put back in the larger bag. Then he moved the whole double-bagged mess into box number four.

"Quadruple protected, if you count both bags," Jin said.

"Works for me," I said. "The more lead between me and a leaking nuclear power source, the better."

We secured box four and went back out to the main silo, locking the door to section F on our way out. Elliot met back up with us in the middle of the room, smiling.

"What's up?" I asked.

"Hey, guys," Elliot said. "Nate, you might want to check on that thing over in section A."

"Right, yeah," Nate said. "There's this thing I was going to look at. Sarah, want to come along?"

"Sure?" Things had suddenly become weirdly vague. Nate led me over to an area near the door where we'd come in. We walked up to the wall of section A: all the boxes were uniform in size, about as big as apartment mailboxes, and there were dozens upon dozens of them.

He pointed at a box labeled with the number "104." "You might be interested in that one."

I looked at him, then at the box. "What's section A for?"

"Harmless stuff. Well, mostly harmless."

"Such as?"

"It's mostly papers and documents, that sort of thing."

"And is that what's in this box?"

"Sarah, I promise. You'll like what's in there."

I looked at the box again. "One hundred and four." Nate knew that October 4 was my birthday, so the box number wasn't a coincidence. I glanced back at Elliot and Jin, who were waiting in the middle of the room, watching us. "You had Elliot put something in this box for me."

"Maybe?"

"Fine," I said. My guts were in a little bit of a knot, because I had a sneaking suspicion that the surprise in the small lockbox might be related to Nate's repeated threats to ask me to marry him. I stepped up to the box and unlocked it. I opened it slowly, fully expecting to find a jewelry box inside.

At first, though, it looked like box 104 was empty. I bent down to look closer, and realized that there was a single sheet of paper sitting in the box. I pulled it out and looked at it. It was a certificate, with fancy scrollwork on the sides and a clip-art cartoon character holding his hands over his head in victory. "Congratulations on Your First Team Lead," it read. All this drama was for a joke gift that had come out of somebody's printer.

"Okay, you got me," I said. "I actually expected—"

I stopped because Nate was no longer standing next to me. I turned all the way around and at first only saw Elliot and Jin in the center of the room, watching me. Then I looked down and found Nate down on one knee, a little velvet box in his hand. I think I gasped, or at least let out a little squeak.

"I have a question for you," he said.

"Oh," I said. I couldn't think of what else to say.

"A guy faces death, it makes him want to ask questions."

"Okay," I said.

"As previously directed, this was purchased from a legitimate source."

"Okay," I repeated.

He opened the lid of the tiny box and held it up higher so I could see. The center stone was black, instead of the usual clear diamond, but I could tell by the way it refracted the light that it was a black diamond, just like the one we'd stolen on one of my first big heists. The setting was simple but perfect.

"Sarah Valentine," he said, "will you marry me?"

"I . . . wow. So you were actually serious." I could feel tears building up in my eyes.

"Very much. But we don't have to do anything right away. We can take as long as we need to figure things out."

"Yes," I said.

"Really?" Nate's face lit up.

"Really, yes," I said. I felt tears rolling down my face. "I've learned that when Nathan Hart asks me a life-changing question, the best answer is always yes." He pulled the ring out of the box and gently slid it on my finger.

"Awesome," he said. "Fantastic."

I waited for him to stand up. A pained expression crossed his face.

"Um." He chuckled and looked a little embarrassed. "A little help here? I didn't expect getting back up to be so hard."

I laughed and gave him both my hands to help pull him up to his feet, touched that he got down on one knee when he was still so sore. He kissed me, I kissed him, and we both wiped tears off our faces. Finally, Jin came running over and threw herself at me in a giant hug. I got a hug and kiss from Elliot and was sure there would be more of that from the rest of the team when we got back to the island.

"All right," Jin said. "Let's get topside so we can all get home."

As we rode up in the elevator, I tilted my hand around, looking at the ring from every angle. I'd never been one for lots of jewelry, but I'd never had a piece of jewelry so perfect before.

We made our way outside, locked up the entrance to the Vault, and went back to the Cessna. Jin insisted that Nate and I sit in the back while she flew the short hop back to Fargo. Elliot didn't look entirely thrilled to be in the front seat, but he didn't say anything about it, bless him. Now I understood why he'd made that cryptic comment about not wanting me to be unhappy today, since he knew what Nate had planned for me in the Vault.

The sun was finally setting as we flew. We'd be getting home late again, but fortunately, most of the work for the job was over. We'd be able to sleep late the next morning and catch up on all of Lucy's news. I was glad Oscar had offered to be with her, to keep her safe and help guide her through dealing with the press and possibly other supers.

Nate twined our fingers together and kissed the back of my hand, near the ring. "I'm glad you like it."

"It's perfect," I said.

I rested my head on his shoulder as we flew on.

THIRTY-TWO

It had been about eighty hours since we'd thwarted the disaster that could have given radiation poisoning to millions of people, and all our side projects were done, so we decided to close the mission by taking Lucy out for dinner and a debrief. She suggested a tiny burger joint in the suburbs northwest of the city, and I knew without asking that it would be delicious. Plus, a burger seemed like an apt way to close the book on the whole job.

She and Oscar showed up together, both wearing disguises. She was already becoming a celebrity, so Rupert had supplied Oscar with a few simple prosthetics to help her go unnoticed. Nate, Jin, and I were also wearing our usual disguises, so at least nobody would feel left out.

It was late afternoon, and we had the place to ourselves. Lucy went up and greeted the man behind the counter, who turned out to be the owner, a gruff but loveable type named Chuck. I realized that the restaurant, Chuck Burgers, was named after him and not a cut of beef. Or maybe he was clever and had intentionally done a name with a double meaning.

Lucy came back to the table. "He recognized me, even with this stuff on my face. But he's known me since I was two."

"I hope he won't call in the press," Oscar said. "It felt like it took me forever to shake those guys from the *Tribune*."

"Oh, no," she said. "Chuck is practically family. He was one of my father's oldest friends."

"Good," Oscar said, sniffing. At least he'd stopped wearing the handkerchief around his face.

"You're sounding better," Nate said.

"Iron constitution," Oscar said. "No cold can keep me down. Especially since we've been so busy."

Chuck came over and took our orders. "Nobody's paying today," he said. "I understand you're the folks who helped get our Lucky the recognition she deserves."

"They sure are," Lucy said.

"So, are you all going to join up with her?" Chuck asked. I wasn't sure what he meant.

"Nah," Oscar said, "we're just regular folks, not supers."

"Well, you're pretty super in my book." Chuck headed back to his grill.

"Join up?" I asked.

"So it isn't in the news yet," Lucy said, "because it's just in the planning stages. As you can tell, word has already passed along through family gossip. I'm thinking about putting together my own squad."

"I saw that you'd been invited to join quite a few groups," I said. "Not interested in those?"

"Not really, no. They saw me as a misfit before; they only want me back because I took on Doctor Oracle and got back what he stole. I'm pretty sure they want my news story to join their group, not me and my powers."

"But that same street cred means she can write her own ticket," Oscar said.

"And being able to tell all of the groups I warned 'I told you so' has been pretty nice."

"I bet," I said.

"How's that fake battery been working for you?" Jin asked.

"Great," Lucy said. "I let them have access just long enough to run a Geiger counter over it, then boxed it back up again. According to a top expert in the field of nuclear science, it can't be repaired, so I offered to dispose of it."

"We did see that bit on the news," Nate said, looking at Oscar. "Nice job."

"It was actually good to be stuffed up. Helped me get into the scientist character and voice," Oscar said.

"Did you guys want it back?" Lucy asked.

"No," I said, smiling. "We have one of our own. That battery is your souvenir."

Chuck brought over hamburgers and fries and topped off our drinks. Everything looked delicious and tasted even better. After checking to see if we needed anything else, he went back behind the counter.

"So," Nate said, "your own squad."

"That's what I'm thinking," Lucy said. "I have good feelings about it. And the idea of being in charge doesn't make me anxious at all. I figure I'll be able to run it all from a central library or something and be able to send teams out to do the fieldwork. Really, I've felt great this past few days, probably because I haven't felt powerless for any of it."

"Any thoughts about how to finance the operation?" Nate asked.

Oscar raised an eyebrow at Nate. "Do I sense that you have some thoughts about it?"

"Well, this might just be a good opportunity to build a bridge," Nate said. "I mean, we have a supervillain whose team is willing to save the world and a superhero who isn't afraid to go against the other super groups and the government and get her hands dirty if necessary. Sounds like a match made in heaven."

"I'm listening," Lucy said.

"If you're looking for an investor, or even just a line of credit, Doctor Oracle might be interested in helping out."

"Told you so," Oscar said to Lucy. "This is right up Oracle's alley."

"Interesting," Lucy said. "But he'd be hands-off as far as running the group?"

"Yes," Nate said. "A total silent partner. However, he might want to suggest that when you're doing your hiring and looking at résumés, you could open up your search to those who are on the other side of the fence. Not the *real* baddies, you know, but there are a lot of young folks out there with useful powers who have fallen to villainy simply because they don't agree with how most super groups are run."

"I think I could agree with that."

We settled on a loose handshake deal, and Lucy even took off her glove to shake with Nate and me. We all thanked Chuck for the delicious meal, then wandered back out into the hot Arizona afternoon.

Jin went to get the car. Lucy and I sat at an outdoor table under an umbrella while Nate and Oscar stood back against the wall of Chuck's, under the awning, so they could talk privately while keeping an eye on us and the surroundings.

"I'm glad Doctor Oracle is interested," Lucy said. "I think this could be the start of something big."

"Well, we'll have to run it by him," I said.

She tilted her head back at Nate. "Oh, I think he'll be in favor of the whole thing."

"I have no idea what you mean," I said, and looked away.

"Of course not," she said. "But unless you're in love with two different men at the same time, the fact that I get the same feeling from you about Nate as I get when you're talking about Doctor Oracle is pretty telling."

"I have no idea what you mean," I repeated, smiling.

"I will remind you, there are probably millions of guys named Nate out there. And I've never seen him without a disguise on, so there's really not much I could say, even if I wanted to." She tapped the back of my left hand, where I wore my new ring. "I guess I'll have to wait for the wedding invitation to find out all the real details."

I looked at her. "You'll definitely be on the list. Though I can't promise it'll be anytime soon."

"He isn't going anywhere," she said. "I think you're stuck with him as long as you want. Which is a shame for me, because I'd put you on my team in a heartbeat."

"Well, I'll keep that in mind if things go south," I said.

"I don't see that happening, but how about this: there's a spot available on my team anytime you want it."

"I'll keep that in mind." Jin pulled up in our SUV. I hugged Lucy. "I'm so glad to have met you."

"Same here," she said. "Take care, Sarah. I'll be in touch."

Nate and I got into the car with Jin, and as we pulled away, I watched Oscar and Lucy walk to their car. He had his hand on the small of her back, a protective move I knew all too well from Nate. But I was pretty sure that in her way, Lucy would be able to protect Oscar, too.

"Are we getting him back?" Jin asked.

"I think so," Nate said. "But I told him to take as long out here as he needs to. He can be a big help in getting her set up."

"She knows that you're Doctor Oracle," I said. "Though she's only seen you in disguise, and she only knows your first name."

"Yeah, I think she's known for quite a while. Decent of her to keep it to herself."

"You aren't worried?"

"Everyone else who has seen Doctor Oracle, what do they take away from it? He's always in disguise, and he's used a hundred names. The only difference here is that Lucy knows that we have a solid team of good people, most of whom she likes, one of whom she seems to already be in love with."

"When you put it that way, I guess I shouldn't be worried."

"Plus, if she's going to become a business partner, there has to be *some* trust. At least a little bit."

We sat in silence for a few minutes, until Jin looked back at me. "So, ready for tomorrow?"

"That's right," Nate said. "You're taking your private pilot test. Nervous?"

"Hell yes," I said. I'd be flying solo out to the Millers' airstrip as a student and hopefully flying back as a licensed private pilot. I'd take the written exam first; then Lee would stay behind to grade it while I took Shannon up in the Cessna. Both Millers were certified instructors and pilot examiners, so they were a one-stop shop. My paperwork might be in a variety of fake names, but I wanted my skills to be tested for real.

Jin and I were planning an evening of hair-coloring in order to take my mind off the upcoming tests, so at least if I failed, I could fail with cool hair.

"Nothing to worry about," Jin said. "I'm confident that you'll pass."

"I'm glad one of us is," I said.

"Well, if you don't get your license, I'll have to change my Sunday plans," Nate said.

"Why, what's up?"

"Some of Rupert's code breakers have managed to crack a little bit of that crazy little book you found."

"Really?" I asked. "They're able to read it?"

"Bits and pieces right now. From the pictures you took of the guy's family photos on his desk, they finally got a match in the database. The owner of your book is a fellow who goes by Mr. Flexible; he's one of those stretchy guys. Once they figured out the glyphs for Flexible's name, they were able to start picking away at the rest. They just needed his name like a sort of Rosetta stone."

"So what have they figured out so far?"

"A lot of numbers and letters and a few words. A lot of the symbols look like shorthand for full words, so there's a lot more to decipher. Some of the numbers look like coordinates, so it might be a list of facilities or items. Kind of like our database, or the list of what we keep in the Vault."

"Interesting," I said. "So what was your Sunday plan?"

"A section Rupert mostly finished has a set of coordinates just outside of Salt Lake City. I figured we could fly out, take a little look around, see if there's anything interesting going on."

"Just a set of coordinates?" I squinted. "There must be more than that."

"Well, a couple of words along with the coordinates. Nothing big."

"And those words were?"

"One of them was *concert*."

I was confused. "So, what, there's a music concert somewhere? Why is that a big deal?"

"The other word was the name Vermeer." He handed me his tablet, open to the Wikipedia article about Vermeer's painting *The Concert*, quite possibly the most valuable unrecovered stolen painting in history.

"You think some supers are holding on to a stolen painting that's been missing for twenty-five years? Valued at over . . ." I squinted at the tablet to make sure I was reading all the zeroes right. "Two hundred million dollars?"

"Won't know until we look, now, will we? I just need somebody to fly me out to Salt Lake."

"Huh," I said. "Well, in that case, I guess I need to pass those exams tomorrow."

"I hope so," he said.

✱ ✱ ✱

The next morning in Albuquerque, I sat in the pilot's seat of the Cessna with Shannon Miller sitting in the copilot's seat next to me. The paper exams were done, and it was time to test my flying ability. They still didn't want to know my real name, and kindly left that space blank on all of my paperwork so I could fill it in myself later.

"Ready to go, boss?" she asked.

"One second," I said. I dug into my pocket and pulled out a tiny toy dinosaur, the kind you get from a coin-op vending machine in front of a drugstore. I pulled out the roll of duct tape from Jin's emergency-repair stash, tore off a small strip, and folded it into a loop. I used the tape to secure the little dinosaur to the plane's dashboard.

"Lucky charm?" Shannon asked.

"That he is. I got him on one of the best days of my life," I said. I'd been disappointed at the time when I hadn't pulled a toy ring from the machine outside of the drugstore, and in a way, that disappointment told me everything I needed to know. And of course, getting the real thing was much, much better.

I pulled the clipboard with the preflight checklist onto my lap, tucked my new kick-ass bright orange hair behind my ears, and put my headset on. Sitting there, I felt something I was still working on getting used to: confidence.

"All right," I said. "Let's do this thing."

ABOUT THE AUTHOR

Missy Meyer is originally from Seattle, Washington, but moved to Florida in order to work for the world's largest mouse. (She's had an amazing variety of jobs, including singing improv comedian, bank teller, game show host, webmaster, pizza chef, accountant, mystery shopper, camp counselor, and casino dealer.) She also draws the web comic *Holiday Doodles*.

Missy is married to Scott Meyer, the guy behind the web comic *Basic Instructions* and the author of *Off to Be the Wizard* and the Magic 2.0 series of books. They currently live near Orlando, Florida, with their two cats.

ACKNOWLEDGEMENTS

A big thank you, as always, to my husband Scott. His encouragement and support have frequently helped me from sliding feet-first into a bottomless pit.

Thank you to all of my early readers: Rodney Sherwood, Kate Jaeger, Amanda Denning, and Cheryl Platz. Their feedback and support are always a huge help. And thank you to my editor, Matt Patin; everything that looks right is due to him, and all mistakes are due to my own stubbornness.

And as always, many thanks to you, the reader!

www.ingramcontent.com/pod-product-compliance
Lightning Source LLC
Chambersburg PA
CBHW060858250626
47159CB00008B/2790